ELVIS THE GUNSLINGER

BY
ROMEY CONNELL

COVER DESIGN AND ILLUSTRATIONS BY THE
REMARKABLY TALENTED GRETCHEN CONNELL

Published by
Elvis the Gunslinger, LLC
346 Southerland Terrace
Atlanta, Georgia 30307-2346
www.elvisthegunslinger.com

ISBN 978-0-9976490-9-3

DEDICATION AND ACKNOWLEDGMENTS

This book is dedicated to the memory of Elvis, the baddest cat ever to stroll the neighborhood, and Daisy, who was his dearest and most loyal friend throughout her life. You were wonderful companions to all who had the pleasure of knowing you and you forever will truly be missed. May you always rest in peace together, knowing that you are remembered by all of us with love and a smile.

The author wishes to extend his sincere appreciation and gratitude to the many wonderful persons whose support, insight and contributions have helped to make this work possible. At the inevitable risk of omitting someone, I would be remiss to not specifically call out James "Raymond" Deason, Janie Bogan, "Captain" Ted Johnson, Darin McAuliffe, Mike Mikula and Deirdre Flint. My brother, Martin, not only for his input, but for his invaluable work creating our web site. And last, but not least, my family – Jerry and Jamie, for all of their input and for tolerating my obsession with this work, and my lovely wife, Gretchen, not only for her never-ending love and support, but also for her immense talent that graces the cover and permeates the design of this book. Much love to all of you and muchas, muchas gracias!

THE COMPLETELY OPTIONAL INTRODUCTION

As the heading suggests, feel free to skip right over this. There certainly isn't anything here that you won't pick up on your own along the way. If you're the type who likes to have a little lead-in, have at it. If you prefer to jump right in and soak it up as you go, please kindly turn to Chapter One.

It's what you likely would recognize as the days of the Old West. In the world that you're pretty much familiar with. Continents, vegetation, bodies of water, animals, the starlit night sky. The usual lot. Except for us. Sorry about that, but I didn't really have much choice. Yes, good ol' Homo sapiens isn't on the lineup card. Somehow, our absence doesn't stifle the whole thing after all. Cultures flourish, technology advances and things move along swimmingly without anyone ever noticing that we aren't around to keep it all running smoothly. It's just that another species got saddled with the responsibility of being in charge of the place.

The sentimental favorite of many might be dogs. They are, after all, man's best friend. And who better than your best friend to look after the joint when you're not around? As much as I have loved my own dogs over the years, I must admit, however reluctantly, that they generally are not the brightest bunch around. Loyal? Fun? Loving? Sure, they're all of that and much, much more. Unfortunately, the ingenuity of the average canine probably is most charitably characterized as less than remarkable.

There are other good candidates. Maybe the primates that anthropologists say are our natural predecessors, or a few of those swimming mammals that many claim are at least as cerebral as we. If I'm here to write about a world ruled by monkeys, then I've probably arrived at the party just a bit late. Not to mention that warding off plagiarism claims isn't at the top of my list of things to do. Were this an undersea saga, porpoises or orcas probably would do just fine, but when it comes to adventuring on land, they have their share of physical limitations.

That leaves us with cats. Yes, the ordinary feline that might be strolling the interior of your dwelling this very moment. Deciding whether it's time for a nap or time for food, or whether it ought to have a momentary change of heart and return to the great outdoors. Never mind that it persuaded you just moments ago to permit entrance via the very door through which it now intends to depart. A species that enough of us are sufficiently familiar with to make our story remotely interesting (hopefully), yet still smug and cunning enough to be in charge of a planet without having to go entirely overboard on the believability scale.

Now that I've come this far, there is one more thing probably worth noting. Maybe you're not such a big fan of the cat. I happen to know many wonderful persons who love animals, but who also are of the opinion that even a talented cat generally is not as useful or as much fun to have around as most any dog. If you do count yourself among that group, please don't let that stop you just yet. If ever you find yourself not enjoying this, then by all means, stop. And feel free to tell all of your friends that you did. Keep in mind, however, that the star of our show here is not your ordinary cat. Every race and generation has its own 007 or someone similar. Given the trappings that we're dealing with here, Jim West (the original one) might be the best human analogy that I can come up with. You should get the picture by now, so I'll get out of your way.

CONTENTS

❧ ELVIS THE GUNSLINGER ❧

CHAPTER ONE

DINNERTIME

Even those with a penchant for the spectacular need to recharge now and then, so he snoozed away early on a calm summer evening. Curled up in the rickety, wooden rocker perched on his country porch, directly in front of an enormous picture window. His dark brown fur contrasted sharply with the weathered gray seat as he rocked gently back and forth.

The fading sun was working its way from yellow to orange and the trajectory of its rays now forced a tight squint whenever Elvis tried to sneak a peek through his emerald green eyes. A slight chill began to set in as the shadows thrown by the pickets supporting the porch railing painted lines over his favorite resting spot. After a drawn-out yawn and a few licks to the white stockings of his forelegs, he casually slipped down from the rocker and strolled through the open doorway of his modest log home.

As he entered, much of the wall to his right was comprised of a brownstone fireplace that reached nearly to the three-foot high ceiling. His grandfather crafted the hulking structure when Elvis was just a kitten – his first memory. Above the mantle was his late father's prized possession, an antique shotgun that had been used in the last great war, when the raccoons (the troublesome ones, anyway) were finally run out of the province. The coonskin rug on the floor below was a product of the first episode that forebode young Elvis' own talents in battle. It conjured up memories of how he nearly bit off a little more than even he could chew that day.

To his left was a round, mahogany dining table encircled by five oak chairs, though only four fit around it neatly. His mother served the family dinner there each night until her passing, almost two years ago now. It held a warm place in Elvis' heart and was his very favorite spot to indulge in his second favorite pastimes, food and beverage. Beams of sunlight shone upon the tabletop through the window's sparkling pane of glass, but the brightest of the light had faded away.

He lazily worked his way over to a small, square cherry table in the corner of the room. On its front was a brass plate, inscribed with a message from the Governor: "To Elvis, a True Statesman." He gazed into the front yard as he raised himself onto his hind legs and slid open a tiny drawer. He plucked out a red-tipped match, struck it across a razor-sharp claw and set afire the wick of an oil lantern centered atop the table.

As he fell back to all fours, he extinguished the match with a quick puff from the side of his mouth, and then he meandered around the dining table and into the kitchen. A bulky cast iron woodstove in the very center of the room warmed the dwelling during the cooler months, but its primary occupation was to heat surfaces. It was there that Elvis practiced one of his hobbies, basic cooking. The wide window above the big porcelain sink provided a great view of the broad side of the faded blue barn that stood northeast of the house. A quick glance reminded Elvis that he ought to take care of the evening feeding while sufficient natural light remained for the task.

He scampered across the kitchen, dashed through the doorway on the side of the house, and swung the door closed behind him, reaching back to snatch his black leather hat off of a hook just before the door slammed shut on his paw. He straightened his headgear as he began to lope, and he quickly traversed the forty or fifty yards separating his abode from the big, sliding doors fronting the barn. Struggling to pry them open, he mumbled to himself for the umpteenth time about how much easier it would be if he would take just a few minutes out of his life to grease the rollers at the top. Some tasks, however simple, never seemed to find their way to the top of the Elvis priority list.

Elvis grunted as he pushed and pulled the doors open as wide as they would go, and then trotted down to the feed chute in the center of the barn. All was quiet for the moment, with the dogs still busy dozing in the back field. Elvis yanked upward on the chute door, releasing a torrent of small, crunchy brown chunks into the little red wheel barrow that he'd used for as long as he could remember to tote feed from stall to stall. The sound of rushing goodies snapped the canines out of their late day semi-slumber.

Simultaneously they rose to stretch, yawn and begin lumbering slowly toward the gate near the back of the barn. All approaching from different areas of the field, as if it had been choreographed. Meanwhile, Elvis made his way to the back doors and slid them open with considerably less effort than he had expended to achieve the same result at the front of the barn.

He bounced across a swath of green grass that was in sore need of a trim, and arrived at the swinging metal contraption that governed admittance to and from the field. By the time he had finished fiddling with the rusty latch (another good candidate for a lube job) that held the gate in place, the dogs had arrived together on cue.

Elvis made an effortless leap to the top of the gatepost and looked out over the field as he held the gate shut with his right forepaw. The fading sunlight gave shimmering highlights to the golden grass, all the way to the foothills at the end of the valley. The flat clouds hovering at the horizon were transitioning from a pale white to a purplish-pink, with a fiery red about to move in for the kill.

He sat mesmerized for a moment, but then was startled by a few crass barks from the troops. They weren't impressed by sunsets under even the most ordinary of circumstances, much less when dinner hung in the balance. Elvis lifted his paw and let the gate swing open to the sound of creaking hinges.

As usual, Amos was at the head of the pack. A young, spirited Catstralian Shepherd who was large for his breed and liked to be first regardless of what he was doing. Shuttling between field and barn, being saddled and bridled for an evening trail ride, even lining up for the weekly application of flea spray. The nature of the activity was of little importance and all events held equal wonder in his wild eyes. He was happy just to be doing something and he seldom found reason to wait for someone else to kick things off.

Jezebel, a beautiful Black Labrador, was next through the gate, trailed closely by her five adorable puppies, who now were approaching two months in age and starting to resemble dogs, not the nondescript balls of fur that they were just weeks before. Although she finally was beginning to show signs of her eight years, Jez still was sharp as a tack and could run circles around most dogs half her age.

Speed (a misnomer if ever there was one) was not too far behind the puppies, moseying like a train whose conductor couldn't loosen himself from the brake. A gentle Collie, she was the perfect mount for Uncle Sam on the infrequent days when he needed to ride somewhere. They were a match made in heaven.

Daisy looked around to make sure that the others had made a safe exodus before rounding out the group, and then moved briskly toward the barn, jumping up to give Elvis a friendly lick on the face as she passed him by. She was slightly smaller than most Golden Retrievers, but the gate was a mere formality for her. She had launched herself over the six-foot, wire fence that surrounded the field on countless occasions, but only for sport, not escape.

Elvis often recounted the day when the cocky trainers at Kleptown Downs stood with their mouths agape after Daisy nearly outran the swiftest greyhounds they had to offer. Had the distance been much greater, they surely would have worn out and left her the outright victor. The day's wagers extended only to whether she could finish within twenty yards of the pack, and Elvis spent much of the train ride home that night counting his absurd winnings from the affair.

He considered taking in more of the sunset, but decided to postpone the matter for a few minutes, knowing that he would enjoy it more if his chores were not left hanging over his head. So, he dashed into the barn while the others proceeded to their stalls. Elvis zigzagged down the aisle with his wheel barrow and water bucket, tossing scoops of feed into shiny metal trays and pouring cold water, fresh from the well located just outside of the barn, into faded black rubber bowls.

Nary two minutes later, was he negotiating the steep roof of the barn in an attempt to improve his vantage point for what remained of the setting sun. His stare was fixed and he seemed unaware of most everything else, as he watched the last of the big fireball creep over the horizon's edge from his choice spot on the apex. Peace and quiet were short-lived, taken in exchange for an inquiring voice.

"Elvis. ELVIS. ELVIS!" His head snapped down as he broke from his trance. He looked to where the road that passed by the front of the house met perpendicular with the pathway extending from the barn, worn over time by the wheels of the Elvis family wagon. He distinctly remembered eight o'clock being the appointed time, not seven-thirty. He hadn't even begun thinking about making a quick sweep of the house, much less setting some food out on the table. Minor inconveniences, though; Calli was stunning.

Elvis trotted along the apex to the front of the barn and launched himself to the ground. He landed soft and silent, and nonchalantly made his way toward her, reached for his hat (in place despite the nine-foot drop) and tipped it slightly, kissed her forepaw lightly and proceeded to escort her over the front lawn, up the steps, across the porch and into the living room.

As the door closed behind, he blindly tossed his hat over his left shoulder, landing it squarely on the hook set upon the back of the door. He then ushered Calli over to the big, worn leather couch in the front of the room, where they dabbled for a few minutes in meaningless small talk. Her ice blue eyes were startling against her sleek black fur. Elvis got up to begin kindling a fire, ostensibly to add light and warmth to the darkening room, but just as much to keep himself from staring embarrassingly.

She pulled the family photo album from the top of the walnut coffee table. Elvis always enjoyed showing it off, and he left her to peruse it while he disappeared into the kitchen to carve some bleu cheese from the pungent block that he'd picked up at Uncle Sam's grocery store earlier in the day.

Calli was new to town and Elvis was intrigued by her. He loved life in Woodville, whenever he had the chance to enjoy it, but it seemed unusual for a young woman of her beauty to take up residence there. On her own volition anyway. The cozy town provided a very peaceful setting for day-to-day life, but there certainly wasn't much excitement to be found.

She had said when they met that she hailed from Albemarle, a coastal town nearly forty miles to the west with a population almost ten times that of Woodville. Elvis was puzzled as to why she hadn't stayed there, or ventured someplace that offered at least a modicum of culture or vibrancy. Her story about wanting to get away from the hustle and bustle, and find a simple place to settle down after struggling to put herself through two years of study at an East Coast university, seemed a bit contrived.

A few bites of the tangy cheese had both of them yearning for a sip of something, so Elvis took her by the forepaw and led her down the hall. It was too dim to see what appeared to be artwork and a few family pictures lining the walls, and they continued to a closed door near the back of the hallway. The damp chill sneaking underneath the door hit Calli with full force as Elvis swung it open and descended into the musty darkness. Being led into a black basement by someone she'd really known for barely half an hour wasn't part of her usual repertoire, but she did her best to ignore the uneasiness.

She made her way down the steps on her hind legs, just behind Elvis, her right forepaw gripped tightly to a smooth banister that she could feel, but not see. The eerie silence hanging in the air as they approached bottom had her rethinking the decision to follow. An abrupt movement just ahead sent her leaping halfway back up the stairwell as she let out a piercing shriek.

She stopped just short of the doorway at the top of the steps as she heard the sound of Elvis giggling and saw the spooky room begin to light up. Elvis tried to steady himself from his own laughter as the large match in his paw burst into flame while he reached for the lantern perched on a small wooden shelf lodged in a corner. Slightly embarrassed, she crept back down and began to look around in amazement as Elvis bounced to the remaining corners, lighting three more lanterns without resorting to a second match.

Elvis had arranged for the cellar to be dug in the fall of '61. Though he still had a ways to go toward rounding out his stock, things were coming together. Elvis was reluctant to admit it, but Uncle Sam's eye for quality imports was improving with every trip to the marina, and Elvis by now had become a respectable connoisseur in his own right. Nearly every eastward journey he'd made during the past few years had included a detour to the heart of wine country to sample the latest there was to offer. Between shipments from noted vintners he'd befriended, and the rare wines and fine Champagnes that Elvis occasionally received as gifts from luminaries, he had amassed what was becoming a fairly impressive store of grape juice.

Because the imported Chardonnay that Calli chose was so exceptional, Elvis didn't bother to mention that he preferred red. They came back up the steps and Elvis made a quick detour on his way to the dining room, breezing through the kitchen to pick up a pair of wine glasses, place settings, candles and a tray of salmon. After everything was situated, they plowed through the fish and the wine. Shortly after they finished, they agreed that it was a beautiful night for a stroll.

CHAPTER TWO

PEACE AND QUIET?

Calli leaned back to relax while Elvis rummaged through the hall closet to find her a light jacket. It was clear and slightly cool outside, and the sky was filled with bright stars and a sliver of crescent moon. They took to a path behind the house that led south, away from the barn. Elvis had opted against bringing a lantern, although he did strap on a faded leather gun belt, just in case an unwanted visitor might be on the prowl looking for its own tasty dinner. As they made their way down the trail, the sound of running water became louder with each step. Limbs and branches of oaks, pines and birches hung over the way, and it all looked very enchanting.

The Rio Albemarle had its beginnings almost due east of the ranch, in the upper peaks of the Slipstill Mountains, the foothills of which began to rise less than five miles from Woodville. It passed through his property approximately thirty-five yards south of the house. There, the water usually ran steady, but not too strong, and was no more than twenty yards across on the average day.

Just short of the river's edge was a log bench with a high back. Elvis had carved it at the age of one from a massive oak tree that was felled by a lightning strike and landed just along the bank. He was very proud of it, and Calli could see as much in his face when he invited her to have a seat with him.

She was plenty warm in the wool jacket that Elvis had found for her, but Calli feigned being chilled as an excuse to slide close up next to him. The sounds of the running river and the night creatures seemed to gather intensity. Elvis pulled a flask from his vest pocket and took a nip of his favorite Catgnac. She did likewise when he offered, but mostly in a show of attitude and enthusiasm; Calli really wasn't much the Catgnac fan. With stomachs full, both were in danger of being lulled into an impromptu nap when Elvis jerked his head into the air and turned to look over his left shoulder.

Calli obviously hadn't heard anything and her face looked up curiously from its perch on his warm chest. Either the years of partnership had him uniquely attuned to the pitch or maybe it was something more instinctual, but Elvis could hear Daisy's bark or yelp from unthinkable distances and above most any distortion. He raised up from the bench, careful to not let Calli's head fall against it, and looked intently back up the path. She reached out as he began to move and asked, "What's the matter?" Her paw found nothing but empty bench, as Elvis had taken off toward the house like a circus clown who'd been shot from a cannon.

Elvis was out of sight before Calli could kneel up and peek her head over the back of the bench. If she had stayed and waited for a few moments, Elvis may well have been able to sneak up on the source of his concern, but she came after him as fast as she could, and her loud cries of "Elvis, come back!" couldn't help but to have startled anything in earshot. Passing by the house and quickly closing in on the barn, he was starting to make out the silhouettes of two, possibly more, animals scrambling out from the front doors of the barn and into the nearby woods. Elvis fired two shots at them as he bolted across the remaining distance toward the barn.

He ran inside and darted toward Daisy's stall, yanked open the door and jumped onto her back as she took off down the aisle. Her right turn out of the barn was sharp and rapid, and her side nearly dragged the ground as she burst toward the woods. As she wended her way through the tree trunks, Elvis emptied the remaining rounds in his revolver toward the branches and bushes that he could see rustling in the distance.

In just a few seconds, Daisy had closed the gap considerably and the shadows were about to take true form. Suddenly, Elvis caught a whiff of smoke and let out with a loud "WHOA!" Daisy slid to a stop and Elvis looked over his shoulder to see a flickering light through the stall window at the back of the barn. Daisy rose up onto her hind legs, spun toward the opposite direction and ran back to the barn faster than she had left it. Even Elvis was having trouble holding on without the luxury of reins or saddle.

At Elvis' urging, Daisy ran down the aisle to the rear of the barn, where a small fire was spreading across the straw bedding in the last stall. Elvis jumped off, grabbed two water buckets that were sitting nearby in the aisle and emptied them onto the base of the flames. Daisy already was heading through the back doors with the handles of two much larger buckets lodged in her jaws. Elvis came running out behind her on his hind legs with the handle of an empty bucket in the crick of each foreleg, and they began working the well rope as fast as they could.

Daisy ran into the barn on her hind legs carrying a full tub in each foreleg, and Elvis was trailing close behind with his smaller buckets. They doused the flames again, but Elvis was uncertain whether they might have to give up the task and get the rest of the dogs to safety before the entire barn ignited. Daisy had nearly refilled her buckets by the time Elvis arrived back at the well, and Elvis took over at the well while Daisy returned to the barn to keep up the splashing.

Amos was banging his body furiously against his stall door, yelping to be let out, and Elvis tried to ignore the cries of Jezebel's puppies, who obviously sensed that something terribly wrong was underway. They could have used Jez's help more than anything, but her paws were full trying to keep her progeny under control, and Elvis knew that they couldn't be left alone at the moment. Amos wasn't the most reliable animal in the barn and there was no time now to be distracted by having to keep an eye on him, but they desperately needed the help. So, while Daisy stayed at the well to fill the third round of buckets, Elvis ran back to the front of the barn to get Amos.

As he opened the stall door, Elvis made it clear that this was not a time for frolic, and Amos could sense that his often light-hearted master was not joking. They ran as fast as they could toward the back of the barn, passing by Speed, who lie asleep in her stall through all of the commotion, and Jez, who stood with a concerned look on her face as she tried to keep the youngins calm. Elvis directed Amos to pick up two more large buckets, and as they were exiting through the back doors, Calli appeared, running toward them from the other end of the barn.

Amos and Elvis went straight to the well, where Daisy already had filled buckets for herself and Elvis, and was about to begin carrying her load. Elvis told her to stay put and fill the new buckets that Amos had brought, and Elvis and Amos rushed back inside, water swishing and splashing from side to side with every step. The flames were reaching dangerously close to the top of the stall, and Elvis threw water onto the walls as high as he could. Amos followed his instructions like a champ and, being nearly five times the size of Elvis, he proved to be far more successful at dousing the high boards.

Elvis knew that the cause would be lost if the bright orange flames were able to reach their way another foot or so to the ceiling and into the straw loft, so they ran back to the well as fast as they could with their empty receptacles. Calli arrived at the well with more buckets, and Daisy was dunking and raising as fast as their eyes could see. Seconds seemed like hours to Elvis, as he could see through the stall window that the flames still were ascending with each lick of the wall.

As Elvis was about to start down the aisle to get the others to safety, Daisy completed filling yet another round of buckets. Elvis stayed to help and all four of them staggered back into the barn with a full complement of water. The stall was lit up like a Christmas tree by now and the smoke was beginning to choke the air from the barn. The puppies were whining and rustling more fervently than ever, and Elvis could sense that Jez was starting to come unglued. Even Speed had awakened by now, and was uncharacteristically jumping and prancing around.

Elvis reached back for momentum to throw another bucketful, but his right foreleg was yanked from behind. Amos snatched the handle from Elvis' paw, wound up and deposited the contents far higher than Elvis could have hoped to. With tears rolling from their burning eyes, Elvis and Calli turned over their remaining buckets to the canines, who launched the water from them and proceeded to do the same with their own larger buckets.

Every splash landed squarely upon its mark and though the flames still licked at the walls, they appeared to retreat for the first time. Everyone instantly returned to the well, where Daisy resumed her work. Elvis and Amos were quickly back at the stall with four more buckets for Amos to throw, and as they rushed back out with their empties, Daisy and Calli passed them going in.

As Elvis began working the well rope, he could see that the reach of the flames no longer extended to the heights of the window, and he started to feel a slight hint of relief. After another full round of dousing, things began to look almost under control. Elvis sternly told Amos that if he wanted to see his next breakfast, he'd better continue splashing the floor and walls as fast as he could until Elvis and Daisy returned. With Amos and Calli appearing fully up to the task, Elvis pounced onto Daisy's back and she again took off down the aisle, out of the barn and into the woods.

The stars shone bright and Daisy's sense of smell was impeccable, but Elvis knew that unless one of his shots had serendipitously landed squarely upon one of the perpetrators, locating any of them at this point was a virtual impossibility. Daisy surely had gotten a good look at them in the barn, and no doubt would recognize any of them that she might encounter again, but providing a verbal description was a bit of a stretch even for her. We already have cats talking here and must live with some constraints.

Daisy meandered through the woods with her nose to the ground, as Elvis stared into the darkness – back and forth, side to side, hoping to find something that might lend a clue. After venturing fifty yards or so into the forest, it was obvious to Elvis that, if anything useful was to be found, the assistance of morning's light would far outweigh any advantage that immediacy of the search could provide. With no serious harm having been done to the barn or the animals, he began to question his own wisdom. Wasting away time on an almost certainly fruitless ride in the dark while one of the most attractive individuals he ever had laid eyes on had been left behind on firecat duty? He promptly steered Daisy back to the barn.

Elvis stomped all around the area where the fire had burned, wanting to assure himself that it was fully extinguished before turning his attention to other matters. A stiff breeze had begun to blow in from the mountains, and it took only a few minutes to almost fully clear the barn air with the doors wide open at both ends. Amos was busy looking around for something new to get into, happy to have an excuse to be out at night. Elvis led him into his stall with a gracious pat on the neck and turned back to do the same for Daisy, but she was taking care of the matter on her own, now back in her stall sliding the door shut for herself. Elvis briefly entertained the idea of returning to the riverside, but decided that he probably would do better to stay nearby and keep a closer eye on things for the rest of the night.

Midnight was upon them and the fire that roared inside the house earlier in the evening had nearly burned itself out. They leaned back into the cushions of the couch and began to kiss, as the last flickers of flame were disappearing in the fireplace. As would any true feline gentleman, Elvis momentarily came up for air to ask Calli if she would like him to escort her home. She looked up with a puzzled expression and asked, "Now, why would you want to do that?" Knowing that it's always best to tell the truth when you can, he replied, "I don't."

CHAPTER THREE

DUTY CALLS

Elvis and Daisy had been rummaging around for clues since shortly after the morning feeding. The woods extended north from the barn for nearly a quarter mile, all the way to Main Street. Elvis was fairly confident that he had determined the escape route of the pack that had engendered the flames the night before. After several passes back and forth along what seemed to have been their path, he figured that he had gathered as much useful information as could be found, and there wasn't much.

He did stumble upon a fresh bloody chunk of white fur in the woods, likely the product of one of the shots that he had fired the night before. That was it. Thanks to some heavy rain that had fallen just a couple of days before, it was muddy at the far edge of the forest, at the bottom of the bank leading up to Main Street. Elvis was able to make out three separate sets of prints and the distance between the hind and forepaws in each stride left no doubt that the trio had been in a great hurry.

Calli was awakened by the closing of the side door of the house, followed by the sounds of Elvis shuffling around in the kitchen. Since Elvis was out and about anyway, he had decided to stop by Uncle Sam's store on the way back to the house. The sound and smell of eggs and bacon crept their way down the hall and into the bedroom, and the enticement was too much for her to resist. She pried herself from the comfy bed and went out to say hello.

Elvis turned and smiled when she stepped from the hall into the kitchen, but then quickly returned his attention to the two pans sizzling atop the stove. She was able to find a mug on her own and poured herself some milk from the bottle on the counter as she offered to help with breakfast. He motioned toward the worn china plates in the cupboard. She grabbed two and he followed her into the dining room, where he slid fried eggs from pan to plates. He stepped back into the kitchen and returned quickly with a plate full of crispy bacon. Elvis hoped dearly that he was only imagining the meter of a very familiar walk making its way up the front steps and across the porch. No sooner did he fall into his chair and reach for a strip of bacon when three loud raps on the front door abruptly dashed his hopes.

He sighed, raised himself up, walked slowly to the front door and swung it open to the sight of a frequent visitor. Frank had a large frame, but he weighed little more than Elvis. Due primarily to a propensity for fidgeting that kept him thin, even though his appetite more closely resembled that of a small dog than one of a cat. His tan fur matched well with his blue-green eyes, although getting a good look at them required fighting through the oft-dirty lenses of his wire-framed, rectangular spectacles. Frank was the oldest and dearest friend that Elvis ever had, although Elvis couldn't have said at the moment that he was entirely glad to see him.

Elvis stepped back inside, rolled his eyes and whispered under his breath, "Really? Ten o'clock in the morning? On a Saturday?" Elvis introduced Calli to Frank, who obviously was impressed, but the meeting was brief, as the boys quickly made their way back onto the porch. Frank had more connections than most gossip columnists, and Elvis was all but certain that Frank somehow had gotten wind of the events of the night before. Elvis was surprised, shocked actually, to hear that the fire and the date all were news to Frank, which really set Elvis' mind to worrying. If Frank was visiting at this hour on a weekend and hadn't come to discuss the barn fire or the date with Calli, then something big probably was up.

Elvis asked Frank if all of this – whatever it was – could wait for just a few hours, so that he could at least enjoy his breakfast and a little more time with Calli before the proverbial hell broke loose. Frank fretted, as usual, but acceded to Elvis' request and agreed that he would return at one o'clock sharp. He put on his battered, black straw hat, trotted down the steps, jumped onto Stella's back and took off southbound down the road, turning back to wave just as he was about to vanish from Elvis' sight. Elvis stepped back into the house, steeped in certainty that the night before and the breakfast on the table soon would be distant memories, and that he would be off in short order to deal with some sort of impending disaster.

Calli waited for Elvis to return to the table before digging into her own breakfast, and she could tell that Elvis was distracted from the moment he sat down. He struggled with whether he should say anything to Calli about the paw prints and fur that he had discovered during his morning ride. Nothing like this ever had happened at home. Sure, he had a few enemies. Many were among the most despicable individuals that the feline world had to offer, but most of them had been hanged or locked away for good. Beyond that, Elvis' adventurous exploits – at least those that might make him an enemy or two – typically took place a considerable distance from the friendly confines of Woodville.

Even if the ranch somehow had become fair game for a gutless pot shot, who possibly could have known that he was not in his house for that brief period of time last night? It all seemed a bit too coincidental, and with each glance at Calli's amazing body, Elvis hoped sorely that it was just his imagination running amok. Still, he thought it best to keep his mouth shut for the time being.

They were so occupied with breakfast that they barely exchanged words until their plates were licked clean. Elvis cleared the table, opened the front door and motioned for Calli to follow him out onto the porch. They cuddled on the oversized bentwood chair that sat next to Elvis' rocker and nearly fell back asleep, as the sun began to warm the air and a light breeze gently shook the leaves of the trees that spotted the front yard.

Elvis said quietly, "I don't know for sure, but there's a good chance I'll be out of town for at least a little while. I can tell when Frank is stopping by to make a social call, and this wasn't that sort of visit. I might be wrong, but if you don't see me for a while, it has nothing to do with you. And if we do leave, we should be back before too long." He paused for a moment and said, "I hope, anyway." Before he could speak again, Calli pulled his body close and covered his lips with hers. With that, they returned into the house and back down the hall, so that they could say a proper goodbye.

- - -

Elvis stood on the porch, looking at one of his most prized possessions. A gold pocket watch passed down by his grandfather just before his death. Just as Elvis was tucking it back into his vest pocket, Frank came around the corner on Stella, a big, beautiful Golden Labrador, and hollered from across the yard, "WHY ARE YOU LOOKING AT THAT THING?" Elvis couldn't think of a plausible reason, not with the feline alarm clock keeping tabs on him. All he could think to say was, "Just making sure this old piece of junk still works. By the way, you're a minute early."

"You'll wish I was a week early after you hear this one, my boy," said Frank. Not only were Frank's saddlebags stuffed full, but Stella also was pulling a small, covered cart that was bulging at the top. Elvis could only imagine what was in there, but he didn't have it in him to ask. With an exasperated look, Elvis sighed and said, "I was afraid you would say something like that. You may as well come in and get on with it."

Frank shook his head back and forth and said, "I don't reckon we've got time for that, partner, not after the time we just gave up so you could roll around with that new friend of yours. You need to get your gear together, pronto, so we can make the two o'clock train. The four-forty-five don't run on weekends and this can't wait 'til tomorrow. I'll tell you all about it on the way to the station. Hurry up now. I'll go out to the barn and get Daisy saddled up for ya."

Elvis yelled, "TWO O'CLOCK! I'm supposed to be at a party in Albemarle this evening. And what about the place? I haven't gotten anyone lined up to take care of it." Frank already had Stella trotting off toward the barn, and even though he was facing in the opposite direction as he rode away, he yelled back at such a high volume that his voice still was audible, albeit fading. "Folks at the party will understand, and I've already spoken to Sam. Everything's covered around here for the time being. I hope you told that new girlfriend of yours that you're gonna be gone for a while. Assuming we even make it back this time."

Elvis went into the house shaking his head in angst, not in the mood for a sudden rush job after what had been (save the previous night's fireworks) a long-overdue stretch of relaxation back at home. He walked to the closet in the middle of the hall, stood up on his hind legs and opened the door. He reached for his large saddlebags with his left foreleg and tossed them out onto the floor, and then threw his black, twin-holster gun belt on top of them with his right.

The belt was one of those nifty models with rotating holsters that lock into three places – one perpendicular to the belt strap, one parallel with it and the third right in between. It kept his gun barrels pointing downward whether he was standing on all fours, up on hind legs or just sitting typical cat-style, with his hind legs tucked under his body. With summer in full bloom, Elvis was happy to pull out a light blanket and forego the musty smelling, oversized bundle of feathers that he called a sleeping bag. He reached in for his deerskin rifle holster, threw it into the hall, fell back down to all fours and used his forepaws to pull up two wide floorboards at the bottom of the closet.

He reached deep into the compartment, barely holding himself up as he hung from his hind legs, and pulled out two extraordinarily beautiful pistols. Each with a gleaming silver barrel and a pearl handle inlaid with an intricate gold "$\mathcal{E}$" on both sides, they resembled art pieces as much as weapons. Elvis set them on the floor, reached back into the compartment and pulled out a long, lever-action rifle. With a cherry stock, a shiny black barrel, and a pewter hammer and trigger, it was nearly as beautiful as the pistols.

After extracting a small bag crammed full with cash, he returned the floorboards to their places. He pulled two boxes of matches and a few hundred rounds of ammunition from the back shelf of the closet, and pushed everything that he had assembled into a pile in the middle of the hall floor. He went to his room and rounded up two blue bandanas (one of which he tied around his neck), a sterling silver flask and a deck of playing cards. As he looked around to see that nothing important was being left behind, he threw those items out into the hall with the rest of his stuff.

Elvis moved quickly toward the front door and bolted it shut, grabbed his hat from the hook, drew the curtains closed in the living and dining rooms, and returned to the pile in the hall. He stood on his hind legs, strapped on his gun belt, loaded his pistols and carefully placed them into their holsters. He loaded fifteen rounds into the rifle and shoved it into its holster, inserted another thirty or so rounds into the small wells that dotted his gun belt, and threw the rest of the ammunition into his saddlebags, along with his wad of money and other belongings.

With his blanket and saddlebags over his right shoulder and his rifle in the crick of his left foreleg, Elvis walked through the kitchen and out the side door. He locked it behind him and wondered to himself how long it might be before he would have the pleasure of going back through it again. The early afternoon sun was blazing, so much that even the grass had become quite warm, as Elvis began to amble slowly toward the barn.

Frank had let Jez and her pups out into the field with Speed, and Elvis was leading Amos down the aisle to join them when Frank interrupted, "Elvis, I think we might need him this time." Amos snapped his head back with excitement as Elvis, nearly at the far end of the barn by now, looked back with a surprised expression and hollered, "AMOS?" Amos looked at Elvis disappointedly, a bit hurt by the backpawed comment, but he quickly regained his enthusiasm as Frank began to speak. "Unless you think those puppies will be all right without Jez around for two weeks, I don't think we have much choice," said Frank. "TWO WEEKS!" Elvis exclaimed.

"Yep" was all that Frank could say, as he reached under Daisy's belly for the cinch to tighten her saddle. It was a special saddle that Elvis had just bought from Weaver, the local leather smith. It had a deep, padded, brown suede seat that he could comfortably hunker down into when sitting with his rear legs tucked underneath. There was a padded, rigid flap that could be laid over the deep seat, which made for a comfortable ride when Elvis needed to extend his legs and keep his hind paws in the stirrups. What Frank envied most, though, were the small wells on each side of the saddle horn and the two directly behind them in the back of the saddle. A soft, secure place for each paw when the rider tired of sitting and opted to stand on all fours to stretch for a spell.

Frank said to Elvis, "When we get back from this one. If we do get back, that is. I'm goin' down to Weaver's first thing and get me one of these. I'm getting sick and tired of sliding all over whenever I need to stand up and stretch for a while." Elvis didn't offer to tell Frank that there already was one in the works, a special present for Frank's sixth birthday, which was coming up at the end of summer.

Elvis turned around and started back down the aisle with Amos in tow. Actually, it was Elvis who was in tow, as Amos trotted quickly back toward the front of the barn with Elvis being dragged behind distractedly, wondering what sort of mess possibly could take two weeks to resolve. Elvis finished saddling and bridling Daisy, and fastened his rifle holster, blanket, saddlebags and lariat into place.

Meanwhile, Frank loaded Amos up with two sacks of supplies large enough to make even Amos start to lose a little bit of enthusiasm. He wouldn't let it show, of course, and somewhere around one-thirty, Stella and Daisy were carrying their riders out of the barn side-by-side. Making tracks toward the front road with Amos trailing close behind.

They turned right at the end of the drive and started toward Main Street. Elvis was mulling over the events of the night before and Frank was sorting through some official looking papers that he had just retrieved from a special delivery to the post office. It was a clear day, and the sun scorched their shoulders and backs as they turned onto Main Street and headed into town, with the foothills of the Slipstills lurching up in the distance straight ahead.

Daisy and Stella were among the most finely trained rides you could find anywhere, and needed virtually no guidance finding their way. The sound of their paws along the hot road was barely audible, washed out by the ruffling sound of Frank lining up his papers just so, in chronological order, careful to create a single new fold. As he pressed them back into his saddlebag, Frank said, "So, what's this you tell me about a fire last night? A fire, did I get that right?"

Elvis nodded his head affirmatively and said, "Yep, a fire. Right inside my barn." Elvis tried to continue, but Frank exclaimed, "IN YOUR BARN? I was so preoccupied with the pups back there, I didn't notice anything. I haven't seen you light a match in there since we were kids. How did you end up with a barn fire? Don't tell me someone was fooling around in there last night while you were busy with Candy, or whatever her name is. By the way, I've seen her somewhere, just can't place her."

Elvis said, "Her name's Calli, and you've probably seen her down at the train station. She just took a job with the rail line." Frank said, "Yeah, that's it. I saw her at the station the other day. How long you known her, anyway?" Elvis replied, "Oh, just a few days. Met her at Sam's and couldn't help but ask her over." Frank nodded and said, "Well, I sure can understand that. Probably would have done the same myself if I'd had the chance. You'd better be careful, my boy. Something tells me she could be trouble."

Elvis was fully aware of Frank's innate ability to sniff out a rat in most situations long before others could. Not being in the mood to jump to a conclusion on this one, however, Elvis responded, "You might be right, my friend, but the way she looks, I'm gonna need a little more than one of your hunches before I just give up on her." Frank knew that he would have a hard time arguing with that sort of logic, so he didn't bother to offer a response.

Elvis unsnapped a pocket on his gun belt, pulled out a small box, opened it up and said, "Look here. I found this clump of fur in the woods. Have you heard any rumblings lately about somebody being upset with me? You know everything that's going on around here." Frank glanced down at the evidence, and then looked back up at Elvis and said, "Sorry, partner, nothing that I know of. You're the pride and joy of this place, in case you forgot. I wouldn't get too caught up in it at the moment, my boy. We've got plenty more than that to worry about."

Frank continued, "Last week, up in the mountains outside of South Sebastian." Elvis exclaimed, "South Sebastian! We're going clear across the country again?" Frank, impatiently tapping his free forepaw on the front of his saddle, nodded and said, "Well, I didn't say that, but if you'd give me chance to finish a sentence or two, I probably would have. What are you worried about anyway? You've been home napping, eating fish, drinking wine and schmoozing for the better part of a month. We do have to work sometime, you know. Now, where was I? Oh, yes, South Sebastian."

"Seems that Clevin Pusserschmott and his wife, Melba, were up at the family lake house last weekend. They were supposed to come back this past Tuesday, but nobody's seen hide nor hair of them. Old man Pusserschmott sent a crew up there to fetch them, and all they came back with was a note demanding five million bucks if they ever want to see Clevin and Melba again.

"Then they get a wire with more instructions. The old man probably feels about the same way as we all do about Melba. Big deal if they keep her. But, they say he's about yanking his whiskers out on the prospect of anything happening to Clevin. He's the only tomcat in the family and I think pops is pretty much finished procreating. Anyway, the wire said that the family has three days to get the cash together."

P-MONEY

You could stand to know a little something about the Pusserschmott clan before you go on. Old man Pusserschmott was one of the wealthiest cats in the country, if not the world. Possibly *the* richest, although the artworks and antiquities that he and some of his contemporaries owned often had values so subjective that no one really knew for sure who was at the top of the list anymore. Suffice it to say that the Pusserschmott family didn't want for much of anything. If they did, it was because they couldn't find it or didn't know how to get it, not because they couldn't afford it.

Back in 525, just after the last spike was driven into the cross-country railroad line, Morris Pusserschmott I (as in the first) surmised that, if he could get his prized catnip fruits – favorites among the locals – to the more populous and affluent West Coast, most everyone surely would love them. And oh how right he was! The maritime voyage around the continent simply took too long, so there was no way to get his goods across the country without them spoiling along the way, but the new rail line changed all of that forever.

After about two years, things had gotten to the point where his workers could barely clear and work crop land fast enough to keep up with the demand. So, he revolutionized the clearing business, inventing an ingenious device that ran on a small steam engine, and chewed up shrubs and small trees like grass on a simple lawn. Once word got around about the Pusshog, every farmcat and landowner in the country had to have one, and before long, Morris Pusserschmott had more money than he could spend. Literally. He shifted his attention to buying companies and did so at nearly every opportunity, and most all of them turned to gold in his paws. By the time he passed away in 534, his business empire reached seemingly into every town in the country, and his son, Morris II, had taken the helm of the Pusserschmott family ship.

Most said that young Morris was even shrewder than his father, but after several years as one of the dominating forces of the feline business world, he grew tired of it all. He sold almost everything that the family owned, except for the original fruit business and an unfathomable accumulation of real estate, and turned to felinthropic ventures. When Morris III arrived in late 542, the family had donated to nearly every good cause imaginable. Unlike his gregarious ancestors, Morris III was a recluse. Beyond the exploits of the Catnip Fruit Company, which continued to roll along awash in cash with little intervention from Morris III, almost nothing was heard of the family or its myriad foundations for several years.

Morris IV was a throwback to the days of his forefathers. Elvis thought that he was an absolutely fantastic character who, even if he really didn't have to work for it, deserved everything that he had. Well, at least the material things. No one really knew for sure how it happened, but he somehow became infatuated with one of the most harebrained individuals ever to grace the feline planet. Elvis was convinced that Carla Baines Pusserschmott had been blessed with more stupidity than her husband had money, and most who knew her agreed wholeheartedly.

Carla and Morris IV had so much money to go around spending that they bothered to have only one litter of kittens, three of whom survived through adolescence. Two beautiful daughters, Sarena and Jeanine, and a handsome son named Clevin. Old man Pusserschmott always hated the "IV" suffix with a passion. He resented the fact that the decision to stick him with it was made during his kitfancy, when he obviously was in no position to lodge a protest. He resigned himself to the proposition that, should the day ever come that he would bring a son into the world, no one would dangle a V at the end of his surname.

Fortunately, the girls took after their father; astonishingly bright and engaging, and destined to keep the family empire on the right track. Clevin, on the other hand, seemed to have inherited a fair bit of his mother's cerebral void. Not that he was an absolute idiot, but certainly no match for his sisters, and always blundering whenever anything important, or unimportant but even remotely complex, needed accomplishing. Pressured by his mother, no doubt, he fell into the marital clutches of Melba Warble, a money-grubbing calico whose sole purpose in life, it seemed, was to complain until all within range of her squeaky voice were enveloped in a cloud of despair. Lost as he was, though, Clevin was quite engaging and as friendly as they came, and was loved dearly by the rest of his family.

The foothills of the great Longtail Mountains butted up against the southern and western edges of the valley that housed the thousands of acres making up the original Pusserschmott Farms. The Longtails boasted the highest peaks in the country and were one of its most beautiful ranges. Over the years, the Pusserschmott family had acquired thousands of acres in the foothills, mostly on the western side of the valley.

One of the few things that Morris III actually did in life (undoubtedly to get a bit further away from civilization) was to oversee the construction of a sprawling vacation home on Lake Claw. It was a marvel that any well-to-do feline family would have been overjoyed to have for a primary residence. To the Pusserschmotts, though, it was nothing more than a convenient, private getaway, located almost ten miles from the family mansion.

That should do for now.

- - -

Elvis said, "Five million! How did anyone make off with those two anyway? Remember when we were out there last summer to visit? They keep enough guards and servants around that lake house to hold off a small army. What kind of gang big enough to get through that force could be sneaking around those hills without being noticed?"

Fiddling with his whiskers, Frank said, "You're reading my mind, Boss. I was thinking the same thing, but apparently, Melba sent all of the help off on hiatus when she and Clevin arrived. Said it wouldn't be romantic enough with them crawling all over the place. I'll bet she's not feeling too romantic right now." Elvis asked, "So, what's all this about us being gone for two weeks maybe? Is there something else we're supposed to be doing after that?"

Frank replied, "That's where it starts to get tricky. The gang at Central think something is going on out there. They admit that they don't know anything for sure, but they've had some agents watching the area. They think there might be some sort of big operation underway and they want us to get to the bottom of it. Central says that they'll dispatch all the help we want once the kids are safe and we find out what's really going on, but they don't want to send in a gang of no-necks to cause a big ruckus just yet. 'Fraid they'll get seen and scare off whoever's behind all of this. And, they don't want to take any chances on something happening to the Pusserschmott kid and his snotty wife.

"Even the President's got his paws in the mix. You know how he and old man Pusserschmott go way back. He told Morris to tell the catnappers that the family will pay, but that it's going to take a little more time to get that kind of cash together. Let's wait and talk on the train. I'm not so sure that we ain't bein' watched around here right now anyways. Not if there's some crowd in town wanting to burn your place up."

The heat was near unbearable and only kittens could be seen in the yards, playing with whatever they could get their paws on and oblivious to the temperature. Frank hadn't stopped whistling and fidgeting since their conversation just a few minutes before, and they now were approaching a large building at the end of town. The big, faded white letters on the sign above read "Woodville Station, Est. 532" and from the sound of the steam engines whirring, it seemed like the two o'clock on the tracks beside the station was almost ready to roll out.

CHAPTER FIVE

HOME AWAY FROM HOME

The train station was one of Woodville's oldest structures. Like most of the town folk, Elvis was very fond and proud of it. Buildings constructed in those days typically were small and simple, but the town's early settlers were intent on erecting something that would impress all but the most worldly of visitors. The broad front doors arched at the top and reached nearly twelve feet into the sky. Faded to gray and splintering slightly in just a few places, but majestic nonetheless to anyone peering up from the stone steps leading to the entryway.

The sign over the ticket booth just to the right of the front doors had been askew for years. Old Mrs. Tabby smiled and waved excitedly from the booth once Elvis had gotten close enough for her waning vision to gain focus of him. He would have loved to stop and chat for a few minutes, and just walk around inside the station for a bit before leaving, but Frank was all business. Guiding Stella quickly around the side of the building toward the stable cars, he tugged authoritatively at Amos' lead line and looked back over his shoulder with an expression clearly insinuating that Elvis was holding things up. Elvis smiled and waved back at Mrs. Tabby, blew a kiss, and hoped to himself that she'd still be around when he returned.

Frank was genuinely enthralled with time. Over the years, he had developed a punctuality obsession that now bordered on the ridiculous. No, Frank never was late for anything unless the situation was *entirely* beyond his control, and that wasn't necessarily a bad thing. However, having grown to treat the whole timeliness thing as an art form, he abhorred being too early for anything just as well.

Whether it be a ferry embarkment, stagecoach appointment, train departure or whatever, right on time was the way Frank liked to be. Nothing perturbed him more than standing around waiting for an event to go off while second hands ran circles around the faces of everyone's timepieces. Although Elvis had become accustomed to the routine, the insistence on arriving at the exact time of takeoff, with absolutely no margin for error, annoyed Elvis to no end.

Today was no different. The two o'clock was ready to pull away, as Daisy, Amos and Stella were being put safely away in their stalls in the stable car at the back of the train. Elvis barely had a second for Daisy to lick him goodbye before Frank began ushering him off of the car and onto the landing, so that they could make their way toward the passenger cars. Not unexpectedly, the train suddenly lurched forward. Elvis and Frank, each lugging a fair bit of gear, were forced to begin accelerating in the hopes of making their car before the big locomotive gathered enough momentum to outpace them. They quickly were left with no choice but to launch into an all-out sprint.

When Elvis jumped aboard the first-class cabin car, he considered staying there to block the entryway, and leave Frank to walk back to the station and wait around for the next train. With Elvis not yet sure exactly where it was that they were going, or who they were meeting once they got there (not to mention that Frank had the tickets), he figured that he'd better step aside and let Frank on, at least this one last time. He wiped some foam from his mouth and then sat idly by as Frank struggled to pull himself up with all of his gear. Elvis shook his head and huffed under his breath, "I swear, Frank. Why we have to go through this every time we board a damn train is beyond me."

They had come a long way since their first cross-country trek together. Stowaways huddled in the back of a smelly stable car, hoping not to be spotted by a porter. Since then, Elvis and Frank had been in agreement that travel accommodations were important matters, and that if they weren't going to be comfortable – very comfortable, then they would just have to find a different line of work. The check writers back at Treasury always swallowed hard at the arrival of Frank's reimbursement requests for official travel, but results were results and no one bothered to argue with them anymore after so many successful missions. The price of having the best, Elvis always said. Thus, the unnecessary hassle undergone to catch an ordinary train soon was forgotten, as Elvis and Frank stepped into their oversized luxury cabin.

Just as they dropped their baggage to the floor, Alley came bouncing through the door. Quite attractive with long, light brown fur and charcoal black eyes, and wearing a bleach-white, tight-fitting apron. She immediately began about the cabin, setting drinks on the cocktail table, pushing Elvis and Frank into their posh leather seats, propping their hind paws up, and shuttling their portage out of the way and into the closet.

As she scurried around picking up pieces of stray hair, she began to ramble, not looking directly at either of them, "It's so good to see you boys! Been so long since the last time, we were afraid you might have finally given up on all of this running around. You know, decided to call it quits and just relax." She peeked up at Frank and said, "I mean, I assume this isn't a pleasure trip. Not with all of those papers stuffed in your bags. Huh, Frankie boy?"

Before either of them could respond, Alley smiled and said, "Now, you boys get yourselves up to the dining car before too long. Lunch ends at three and our new cook, Calli, hates to go over. Likes to get that kitchen cleaned up so she can start getting ready for dinner."

Elvis and Frank looked at each other curiously, and Elvis quickly turned to ask Alley, "This Calli, is she black with pretty blue eyes?" Elvis held his forepaw out and said, "About this high at the shoulder?" Alley responded, "Yep, I think that's her. And a body to die for. Every tom we've had on the train starts foaming at the mouth when she gets within ten feet. You know her, slick? I'm not surprised, figures you would."

"Let's just say I think we've met," Elvis replied. As she stepped into the aisle and started to slide the door shut, Alley smiled and quipped, "Some things never change." Frank tossed a large coin in her direction and Elvis hollered toward the door, "Thanks for everything, beautiful! We'll see you in a little while." Alley caught the coin in her teeth and dropped it into her front apron pocket with a wink. "Well I sure hope so," she said as she closed the door.

Elvis pulled himself out of his chair, walked across to the big window, stood up on his hind legs, pulled back the curtains and stuck his head out for a moment to cool off in the breeze generated by the speed of the train. The sky was crystal clear, the sun was past its peak and the green tree-covered foothills of the Slipstills were fast approaching. The train soon would make its inevitable zigzag through Maloney's pass. He pulled his head back inside, but kept his stare directly at the mountains and said, "Isn't this beautiful, Frankie?"

There was no response. Sitting still and relaxing for a few moments wasn't in the cards for Frank, who already was spreading maps and documents all over a big, red velvet couch and a glass-topped, wrought iron coffee table. The familiar sound of rustling paper obviated the need for Elvis to turn and see what was happening. Still staring out the window, he pleaded with calm exasperation, "Frank, do we have to go through all of that right now?"

Frank was busy lining things up on the table and barely looked up as he responded, "Elvis, don't you think I know you well enough by now? We haven't had five minutes to talk about exactly where we're going or what we're doing, and I'm not that clear on all of it myself. We go down to the dining car and get caught up in that scene, and I'll be lucky to see you alone again before we get to Littermark Station." With that, Elvis sat down, and he and Frank began flipping pages.

CHAPTER SIX

COULD HAVE, SHOULD HAVE

The Tin Roof Gang had wreaked minor havoc off and on for over two years now, popping up sporadically at various locales up and down the East Coast. Until recently, the operation hadn't become pervasive enough to warrant a major initiative by the feds, but the brain trust at Central had been wary for some time that things might be coming to a head. Elvis and Frank had heard a few stories, but never were that impressed, and always thought of the Tin Roof Gang as a disorganized, ragtag bunch not worthy of much attention. Any decent local law enforcement outfit should have been able to deal with them without much fanfare, they thought.

This sentiment grew primarily out of the fact that the Tin Roof Gang apparently were led by Harold Fatscat, a fleabag who had busted out of San Catin prison a few years back, not long after he had been thrown in for assassinating a mid-level government official. Elvis had gotten the call on that one – his first cross country mission – back in the winter of 560. He found Fatscat with minimal effort, hiding out in some hills about fifteen miles from the prison with three other murderers who had escaped with him.

Elvis casually sat down by their campsite early one morning and began to whistle a tune. Fatscat snored so loudly that it probably drowned out his chance at hearing the ruckus that was about to brew. His unkempt colleagues, courageous in their numbers, woke up and snidely told Elvis that if he didn't leave on his own right away, they'd find a nice hole for him to rot in. Fatscat awoke quickly enough from the staccato sound of a trio of gunshots, followed by the sequential thuds of his cohorts falling to the ground as they reached hopelessly for their pistols.

Fatscat didn't bother to look back as he ran from the clearing toward the forest in a blur, but before he could get behind the nearest tree, Elvis had shot his right ear and left foreleg clean off. Elvis would have finished the job then and there, but the higher-ups back at Central had wanted Fatscat to be taken alive. As the sordid reality of making a cross-country return trip with a bloody Fatscat cuffed to his leg began to set in, Elvis' mind wandered for a superior alternative.

As he tried mightily to convince himself that there must be a suitable option, Elvis thought to himself, how much of a threat could Fatscat really be at this point? Seriously! Bleeding heavily, limping around the woods with three legs, one ear and zero friends. He'd suffer far more in the wilderness than he would anywhere that the folks at Central would want to put him. Elvis promptly wrapped up the ear and leg, threw them into his saddlebag, rode Daisy back to Littermark Station, and sent the souvenirs to Central on the next train out with a note that read:

14 January 560

Ladies and Gentlemen:

Enclosed you will find the right ear and left foreleg of the "formidable" Harold Fatscat, whom you sent me all the way across this great country of ours to capture. His three scummy cohorts lie here dead in a pile, not twenty strides from where I presently find myself situated, and I soon will inform the local authorities of their whereabouts. The sound of Fatscat limping through the woods still is audible, and were it not for the obnoxious odor emanating from his filthy body, I probably would retrieve him and return him to your custody, as you had requested. It is not worthy of my effort, and it is in any event quite doubtful that he is in much of a position to harm anyone. He will be lucky to live, and I find it a fitting punishment that he should suffer here among the elements and the local predators.

Please know that, should you not go too overboard in your desires, I stand ready to help your cause whenever and wherever I am needed. That said, I do request that you please not again send a cat to do a kitten's work. Not me, at least. I well know that this is my first mission all the way across our fine land. Maybe you considered it to be some sort of a test. Thank you so much for conducting it in the dead of winter! I do not harbor any ill will at this point, but I trust that you will call on me in the future only when there truly is a need for someone of my ability.

Faithfully Yours,

Elvis

Having dispatched with Fatscat's pieces, Elvis embarked on his own train ride, straight to Catson City for three days of gambling and entertainment. He was unstoppable on the craps and poker tables that weekend, and returned home with what was to him in those years a very tidy sum. The company of Catrina Wildsen, a gorgeous red-haired who introduced Elvis to the pleasures of fine wine and whose family owned the best restaurant in town, wasn't bad either.

As for Fatscat, Elvis and Frank deemed him not worthy of much respect, but they were not so stubborn as to completely rule out the possibility that things may well have changed. If there was one lesson that they had learned in dealing with their rivals over the years, it was that those who rank among the scum of the feline universe often are capable of surprising feats and unexpected resurgences.

Unlikely as it once may have seemed, it looked like Fatscat just might have pulled one off this time. As Elvis read further, he began to regret that he hadn't blown off another one of Fatscat's legs when he had the chance and just left him there for certain death. Not to mention that he now was feeling a tad foolish for the patronizing tone of the note that he had enclosed with Fatscat's body parts.

According to the limited intelligence that was available, the heart of the Tin Roof Gang was holed up somewhere in the highest elevations of the Longtails. Down below, it appeared, a full-blown crew of sleaze had been assembled along a sizable chunk of the Eastern Seaboard. In the earlier days of the enterprise, the only useful tools that the Tin Roof Gang had at their disposal were force, intimidation and trickery. They now were able to couple those tactics with handsome bribes, and were having less and less trouble obtaining cooperation from all but the most principled and well-off shippers, traders, mariners, bureaucats and policecats.

Unfortunately for Fatscat, Collarsport and Leashing, by far the largest East Coast port cities, remained essentially free from Tin Roof influence and seemed hopelessly out of reach. Their powerful businessmen were far too wealthy to be extorted for the "cooperation" and "assistance" that a cruddy gang might try to impose upon them. To make matters worse, their public officials were too highly compensated to be enticed in any meaningful way by the bribes typically passed out by the Tin Roof Gang. The same was true for top law enforcement officials, whose substantial outfits were more than worthy of repelling any attempt to take something by force.

It was at this point that the intelligence got murky. Fatscat reportedly was working with someone in the area to assemble a large group of thugs for something, but no one knew what for sure. Some of the brass at Central thought that Fatscat might try to make a move on something in one of the big towns, but Elvis and Frank knew that to do so would require a cadre of experienced fighters. Something that even the most organized band of outlaws would be hard-pressed to accomplish unless they had the money to buy off virtually an entire police force, and that just couldn't be done at Collarsport or Leashing. Well, anything might be possible with five million, but with all of the dirty cash that the Tin Roof Gang was handling by now, what was the urgency? And why catnap a Pusserschmott and chance getting the feds all up in their business?

CHAPTER SEVEN

STUDY BREAK

As the train emerged from the mountain pass and the rails began to straighten, Elvis picked up his glass from the table, only to see that his drink was approaching near empty. He said, "Frank, let's just grab a bite while we've got the chance. I promise we'll make it quick. Dinner's too far off." Skeptical as he was, Frank was nearly famished himself and he had little choice but to reluctantly acquiesce.

Nearly all of the passengers on the train had finished their lunches by now and the dining car was almost empty. Elvis and Frank went straight to their favorite table, a small roundtop in the back corner of the room, with a view that currently looked out over a small river. No sooner had they seated themselves was Annie standing right in front of them on her hind legs, with a smile as big as her fluffy, white belly.

Frank started to say, "I'll have a," but before he could get another word out, Annie finished his sentence, "Gin and tonic with a lime wedge?" Frank nodded affirmatively while Elvis, having witnessed the foregoing exchange, simply looked up at Annie and smiled. Annie veered her eyes toward him without lifting her head and continued, "And a bourbon and ginger for you, I assume?"

Elvis nodded and said, "I really don't know why you waste your energy walking all the way over here to ask." Annie, still smiling, patted her tummy as she replied, "Can't argue with you there, kiddo, but this little girl needs all the exercise she can get, if you know what I mean." Elvis and Frank looked at each other and chuckled as she turned around and waddled toward the service bar only a few steps away.

Annie returned in the blink of an eye with large tumblers and a big block of cheese with crackers. As she set them down, she said, "That's Muenster. Our new cook heard y'all are on board and said you'd probably like this. How'd she know you guys are so . . . cheesy?" Annie snickered and snorted, as she usually did when she let loose with one of her stupid jokes. "Just a lucky guess, I suppose," said Elvis, as Annie hustled across the room and disappeared through the double doors leading into the kitchen. Unlike most of the staff, Annie never went through just one door at a time, and they both swung rapidly back and forth in her wake.

Elvis and Frank reached for their drinks in tandem and looked out over the river. Elvis said, "So, we're going to the end of the line, I assume? Pulling into Littermark about this time Monday?" Frank replied, "Yep, two-thirteen if everything goes according to schedule. So, we've got a couple of days to figure out how we're going to handle all of this before old man Pusserschmott's boys come to the station to get us."

Elvis said, "Is it me or are you starting to slip? I don't think I can remember us leaving town together without you knowing exactly where we're going, what we're doing and when we're gonna do it. It's not like you." Frank said, "I don't like it any more than you, partner. This happened so fast, and the brass was so all over my furry ass to get going, that I just didn't have time to look at everything. Anything, really. It was all I could do to get those maps and papers together, and get to your place in time to make this train. Did you see all of that crap I've got? I'm worried this time, E. I really am."

Nary another word was spoken as a pair of swordfish sandwiches disappeared into their stomachs even faster than Annie had whisked them out to the table, and Frank was taken by surprise when Elvis suggested that they return to the cabin and get back to work. Unless there was some sort of emergency underway, Elvis never left the dining car without stopping at the bar for a windup beverage. Frank certainly couldn't recall it anyway. "Are you sure?"

Frank said in a surprised voice. Elvis replied, "I'm sure. I said we'd get right back to it, didn't I?"

They walked back through the dining car and, just as they were about to exit, a voice rang out from the kitchen doors: "Where are you two going so fast?" They turned around to see Calli stepping behind the bar in a messy apron and a white chef's hat. She said in a sarcastic tone, "Too busy to chat for a few minutes before I have to get back to work?"

Elvis replied, "You didn't say you were working this trip." She smiled and said, "I wasn't planning on it, but after you ran me out of the house today, I figured I may as well come pick up a shift. The other cooks always are looking for time off during the summer." Elvis said defensively, "Run you off?" Then he pointed at Frank and said, "That was his idea, not mine." She said, "I understand. Duty calls when you're Elvis the Gunslinger, doesn't it?" Elvis began walking back toward the bar and said, "My only duty at the moment is to have a drink here with you."

Frank quickly got back to more worrying. Something about Calli bothered him and it wasn't simple jealousy over the attention of his best friend. Just being associated with Elvis had landed Frank in more romantic interludes than he ever could recount. No, Frank approved of the activity in general terms; he just had an uneasy feeling about this one.

Why Elvis was occupied with her and away from the house when a fire sprang up in his barn was intriguing at a minimum. Suspicious was more like it. No one ever had chanced arson at Chez Elvis. Ever. Anytime. While he was home? Right there under his whiskers! Then she runs straight from Elvis' house to the train this afternoon to pick up an extra stint. Five days round trip, without even bothering to stop at home? Something definitely was up, or at least Frank sure thought so.

"I've got to get started on dinner soon, but I guess I can have one with *you*," Calli said, as she walked to the far end of the bar and began pouring some vodkat and catnip juice into a tall glass. Neither

Elvis nor Frank could take his eyes off of her as she walked around the other end of the bar, took the glasses from their table, refilled them and set them on the bar. The three of them then proceeded to ramble on pointlessly for nearly half an hour.

With the tops of their drinks having sunken to the bottoms of their glasses, Calli announced that it was time to get back to the kitchen. Elvis kissed her paw and told her that he hoped to see her again before the night was over. "I don't think you have to worry about that," she said, as Elvis turned and sped up to catch Frank, who already was out the door and back into the first-class car.

As soon as their cabin door shut behind them, Frank said, "Something bothers me about her, my man. It sure would be easier to not like her if she wasn't such a knockout." Elvis squeezed himself onto the only space on the couch still uncovered by clutter, looked up at his colleague and said, "I'm surprised at you. I've really known the lady for barely a day, and you've spent all of half an hour with her. I'll admit that a couple of things might seem a little strange, but I sure don't see any reason for getting all worked up like you are."

Frank pulled one of the leather chairs up to the coffee table and said, "You wouldn't know it from the way you act around her. You look like a schoolboy on his first date." "Don't worry about me," Elvis assured him. "Don't you think I can handle this sort of thing by now? If she *is* up to something, a lot of success I'll have figuring it out if I start acting suspicious around her. And that goes for *you*, too. And, if I'm going to be acting like nothing unusual is happening, don't you think I should have at least a little bit of fun while I'm at it?"

Frank replied, "I guess you're right, E. Tipping her off certainly isn't going to do us any good. Be careful, though. Some of us like having you around, and I don't want to think about what they'll do to me if I ever come back to town from one of these crazy trips with you in a box."

Just as he was about to walk Elvis through some of the papers on the coffee table, Frank paused, stared down quizzically and said,

"E, did you move any of these?" "Haven't touched them," Elvis replied. Frank looked up seriously and said, "You're sure?" Elvis looked funnily at Frank and replied, "I'm positive, Frank. What's the big deal?" Frank shrugged his shoulders and said, "Oh, I guess it's nothing."

Frank didn't *think* anything was amiss. He was sure of it. But, he thought better to not start raising his eyebrows at the moment. Nothing important appeared to be missing, and after the discussion that they had just completed about being careful around Calli, another suggestion that things were out of whack undoubtedly would have Elvis harping on Frank again about his paranoid tendencies.

Someone definitely had been in the cabin. The two pages on top of his pile were dated later than the one below them. Not an unusual occurrence for regular folk, but Frank was anal about his work and especially official papers. He *always* kept his documents in chronological order whenever he was about to review them to plan for a mission, and he knew with certitude that he had left them that way before leaving the cabin for lunch.

Alley? Not likely. She always was a little too nosey about what they were up to, but she also knew how Frank hated anyone interfering with the order of his documents. She certainly would have put them back exactly as Frank had left them. Not to mention that their empty glasses still were on the cocktail table; Alley surely would have taken them with her if she had stopped in. Frank couldn't help thinking that Calli's sudden appearance at the bar when she should have been cleaning up the kitchen must somehow have been related to the intrusion.

Frank reached back into his bag, pulled out a map of the entire East Coast, got up and began walking toward the closet. He reached in and pulled out a large, wooden easel, set it in front of the coffee table, spread out the map on it and then returned to his chair. Nervously twitching his mouth right and left, and licking his forelegs clean every few seconds, Frank was pawing through all sorts of documents, raising his eyes up at the map from time to time to get his bearings. Elvis was busy staring into his own little pile of paper.

CHAPTER EIGHT

MORE SNOOPING

When his head finally began nodding under the weight of information overload, Elvis proclaimed, "I'll be back in a few minutes. I want to give my eyes a little breather, and go back and check on the pups. Wanna come?" Frank said, "Naw, you go ahead. I wanna get through a little more of this." Frank actually was dying for a break, probably more so than Elvis. Sitting in one place for more than ten or fifteen minutes was a chore for nervous Frank, much less hours at a time. After what had happened when they stepped out for lunch, however, he was intent on not leaving the cabin unoccupied unless there was absolutely no way to avoid it.

As soon as the door closed behind Elvis, Frank seized upon the opportunity to search around for clues about who had been thoughtful enough to drop in for a visit while they were out. There was little to be gleaned. The guns and ammunition appeared to have been untouched, and it didn't look like anyone had been in either of the saddlebags, especially since the wad of cash that Elvis had brought along seemed to have been completely untampered with. Your average burglar would have been far more interested in that than anything else in the room, but Frank was convinced that this was not your day-to-day intruder. Giving up for now on his search for clues, he poured himself a glass of water, sat back in his chair, stared out the window and waited for Elvis to return.

Moving quickly through the passenger cabin cars was not Elvis' forte. He always was friendly, and made time to stop and chat for at least a moment whenever he could. Usually for longer if an attractive female was involved. It took him almost five minutes to get to the back of the first-class car and another ten to make it through the two second-class cars, and he considered himself lucky to have been able to do it that quickly. Good fortune for him that many passengers still were mired in their post-lunch naps, a traditional feline pastime.

The cargo car didn't carry with it the same sorts of distractions and Elvis sprinted through, dodging bags, boxes and assorted other containers. When he finally reached the stable car, the first thing that he saw was the back of some worn brown coveralls and a faded red straw hat, with nothing but a pair of fluffy white paws and the gray hairs of a big head sticking out of them. Elvis stood quietly in the car's entrance, as the train's wheels chugging along the tracks sounded loudly in the background. Then he screamed at nearly the top of his lungs, "TOMCAT, MY FRIEND, HOW ARE YOU?"

The fact that he had long since passed retirement age no doubt played a part. Consider also that he'd worked in that open-air stable car for the better part of his life, and it was no surprise that Tom really couldn't hear all that well. Nevertheless, he turned his head quickly in response to Elvis' high-volume greeting. A big smile came over his face, as his eyes focused through his thick glasses and the sight of Elvis became clear. Clear for Tom, anyway.

Tom replied, "Well, well! I thought that sounded like you, my boy. Can't be too sure anymore these days, you know. Old ears ain't as sharp as they used to be. Figured you was with us, though, once I saw Daisy back there. And Stella, too, so's I guess ya got Frankie with ya, huh?" Elvis replied, "Yep, he's here. And I assume you saw Amos? Behaving himself, I hope." Tom said, "Naw, he ain't no trouble. Matter of fact, last time I came back here to look in on things, somebody was over there checkin' him out."

Elvis looked at Tom inquisitively and Tom continued, "It seemed like he was mostly looking around at the bags, not Amos, but my eyes ain't what they used to be, even with these here glasses. By the time I made it over there, he was just pettin' Amos and sayin' how handsome he is. Young Amos wasn't too happy about it, either. Shakin' his head all round and round, and barkin', so I told the guy he'd better just leave Amos alone. Even Daisy barked at him a couple of times from across the car. He was a big, big guy with white fur."

"Anything else?" Elvis asked. Tom replied, "No, nothing that I can think of. He was just your typical real big male." Then, Tom blurted, "Wait a minute, Elvis. There was one more thing. He had a pretty good chunk missing off of his left shoulder. Nothin' permanent, I don't think. Just looked like he'd been in a scuffle or something. Big as *he* was, though, I'd hate to see who it was that he was scufflin' with. Unless he was tangling with somebody like you, of course." Tom smiled and laughed, and patted Elvis on the back as they walked toward the rear of the car.

Elvis looked at Tom and said, "A big guy with white fur and a chunk out of his left shoulder?" Tom nodded his head and Elvis continued, "No, he wasn't tangling with me. Not this time, anyway. Have you seen him back here since?" Tom replied, "Nope. That's the last I seen of him, but I'll get word up to you right away if I do."

"Thanks, Tom," said Elvis. Elvis walked over to Daisy and Stella for a moment, gave them each a pat on the chest and hollered back at Tom, "LOOKS LIKE YOU'VE GOT EVERYTHING UNDER CONTROL AROUND HERE AS USUAL." He walked over to Amos, looked around to see if any of the gear had been fooled with, and continued, "DO LET ME KNOW IF YOUNG AMOS OVER HERE STARTS ACTING UP ON YOU." Elvis looked at Amos with a wink and a smile and continued, "I'M GONNA GET BACK AND CHECK ON FRANKIE. YOU KNOW HOW FIDGETY HE GETS WHEN HE'S STUCK IN A ROOM WAITING ON SOMEONE."

Elvis walked back through the car and toward the front door, and Tom said, "Don't worry, Chief. They're in good paws. Good to see you, Elvis. Don't be such a stranger, okay?" Elvis smiled, looked back over his shoulder and spoke semi-loudly, "Don't worry, we'll see you before we go."

Elvis pulled down the front of his hat and kept his eyes fixed on the floor as he cruised through the passenger cars. He wasn't able to avoid everyone, but his passage back was far more efficient than the opposing trip that had preceded it. The sound of the door opening and closing startled Frank, who was about to doze off, and Elvis walked over to the couch and sat down with his forelegs crossed in contemplation. Frank immediately knew that something was up.

"What is it?" Frank asked. Elvis looked over and replied, "Tomcat said someone was snooping around by Amos, near our gear, a little while ago. Also said that Amos wasn't liking it one bit, even when the guy started petting him. You know how Amos loves to make new friends. And Daisy was barking at the guy from across the way. When's the last time you've heard her do that, except when she was really upset or trying to get our attention for something? I can't believe I didn't hear her myself. Must've been when we were eating lunch."

Frank said, "Or when we were having that drink with Calli. Did Tom get a good look at him?" Elvis replied, "Yeah, Tom saw him go right by. And guess what else?" Elvis paused for a moment and Frank said, "Well . . . what?" Elvis replied, "Tomcat said he was big and white, with a chunk of flesh ripped out of his shoulder. Remember that bloody chunk of white fur I found in the woods this morning?" Frank nodded and Elvis said, "That's a little too much coincidence for my blood."

Frank said, "I hear you, partner. And since you brought it up, I've got a little more news for you." Elvis cocked his right eye and looked curiously as Frank continued, "Somebody paid our cabin a little visit while we were at lunch. Nothing seems to be missing, but my papers were a bit out of order when we got back, and I know exactly how I left them. Whoever it was had to be looking through them." Elvis got up and started for the closet, but Frank interrupted, "Don't worry. I said they didn't take anything."

Elvis stopped in his tracks, spun on his left hind paw and went back to the couch, where he sat for a moment with a disturbed look on his face. He leaned back, put his forepaws behind his head, looked up at the ceiling and said, "You know, I expect some hiccups once we get out there, but trouble in my *barn*? Trouble on the *train*? I think somebody knows we're coming, my friend, and I'd sure like to know how, because *I* didn't even know until you showed up at my door this morning."

CHAPTER NINE

VERY SAFEKEEPING

The sun had dropped out of sight behind the train long ago, and not a peep had been heard out of their cabin. The hardwoods that once were the floor had been supplanted by what now looked to be one big piece of paper, a collage if you will, and Elvis and Frank were crawling back and forth over it like little kittens.

Elvis was amazed at how Frank had gotten all of it into his saddlebags. Where there weren't maps, there were orders, memos, reports, notes, letters, drawings, receipts. No surface was safe from pulp. On tables, on ledges, on the seats and arms of chairs, even balanced on cups and glasses. And every scrap that didn't have a place to sit was somehow gummed or glued to a wall or window. Even Frank, the high priest of organization, often found himself trying to locate a misplaced document. It appeared to be more complex than the usual mission, but Elvis and Frank loved the game of it all, and they tackled their work with great enthusiasm.

Regardless of how enthused they may have been, stomachs were starting to growl with nine-thirty racing upon them. Another thirty minutes and they'd miss dinner altogether. Already victimized by an unannounced visit during their previous meal, they couldn't very well leave the room in its present state, and Elvis was worried that they might exhaust the entire thirty just gathering the mess and putting it someplace where it couldn't easily be found. Frank, on the other hand, was buoyed by what he considered to be near-starvation, not to mention the opportunity to get his disarrayed materials back into their proper place and order.

Frank's excitement was almost humorous as he ran around the room in a whirlwind, snatching, unsticking, folding, piling. Elvis wanted to assist, but his desire to help straighten things was so dwarfed by Frank's obsession, that Elvis felt he would be more in the way than anything else. So, he plopped onto the couch to watch the cleaning tornado that was Frank. It couldn't have taken five minutes and he had transformed an entire roomful of clutter into a neat little pile, barely higher than his belly as he stood on all fours. Finally, a legitimate opportunity to put one of the mighty Sabertooths to use!

It had been almost two years since the day when the eyes nearly popped out of the big, fat head of Kit Cashen, the crotchety Secretary of the Treasury. He stared down with a facial expression that at once combined the elements of horror and amazement, peering at a pawwritten note brought to him by one of his minions.

11 July 561

Dear Mr. Cashen:

> *Please accept my apologies for taking your time with this matter, but surely you will remember specifying that I should send directly to your attention all requests of this nature.*

> *You may know that I recently returned from a long mission in the North, the result of which will save our fine country several million dollars. Given your position, I thought that you would find this particularly comforting.*

> *Fear not for your time, though, as I will get to the point. On this mission, I had the pleasure of encountering one Cena Sabertooth, the founder of the esteemed Sabertooth Lock and Safe Company. Mrs.*

Sabertooth has made to us a proposition that I feel we cannot refuse.

I often encounter the need to safeguard important documents during my travels. Many of these documents are among the most classified that my agency maintains, often relating to the very security of our nation. It is for this reason that I respectfully request that the government purchase two Sabertooth Model 9L safes, one for each train cabin on which I travel for official business.

The Model 9L is of an ideal size for my use (an interior of 8.5 inches wide, by 6 high, by 4 deep) and possibly is the most technically advanced safe in its class. It is fireproof, impact-proof and, literally, uncrackable. Although it sells at a list price of $550, Mrs. Sabertooth has offered to sell to us two brand new Model 9L's for only $650 - a savings of $450!

I would appreciate it if you would send to me as soon as possible a draft, payable to the Sabertooth Lock and Safe Company, in the amount of $650. I will see that it is directed to the appropriate persons and that the safes are properly installed in the cabins where they are needed.

Faithfully Yours,

Elvis

Cashen belted out a roar that rang through the Treasury building like church bells on a Sunday morning. His monthly salary didn't approach $650! Worse was the fact that, had he refused it, Elvis likely would have gone over Cashen's head and almost certainly would have succeeded in getting what he wanted. So, after he cooled down a bit, Cashen bit down hard, wrote the draft himself and sent it along with a note, pleading for Elvis and Frank to refrain, at least for a while, from furniture shopping.

As useful as Elvis and Frank thought the safes would be, however, there seldom was a legitimate need for them. If Cashen had known what kind of dust they were collecting, he would have been doing backflips from the top of the Capitol building. Sure, Elvis and Frank put things in them from time to time, but only for novelty, really. They always *thought*, until now anyway, that no one other than trusted attendants such as Alley entered their cabin during a trip.

Nothing ever had been stolen or tampered with, and Elvis and Frank routinely left official documents, weapons and large amounts of cash in plain view when they stepped out. The disappointment that they felt about having to abandon their casual habits, however, was far outweighed by their excitement about having a bona fide reason to take advantage of the security offered by one of the Sabertooths. This one use alone could be worth more than scores of $650 checks, Elvis thought, as he smiled and whispered to himself, "Damn, if we weren't right again!"

Both safes had been fitted to work on the same key, and Frank and Elvis each had one of the three copies that existed; the other was tucked away safely at Central Headquarters. Elvis stooped down in the back of the closet, unlocked the safe and slid Frank's neat pile of maps and papers inside. He shut the safe, started for the door, and said to Frank with a wink and a smile, "Maybe you'll get the chance to work the safe sometime."

CHAPTER TEN

MR. HAPPY!

"TWO THOUSAND!! What kind of operation do they think I'm running? Does it look like we're growing money trees up here? The guy doesn't make that in a whole year. Who offered him that much? Lancer, I'll bet, that little sonofabitch. They ought to lock me away for sending a nitwit like him down there in the first place. I knew better. Try to give a crumb a chance and this is what I get. Do I have to do everything myself?

"You get word down there for him to get his measly tail back up here right away. I'll send someone down there who knows how to get the job done. Two thousand dollars for him? IT'LL TAKE US THREE MONTHS JUST TO BREAK EVEN OVER THERE AT THAT RATE. And we haven't even gotten to the merchants yet. What does he think, that they all get on board for free? I'm going to fry Lancer's little hide if he's not afraid to come up here and show it."

- - -

And so it was, another sunny day in the life of Harold Fatscat. He was venting to his right paw man, Treeclimb, late in the afternoon about a request for money to bribe a mid-level local official in a town where the Tin Roof Gang was trying to make new inroads. Unless you fell asleep earlier on, or you think that mammals re-grow appendages in our story, you know a little bit about Fatscat. That he hops around as best he can on three legs and that there is a hole on the right side of his head where most cats display an ear.

Beyond these maladies, Fatscat also carried with him a few random scars, testimony to a much-rougher-than-average life. His general aversion to any sort of bathing wrought a fairly strong malodor that kept even his most trusted colleagues from maintaining sustained proximity to him for anything more than a pawful of seconds. Throw in for breath enhancement the ubiquitous cigar or cigarette that stuck out of either side of his mouth or the forepaw that he still had possession of, and you can imagine the rest for yourself.

Don't let appearances fool you. Fatscat was an extraordinary individual in his own right and was not to be taken lightly. One on one in a shootout with someone the caliber of Elvis the Gunslinger? Well, that might be a different matter, but Fatscat was careful to avoid situations like those. And for all of the cowardice that lived within him, there was a corresponding amount of cunning.

To be sure, all he had created was borne of underhandedness and sleaze, but then again, architecting a complex and successful criminal enterprise often is a more difficult task than building one on the up and up. There may be fewer rules to abide, but there also are a lot more cats out there trying to stop you and no one useful to turn to for recompense or assistance when you are wronged. Not to mention that finding and keeping good help is an arduous task when the candidates treading in the applicant pool almost uniformly are not the best and brightest.

Somehow, he seemed to have pulled it off, at least for the time being. From that dreadful (for him) day when he crawled through the woods bleeding nearly to death and with the loudest ringing in his head that he ever had experienced, he scratched and clawed – no pun intended – his way back to the top of his rotten field. From a strategic hold high atop Mount Aracat, Fatscat worked tirelessly. Issuing orders upon orders to a low-life group of rowdy and occasionally uncontrollable "officers" who were charged with overseeing the rapidly expanding day-to-day operations of his smelly empire. Plotting the course of the Tin Roof Gang was not easy business, but someone had to do it.

He spent the majority of his waking hours seated in the big oak chair behind the industrial-looking metal desk in the rear of his unkempt office. The earthen floor was dark and the lone window was small and faced due east – to Fatscat's right as he looked out from his perch. The desk was not particularly cluttered with paper, but cleaning was not a high priority for Fatscat. So, where there was not paper or an ashtray, there was dust. Lots of dust. A small, grimy wooden table was situated against each of the side walls of the room, and a few rusty metal chairs were scattered about. Places for his minions to settle momentarily while he barked out orders or listened to reports of the latest activities.

Fatscat liked to keep the chairs close to the front of his desk, although his underlings frequently came into the room when he was absent, surreptitiously sliding chairs away from his desk and nearer to the small tables. Any trick to distance themselves from the mixed aromas of Fatscat's grimy fur and untoward breath, should one of them end up stuck in the office for an extended period.

Fatscat often could be found staring up at the Tin Roof empire, depicted on a huge map that took up nearly the entire wall behind his desk. When he wasn't busy just perusing the kingdom, he was adjusting the tacks, pins and other objects that he used for symbols to track the elements of Tin Roof commerce. He paced around occasionally, but his confrontation with Elvis in the woods a few years back understandably had made routine walking – simply for sport anyway – usually more trouble than it was worth.

Tomboy, the telegraph operator, was in the unfortunate position of having to make constant appearances in Fatscat's office, although she tried to keep each visit as brief as possible. Whether delivering the latest news or jotting down the next order for transmission, her foremost endeavor each time was to hold her breath for the duration of her stay. Treeclimb also was a frequent guest, though he had mastered the art of staying close to the door at the far end of the office while appearing attentive and involved in whatever one-sided discussion might be underway.

Fatscat always intended to keep the operation at headquarters to a bare minimum, something that would be tough to spot if anyone started to catch on. But, as the gang's reach began to extend and its members began to multiply, it became impossible for Fatscat to keep things under control with one small office and a pair of staff. Over time, he reluctantly allowed what once had been nothing more than a lone, tiny shack to transform into what now would be best described as a small compound.

Below Fatscat's office and the telegraph room that stood behind it were three medium-sized buildings. Simple, nondescript, rectangular structures that resembled military barracks more than anything else. They were unimpressive for the most part, but since most of the labor had been provided by career criminals whose skills generally did not include construction and architecture, Fatscat was thrilled that the buildings stood at all. The interior of each building was barren, save for some beds, each with a small wooden table and lantern set beside it.

Just below these buildings was a recently-expanded mess hall, complete with a rudimentary kitchen, and a bit farther down the northern side of the mountaintop were a fairly large barn and paddock for keeping the dogs of those who occupied the compound, both permanent residents and those on visitation.

Above all of this, but still below Fatscat's office, was a small building where Fatscat, Treeclimb and Tomboy resided. Fatscat originally had ordered that a smaller, one-room structure be built for the purpose, but in an effort to put some space (and fresh air) between them, Treeclimb convinced Fatscat that an individual of Fatscat's nobility should have his own quarters, and that Treeclimb and Tomboy (who was quite attractive) should share an auxiliary room in the building. Fatscat's unbridled ego would not allow him to refute the suggestion, and so it came to be.

Most of the compound's occupants were part of Fatscat's sleazy corps of mid-level "officers." A place to report their doings, get new orders, and rest themselves and their dogs for a day or two before going back out to help wreak more havoc. There were at least fifteen, probably twenty, in total, but seldom did more than six or seven stay at the compound at any one time. One of the residence buildings housed semi-permanent guests. Mostly big, scuzzy thugs who carried around rifles and took turns keeping watch over the place (when they weren't busy eating, that is), and Calvatore, who hailed from Cataly and had been the resident cook almost since the kitchen had been built.

The only woman that anyone could remember entering the compound other than Tomboy was Felaine, whose job it was to oversee the stable and take care of the dogs, including those who were in for a visit. She had lived in the nearby woods all of her life and her husband had run off a few months ago. Although she was nothing like Fatscat and his minions, most of whom she despised, she loved dogs and needed the money badly to support her six kittens. Paying work was not easy to find high up in the Longtails.

Since the day he lost his leg and ear, Fatscat understandably had been nervous about the possibility of an ambush, so a few thugs constantly scoured the compound and the surrounding area, on the watch for intruders. Or at least Fatscat thought so. At any given time, one if not more could be found napping under a distant tree. Being caught always resulted in a few lashes or sometimes a worse fate, but it still happened not that infrequently. Fatscat's paranoia dictated that one of the guards follow him personally at virtually all times, wherever he went. The latest to be caught in an unauthorized slumber was the one who did the honors until the next violator was discovered. Heinrich currently was the unfortunate one.

Now, where were we?

- - -

After Fatscat finished his tantrum about Lancer offering an excessive bribe to the top assistant of a small town mayor, he hopped into his chair, leaned back, took a puff from his sloppy, chewed up cigar and looked across his office at Treeclimb. Treeclimb was without a doubt the cleanest and most urbane cat in the entire lot, although that wasn't saying much given the level of competition. He was medium-sized, brown and tan, with dark eyes and a strong build, and although he basically was as rotten as the rest of the gang, he fancied himself a sophisticate and sported nearly perfect diction.

"Harold," Treeclimb said in an uppity tone, "I couldn't agree more. Two thousand is outrageous and we shouldn't pay it, but is there some purpose to your jumping around like that? It certainly isn't helping me think through this. I'll talk with Tomboy and we'll get someone down there to take care of it, but I would be ever so appreciative if you would restrain yourself once in a while and quit acting like a distressed kitten."

Fatscat leaned forward in his chair, glared at Treeclimb for a few moments and then burst out, "SINCE WHEN DID YOU START TELLING ME WHAT I CAN AND CAN'T DO AROUND HERE? Just who is in charge of this shindig anyway?" He picked up a small wooden nameplate that sat near the front of his desk, opened his eyes wide and said in a feigned tone of surprise, "Well, lookey here. H-a-r-o-l-d." He pretended to stutter, "Har, har, uh, Harold. Yes, Harold. Harold F-a-t-s-c-a-t. Fats, uh, Fat-scat, I think. Harold Fatscat. That's it, Harold Fatscat. This must be Harold Fatscat's office. Does that sound right, BONEHEAD?"

He put the nameplate back on the front of his desk and continued, "I'll jump around in here when I damn well please. If you don't like it, then get the hell out! You got a problem? Pack up your bags, go back to that penny-ante swindling game you were playing when I found you, and pick up your miserable little life where you left off. What've you got to think through anyway? You and Tomboy get on that fancy little machine of hers, tap out a message and get somebody on this right away."

He continued, "Seven hundred fifty is way more than enough. YOU HEAR ME? One thousand tops. Not a dime more. Two thousand bucks? If that's what we've got to spend, I'd just ride down there on my own time and pay off the Mayor himself. If that little dirtbag assistant of his balks, then to hell with him. He's probably keeping half of it anyway." With that, Fatscat jumped up and said, "I can't fool with this anymore right now. JUST TAKE CARE OF IT, OKAY?"

Fatscat lowered his voice and said, "Hey, get over here and get a look at this first. Tomboy said it came over the wire late this morning." Treeclimb had no choice but to walk over and stand right next to Fatscat. He held his breath and looked down at a note that read: "No luck with fire. Had to run. Will try to make mark on train back."

Treeclimb said, "Harold, is this from who I think it's from?" Fatscat replied, "Of course it's from Tony. Who else would it be from? Hardcrass and his bright ideas. 'We'll burn up his barn and all of his dogs.' Yeah, right. What was I doing listening to that idiot in the first place?" Fatscat slammed the note down on his desk as Treeclimb quickly moved away for air.

CHAPTER ELEVEN

FRIENDS, OLD AND NEW

Frank was shaking his head, chuckling to himself about Elvis' obsession with the Sabertooth, as they left their cabin and started down the aisle. There would be no peaceful dining experience at this point. The serenity that they left behind in the dining car earlier in the afternoon since had evolved into mostly commotion. Getting a table in time for the last serving was out of the question, and they considered themselves fortunate to find two stools together at the far end of the bar. It was as crowded as they ever had seen. One of the vagaries of traveling during vacation season.

Willis might possibly have been the fastest bartender ever to board a train, but even he was having trouble keeping pace with the orders. Even so, he paused for a brief moment when he caught sight of Elvis and Frank out of the corner of his eye. The distressed look on his face was replaced with a wide grin as he hustled toward them, wearing his trademark black bow tie, and asked in his Catstralian accent, "What can I do for you fine gentlemen?"

Elvis and Frank reached across the bar to rub paws with Willis and, with a big smile, Frank mimicked the accent and said, "I am sure that whatever it is that you're mixing most certainly will suffice for us, mate." Elvis said, "And a couple of menus, straight away, please."

Willis returned quickly with filled glasses, but no menus, and said, "Regretfully, sirs, all that remains of the entrees is the sautéed chicken in a spicy milk sauce. It is rather good, I must say, though." Elvis took his turn at adopting the accent and replied, "No worries, mate. That will do just fine." "Excellent," said Willis, before he scampered away and disappeared into the kitchen.

Elvis sat there with his mouth agape, staring toward the far end of the bar, where an absolutely stunning Siamese was busy cavorting with a group of tomcats who were huddled around her. Frank looked down to see what had caught Elvis' eye. With his gaze still fixed toward the other end of the bar, Elvis said, "Would you look down there?"

Frank shook his head and said, "I'm not blind, E. I can see her just as well as every other guy in the room." Elvis said, "No, not *her*. The guy next to her, the big one." Frank inquired, "White fur, gray jacket?" Elvis replied, "Yep, that's gotta be him, don't you think? Tom said he was big and white. I'm going to keep an eye on him. Do me a favor, if you don't mind, and run back into the kitchen. If Tom's still back there, ask him to take a peek out and see if that's him. Quick, you know how old Tom likes to hit the hay early."

Without a word, Frank got up and began bobbing and weaving, contorting his tall, thin body to wade through the crowd like a seasoned waiter in a busy nightclub. He made it to the kitchen doors just as Annie came blasting through them with a full tray high over her head. Frank twisted out of the way just in the nick of time and Annie breathed a sigh of relief before she said, "What's up, Frankie? You and the big E need something?" Frank said, "Actually, I was looking for the Tomcat. Is he still back there eating?" She said, "Just saw him not two minutes ago, dear. I think you're in luck."

Frank hustled with his long strides toward the back of the kitchen, and just as he got to the staff table, Tom looked to be getting up to take off. Frank said, "Tomcat, I'm glad I caught you before you went to sack out. Can you help me out with something for a minute?"

Tom lifted his head, put on his glasses as he wiped his mouth, and slowly got up from the table. He said, "Frankie boy. My, it's good to see you! Help you out with somethin'? Sure, you know that. Like to do it quick if we can. You know how us old folks need more nap time than you young whippersnappers. And I got me an early mornin' comin' up."

Frank chuckled as he put his foreleg around Tom's shoulders and said, "Shouldn't take but a minute and then you can get started on your napping." Tom was about to push his way through one of the kitchen doors, but Frank grabbed him by the shoulder and said, "Just a second. That's why I came back to see you. You might need to wipe off your specs for this one if you don't mind."

Tom took off his glasses and wiped them with his torn pawkerchief, and Frank pulled Tom up to one of the door windows. He said, "Over there, just on the left edge of the bar. See the big guy with the white fur, gray jacket?" "Yeah, I think so," said Tom. Frank said, "He isn't the guy you saw snooping around Amos and our gear earlier today by any chance, is he? You know, the one you were telling Elvis about."

Tom squinted and stared for a moment and said, "Sure looks like him from here, Frankie, but I can't say for sure. Can we take a walk on through and get a little closer?" Frank said, "Yeah, but I don't want him to think something's up. I'll go first and you follow me out. Act like you're not with me. I'll peel off just after we pass him and you tell me one way or the other, and then you just keep on walking straight ahead."

Tom said, "Got it. Hey, Frankie, you guys aren't going to start something here in the dining car, are you?" Frank said, "No, don't worry about that. We just need to know who's been snooping around. And let's not say anything to anyone about this, okay? Even Alley." "You've got my word," Tom said, as he followed Frank through the kitchen doors and out into the dining car.

Just as they passed the crowd hovering around the Siamese at the end of the bar, Frank started to the right and he could hear Tom whisper, "Yep, he's the one. Couldn't forget him if I tried." Frank looked back over his shoulder, winked and waived inconspicuously at Tom, who was headed toward the door at the back of the car.

By the time Frank had worked his way back to the other end of the bar, Elvis was busy chatting with a young lady who apparently had assumed ownership of the bar stool that Frank was occupying just a few minutes before. Frank snuck his head in over Elvis' right shoulder and whispered, "You were right, partner, that's him."

Elvis stopped at the first conversational pause and said, "Melissa, I'd like to introduce you to my very good friend, Frank." Elvis turned his head toward Frank and asked, "Do you mind if Melissa joins us for dinner?" Frank, looking around in vain for an empty stool, said, "Of course not. We'd better order for her quick, though, if she's going to have a chance at some food." Elvis replied, "I was sure you wouldn't mind, so we just went ahead and ordered one more. And don't you worry about your seat. Willis is bringing another one out for you."

As if on cue, Willis appeared, walking in back of the bar on his hind legs and carrying a stool over his head. He said, "Here you go, mates. Food'll be out before you know it. Let me know if I can do anything else now, you hear?"

Elvis squeezed to his left, toward Melissa, to make room on his right for Frank, who was reaching across the bar to take the stool from Willis. Only a few seconds after Frank had re-situated himself, Melissa excused herself to go to the ladies room before dinner arrived. Frank and Elvis couldn't help but watch as she strode away, and Frank said to Elvis, "You don't know if she's got a friend that looks anything like her, do you?"

Elvis smiled and said sarcastically, "Is that all you can think of? Isn't this supposed to be a work trip?" Then he took another sip of his drink and said with a chuckle, "Actually, I don't know whether she knows anyone who looks just like her, but that Siamese at the end of the bar." Frank said, "Yeah, the one sitting down there next to Snowball?" "Uh huh, you got it," said Elvis. Elvis paused for a moment and then continued, "Her name is Kelly, and she and Melissa are traveling together. They're picking up the southbound tomorrow to go to the beach for the week, somewhere near Catpus Christi. She already asked if we want to come along, but I told her that we've got plans to be somewhere out east and can't break them."

CHAPTER TWELVE

A SPLASH OF UNCOMFORTABLE

When Melissa returned, Willis was standing across the bar from them with three large plates in his forelegs and a wine list jammed between his teeth. He pointed his eyes toward Elvis and mumbled through his teeth as clearly as he could with the list still in his mouth, "I assumed you would want to have a look at this, mate?" "By all means," Elvis said, as he reached across the bar and pulled the list from Willis' mouth. Then Elvis said with a big smile, "Why thank you, mate."

Elvis glanced down at the list, quickly looked up and asked, "Number thirteen, the Caternet, is that new?" Willis responded, "Certainly is, mate. Our first one from that vineyard. Everyone has been saying such good things, we thought we'd give it a try. Have a white from them, too, if you'd rather." Elvis said, "No. I've also heard good things about them. Trying to get my uncle to pick some up, but he keeps hemming and hawing about it. Says he's already got too much of the high end stuff in the store. Let's stick with thirteen."

Willis nodded and was off in a flash, and all conversation ceased as Elvis, Frank and Melissa directed the whole of their energies to food consumption. After they had given their entrees undivided attention for a few minutes, Elvis finally spoke up, "So, you and your friend, Kelly. You're traveling alone?"

Melissa spoke quietly, "Just us. Too many of us all at once and we never get a chance to relax." Elvis took another bite and said, "Her suitors down there. Just folks you've met on the train?" She replied, "Yes, all from the train. Kelly usually attracts a crowd. I just wanted to get away for a few minutes and get a little breathing room. Wasn't expecting to find food, though. This is delicious! Maybe I'll save some for her if I can't eat all of it. Do you two know the chef? You seem to know the bartender quite well." Frank looked to his right, near the middle of the bar, and said under his breath, "Well, well, speak of the devil."

Calli was slithering along the back wall of the bar, carefully trying to avoid taking a blow to the head as Willis fervently shook a fresh concoction. She was coming toward them with a bottle of wine in the crick of her left foreleg. She made it over to their end of the bar, turned the label toward Elvis and said with a wry smile, "Your selection, sir?" Elvis said, "Why thank you very much, it certainly is. We didn't expect you to drop what you were doing and make a personal appearance to serve our wine."

Calli poured a small amount into Elvis' glass for him to taste and said to him with a serious look, "Obviously not." Elvis took a quick taste, nodded toward Calli, held up his glass and said, "Excellent." Then he motioned with his forepaw for her to go ahead and fill the glasses.

Elvis looked at Calli as she filled Melissa's glass and said, "Calli, meet our new friend, Melissa. She and her companion are traveling to Catpus Christi." He looked at Melissa and continued, "Melissa, this is Calli, the chef you were just complimenting." Melissa replied, "The chicken, it's absolutely fabulous!" "Why thank you," said Calli with a semi-feigned smile.

Calli looked at Elvis and Melissa together and said, "You two should come down in the morning for breakfast. If you aren't too busy, I mean. I have a great new recipe for fish crepes that I've been planning to try." She filled the remaining glasses (Frank first, then Elvis) and said, "Well, I need to get back to the kitchen for a while." Then she started toward the other end of the bar, flashing a less than cordial glance at Elvis out of the corner of her eye as she went by.

Before much time had passed, Elvis and Frank had shined their plates clean, and Melissa had eaten what she could, pushing the rest aside to save for Kelly. Most of the wine had been consumed and the three of them now were relaxing contentedly against the backs of their stools. Though much of the bar crowd had made their exit and most of the tables had emptied, the horde in Kelly's vicinity remained thick. Melissa excused herself to take her dinner leftovers down to Kelly, and Elvis told her that he and Frank would be down to join in a moment.

Elvis asked Frank, "You've got your little bag of tricks on board, don't you?" Frank replied, "Of course." Elvis said, "What do you think about running back to the cabin to get some ZxZ and meeting me back here at the bar? I'll probably be down at the other end." "What a surprise," Frank said as he hopped off of his stool. "I'll be back in a few," he said as he started making his way through the tables in a diagonal path across the room to the door in the back.

CHAPTER THIRTEEN

A TIGER BIDS HELLO . . . AND ADIEU

Frank was worried about what he might discover when he entered the cabin, as he slid the door open with trepidation. Happy he was to see that nothing appeared to be out of place. He went into the closet and began rummaging through his saddlebags until he removed what looked from its exterior to be a small, black leather pawicure kit.

He pulled back the zipper to expose its contents, but there were no tools for clipping or filing, or any other sort of pawicuring for that matter. Instead, there were tiny metal devices of various sizes for picking locks, matches, detonation fuses and a few small vials. Frank slipped one of the vials into his vest pocket, zipped up the kit and threw it back into his saddlebags, slid the closet door shut, and busted a move back to the dining car.

Elvis barely had worked his way to the front of the crowded end of the bar before Frank had returned. A phenomenon brought on by the concurrent forces of Frank's unrivaled efficiency and Elvis stopping several times to chat along the way. Frank didn't bother an attempt to wade through the mass of felinity at the bar, opting instead to walk around, climb in behind the bar like one of the help and take his place in the conversation from there.

Melissa encountered little resistance working her way to the bar front. She had taken a seat next to Kelly, on the stool that had been monopolized for the preceding hour by the big white cat who Tom said had been snooping around in the stable car earlier that day. He had given up his stool for Melissa in gentlemanly fashion, although he still was squeezed up about as close to Kelly's face as he could get without being on top of her. Elvis worked his way between Kelly and the stool on the other side of her, and they began to converse, somewhat to the chagrin of Snowball (as Frank had dubbed him).

Frank felt the awkwardness of the moment and interrupted from behind the bar by saying, "You must be Kelly. I'm Frank." Then he looked over at Snowball, held his right forepaw out and said, "Frank." The big guy reached out, rubbed Frank's paw with a heavy push and said in a deep voice, "I'm Tony. Tony the Tiger." Frank was afraid that if he didn't quickly speak or find another way to occupy his mouth, he might start to giggle. He reached over as fast as he could to tap Elvis on the foreleg, and said, "Elvis, this is Tony. Uh, I mean Tony the Tiger." Elvis said, "I know. We just met."

Still trying to suppress his amusement with Tony's moniker, Frank began talking with Tony and Melissa, speaking loudly to overcome the collective roar emanating from the crowd. Fortunately, Frank and Melissa didn't have to speak much. Tony had more than enough to say, even if most of it wasn't worth hearing. Good after-dinner entertainment, Frank thought to himself. Elvis and Kelly continued to chat away. Willis was pouring and mixing and shaking and hopping around at a furious pace, and before long, eleven-thirty rolled around and he hollered his familiar, "LAST CALL, MATES!" Within fifteen minutes, the room was empty, save for a few die-hards.

Elvis suggested that they all go back to one of the cabins for a nightcap, but lamented that his and Frank's cabin was too much of a mess for the occasion. That could not have been further from the truth after the janitorial miracle that Frank had executed just before they left the cabin for dinner. Frank knew better than to dispute Elvis' assessment, though, knowing that Elvis must have something in mind.

Kelly interjected excitedly and offered her and Melissa's cabin for the event. Then she said to Melissa, obviously as an afterthought, "You don't mind, do you?" Melissa replied with a smile, "Of course not." Tony roared, "There we go then. The party is moving to Kelly's."

At the sound of Tony's pronouncement, Melissa looked at Frank somewhat alarmed, and Kelly fired a similar expression at Elvis. The boys ignored them, appearing completely unconcerned about Tony simply assuming that he was invited to join. Elvis pulled a $50 bill from his pocket, set it on the bar and said, "This should cover all of us, Willis. Don't you think?"

Willis exclaimed, "And a lot more! Let me get you some change, mate." Elvis said, "No, keep it, and make sure you give some to Calli. Everything was superb, as usual. One more thing. Would you mind asking Alley to bring some Port and Catgnac to Melissa and Kelly's cabin before she hangs up her apron for the evening?" Willis said with a big smile, "Will do, Boss, and thanks again. Cheers!"

Kelly and Melissa thanked Elvis for picking up their tabs, as did big Tony, and they all drained their glasses and headed for the back of the room. They walked out of the dining car and through the first-class car, and stopped as soon as they crossed into the second-class car. Kelly pulled a key from her purse, unlocked the door to the very first cabin and slid it open. Not the furnishings that Elvis and Frank enjoyed in their super-suite, but certainly comfortable and more than roomy enough for all of them.

Everyone barely had gotten seated when a knock came at the door. Elvis jumped up and slid the door open. Alley came through without hesitation, went to the table in the back of the cabin and set down a tray filled with glasses and two bottles. She said, "You kids behave in here now, okay? There's lots of cats sleeping on this car. Little ones, too, and we don't need them up all night meowing and hissing."

Elvis followed her back to where she had set down the tray and said, "Don't worry about us. I'm not sure how much behaving we're going to do, but I promise you that we'll keep it down." Then he put a $20 bill in her forepaw and gave her a kiss on the cheek. Alley just shook her head as she walked out of the room and said, "I'll see you all tomorrow. If you haven't been kicked off by then."

Elvis inquired with everyone about their preferences and motioned Frank over to the table to help pour the drinks. After the orders were confirmed, Elvis turned around, pulled the cork from the Port bottle and began to pour. He turned his attention to the Catgnac and, as he began to slowly fill the first glass, he looked at Frank and nodded toward it. Frank had his back turned to the others and kept his forelegs in front of him, so that none of them could see his forepaws. He pulled the vial from his vest pocket, unplugged the top and emptied almost half of its white, powdered contents into the glass.

Elvis whispered, "Damn, Frankie! You think that's enough?" Frank just snickered and whispered back with a smile, "As big as he is, I'm not taking any chances." While Elvis filled the remaining glasses, Frank swirled the special beverage about with a stirrer until the powder had dissolved into invisibility. When they were finished, Elvis carried the tray over to the crowd and Frank began passing out the refreshments, careful to make sure that Tony got the drink that no one would be able to handle.

Tony the Tiger apparently considered his talent for rapid beverage consumption to be very impressive. At least to the ladies, if not to everyone. So it seemed as if only a few seconds had passed before his glass had been emptied and he boldly announced to the room at large his desire to have another. Less than impressive he was, though, when he raised himself from his seat, took two steps toward the beverage tray and fell face first to the floor, akin to the final domino in a row that had suffered collapse.

If their collective babble hadn't yet awakened the nearby sleeping passengers whom Alley had spoken of, it was a sure bet that the thud of Tony's massive body hitting the floor and the piercing shriek that Kelly let out in response were enough to finish the job. Elvis and Frank did their best to act surprised while Melissa sat speechless with her jaw dropped open. All stared down at Tony the Tiger. Sprawled on the floor with an empty glass rolling slowly on its side, back and forth between his face and his right forepaw, as the train rocked softly along the tracks.

Elvis and Frank jumped from their chairs, rolled Tony over and feigned concern as they ostensibly checked to see whether his heart still was beating. Of course it was. The big fellow simply was mired in a deep sleep. One that probably would last for at least ten hours, if not fifteen, given the hefty dose that Frank had administered. Elvis looked up at Kelly and Melissa and said, "I think he'll be okay. Probably just a little too much to drink for the big guy tonight."

Kelly and Melissa were visibly shaken and Kelly said excitedly, "We have to do something. Shouldn't we get a doctor?" Elvis looked up calmly as he patted Tony on the side of the face and said, "No, I think he'll be fine once he comes around. It probably was the Catgnac. That stuff really packs a wallop if you're not used to it. Doesn't it, Frankie?"

Frank looked over at Elvis with a wink and said, "Sure does, E, especially that brand." Frank looked at the girls and continued, "I'll tell you what. If one of you wouldn't mind getting the door, we'll get the big guy back to his cabin and set him on his bed, and he can sleep it off. His key is right here in his pocket. I'm sure he'll be fine by morning. Or, maybe the afternoon. Well, certainly by early evening. And I hate to say it, but we probably should call it a night. Alley was right. If someone complains about this racket, we're all liable to be standing at Fallston Station first thing in the morning with our bags, waiting for the next train to come by. You girls hurry up and put those bottles away, get in bed and just act like you've been sleeping if anyone comes around, okay?"

Frank and Elvis each took a side and struggled to lift the dead weight of Tony's big body from the floor. They began dragging him toward the door when Melissa stood up, obviously upset. She said, "This is terrible, just terrible. Are you sure he's going to be all right? And can they really leave us behind for making a little noise?"

Frank started to respond, but Kelly dutifully jumped in to handle the job for him. She walked to the door, readied herself to open it, fixed her eyes on Melissa and said, "A little noise? Did you hear him hit the floor, Melissa? And the scream I let out? I'd be surprised if the porters aren't on their way right now. We most certainly *can* get kicked off! Did you read the notice in the closet?" Then she turned back to Elvis and Frank and said, "You boys are right. Get him out of here now. We'll see you at breakfast."

Elvis and Frank kept moving toward the door as quickly as they could, and Elvis looked back at Melissa and said, "Don't worry about Tony. He's going to be all right. We'll see you two tomorrow."

Struggling to shuffle sideways through the door with big Tony between them, Frank and Elvis somehow got out of the cabin and into the aisle. Kelly shut the door behind them quickly and quietly, and Elvis and Frank dragged Tony the Tiger through the car as fast as they could. They sorely needed a breather, but the possibility of being discovered by a passerby was enough motivation for them to continue staggering non-stop through the next second-class car and, finally, into the storage car. There, with the help of his new friends, Tony promptly made his second drop to the floor.

Elvis pulled a gun from inside of his vest, handed it to Frank and said, "Keep an eye on him. I doubt seriously he's going to be doing much of anything for a while, but you never know. He may have a buddy or two on the train as well, so be careful." Elvis took off back through the second-class cars and quickly was back inside his cabin, pulling his gun belt from the closet. He popped open a small compartment and pulled out the box that held the tuft of white hair and flesh that he had found early that morning in the woods. So much had happened, it seemed like days ago when he had discovered it.

He took off back through the aisles of the passenger cars and quickly returned to find Frank sitting on a box in the storage car, holding Elvis' gun and looking down at Tony. He was dead to the world with his jacket pulled down from his shoulders, trapping his forelegs awkwardly behind him. Sort of a makeshift pair of pawcuffs. Elvis said to Frank, "You never cease to amaze me, my friend," as he knelt down next to Tony's left shoulder, took the piece of flesh and placed it into the spot where Tony had been gashed.

Elvis looked up at Frank and said, "Yep. Looks like it's him." Elvis stood up, kicked Tony hard in the side and continued, "I guess we can't be totally sure, so I won't put a bullet through his dinky little brain. It'd make too much noise anyway. But, I'd make a hefty wager that he's one of the gang who tried to flambé my barn last night. If he is, you know that Fatscat or one of his mangy buddies must have sent him."

Frank said, "Well, what do you think we should do with him, E?" Elvis looked up and asked, "Is he carrying a gun?" Frank smiled and held up a pistol as he replied, "Do you mean this one?" Elvis shook his head with a smile and said, "Give me a couple more minutes." Elvis went bouncing back through the storage car, soaring over and slipping between crates, and then went into the stable car.

Daisy barked quietly when she caught sight of Elvis and he darted into the back of the car to say hello. As he petted her on the top of the head, he said, "You be a good girl. We'll be back to see you in the morning." Elvis walked by Stella and Amos, who were fast asleep like the rest of the dogs in the car, and went into the back storage room. He emerged right away with a burlap bag and a paw full of twine, and he dashed back through the stable car, out the door and into the storage car.

Unwieldy as he was, Elvis and Frank eventually were able to squeeze Tony the Tiger into the bag, which they tied tightly at the top with the twine that Elvis had appropriated. They dragged him over to the sliding door on the side of the storage car and opened it as wide as it would go. Fortunately for Tony, the train had slowed to nearly half speed to negotiate a bend. With a big heave-ho, Elvis and Frank tossed out a bag full of Tony, not unlike a pair of airline employees might toss your oversized baggage into a cargo bay. Elvis and Frank looked out behind as the bag bounced and tumbled under the light of the stars and moon, down the slope that led up to the tracks and heading for the edge of the nearby woods.

Pulling the door shut, Frank said, "I don't think he'll be lighting more fires anytime soon, partner." As they walked into the adjacent second-class car, Elvis said, "Not if he knows what's good for him." Poor Tony; he had done such an admirable job of looking innocuous. You never would have known that his plan all along was to get Frank and Elvis liquored up, follow them back to their cabin after the nightcap with the girls, and put a bullet in each of their heads. Not that they wouldn't have had their guard up, or that he could have pulled that off even if they didn't, but even Elvis and Frank hadn't really suspected that he might try something that bold. The big guy, he just never saw this one coming.

They were anxious to get to their cabin and wind down, but there was one more stop to make. Frank started to slow down and look at door numbers midway through the forward second-class car. Then he stopped and pulled from his pocket the key that had been Tony's just minutes before. They knocked a few times to be sure, but no one answered. Frank unlocked the door, slid it open, stepped inside, struck a match and fired up the lantern beside the couch. Elvis looked up and down the hall to make sure that the coast still was clear, and then eased the door shut behind them.

There was little to be found. Some large clothes, a hat, a few bullets for the gun that Frank had lifted and some miscellaneous personal items. Being the good guys, though, they of course found one item of interest – a small, black bag stuffed full with a pile of papers. They searched around the room a bit more without success, grabbed the bag, extinguished the lantern and made a quick exit back toward their cabin.

As soon as they were inside, Frank mumbled a barely audible "goodnight" and went straight for his bedroom. Elvis plopped onto the couch, lit one of the lanterns aside it, and began to look through Tony's bag. The jackpot it was not, but it certainly was more serendipity than either he or Frank possibly could have hoped for. Letters to merchants – most likely having to do with some sort of Tin Roof Gang business, and a note from someone written on the letterhead of the City of South Sebastian. Most interesting by far was a map of trails in what looked to be the uppermost reaches of the Longtails, although Elvis couldn't tell for sure.

He got up and started for the Sabertooth to consult some of Frank's maps. As he crossed the room, Elvis could hear the sound of pawsteps softly approaching the cabin door. He quickly put Tony's papers back into the bag, set it in the closet, grabbed his pistol and quietly backed up against the wall, just next to the cabin door. He stood there silently for a few moments and was somewhat startled at the sound of two soft knocks. With a cocked pistol in his right forepaw, he slid the door slowly with his left, stepping back along the wall as it opened to keep himself hidden from sight.

There in the open doorway stood Calli with a sneaky smile, looking marvelous, despite having been toiling away in the kitchen for the better part of the past twelve hours. She didn't say a word as Elvis exhaled, lowered his pistol and set it softly on the couch. He smiled back at her, pointed to Frank's room and whispered, "Shhh, Frankie's asleep. I think." He took Calli by the forepaw, pulled her inside and kissed her on the cheek as he closed the door. He went to the side of the couch, put out the lantern, and then led her through the darkness and into his bedroom.

As the door closed softly behind them, Frank mumbled quietly to himself, "And he says *I* never cease to amaze *him*."

CHAPTER FOURTEEN

"OFFICIAL" VISITORS

Elvis accompanied Calli out to the cabin door as she rubbed the sleep out of her eyes, dreading the task of readying the kitchen for the seven o'clock breakfast rush. Elvis went straight back to bed and was fast asleep, not budging until he heard Frank fumbling around in the living room not long after ten o'clock.

As Elvis entered the room, Frank said, "I trust that you slept well?" Elvis replied with a mischievous grin, "Of course. Once I got to sleep, that is." Frank shook his head with a smile as he carried Tony the Tiger's little bag over to the cocktail table and said, "I hope you kept an eye on her while she was here. I'm still not sure about that girl." As Frank began flipping through Tony's papers, Elvis said, "Never let her out of my sight."

Elvis walked over behind Frank's chair, looked over his shoulder and said, "We've got some pretty interesting stuff here, don't you think?" Frank, playing nervously with his whiskers, said, "I'll say." Frank held up a couple of letters and said, "Wait until the Barncat and her crew drop in on these shippers and tear their places apart." Then he held up a note and said, "I wouldn't mind being a flea on the wall when she stops in to visit this little town manager either." Elvis said, "You and me both, brother." Elvis pointed at Tony's bag and said, "And check out that map in there. If that's what I think it is, ol' Fatscat might be in for a little surprise before long."

Frank dug the map out of Tony's bag and started to look as Elvis continued, "See all of those trails? I've been up in that direction a few times, but I've never seen anything leading way up into there.

You know how thick all of that is. And, there's a big clearing at the top of Aracat. That's exactly the kind of place for that paranoid little scumbag and his gang to hole up in, so they can run in any direction if trouble starts down below somewhere. If all of that's for real, you know that's where they're keeping Clevin and his lesser half."

Frank said, "I don't know about you, partner, but I'm too hungry to talk about it. Let's get down to the dining car. Those two Albemarle ladies probably are down there, too, and I wouldn't mind seeing them once more. They'll be getting off to go south in a few hours." Elvis just smirked at Frank as they grabbed their vests and hats, and started for the dining car. Melissa and Kelly were seated near the back of the room and Frank spotted them instantly.

When Elvis and Frank made it over to them, Kelly asked, "Did everything turn out okay with Tony last night?" Frank replied, "Yeah, but he sure had a load on. I don't think he'll be waking up anytime soon." Melissa said, "Did you know a couple of guys were banging on his door at the last stop? I don't think he answered. He told us last night that he was traveling alone, so I don't think they were friends of his. They looked kind of official, too. Like they were with the rail line or something. We told them that they'd probably need to bang pretty hard with all that he had to drink last night."

Elvis and Frank exchanged glances as she spoke and Elvis, trying to appear unconcerned, asked, "Did you tell them that we had to carry him back to his room?" Kelly leaned forward, and said seriously and quietly, "Of course not. We were afraid that they might put two and two together, and start asking about all of the noise in our room. We'll be at our stop in a few hours. We don't need to be getting into any trouble now."

"Good thinking," said Frank, as Annie arrived at the table with a loaded tray of fish crepes and large glasses of milk. After everyone at the table had finished what they could, they sipped coffee and talked for a while about the ladies' vacation. Neither of them had been to Catpus Christi, and Elvis and Frank were full of suggestions about places to go, things to see and friends to say hello to if they had the opportunity. As Kelly and Melissa were about to go, they wrote down their addresses at home and at work, and asked Elvis and Frank to please come visit before too long.

When Elvis and Frank returned to their cabin, Elvis said, "You wanna go find out who that was at Tony's door this morning, or should I?" Frank walked into his room, grabbed the gun that he had taken from Tony the night before, slipped it inside his vest, came back out and said, "Why don't you see what you can find out, Chief? I think it's my turn to check on the pups."

Elvis nodded, turned and went back out the door with Frank on his heels. As Frank made his way toward the back of the train, Elvis went back to the dining car and then quickly through it. He vanished into the kitchen doors, smiled and waved at Calli as he passed through, and went out the door on the back side of the kitchen. The late morning air blew warmly in his face as he adeptly climbed his way over the coal car, toward the locomotive. Hank, who had been hijacked more than once in his time, had seen someone approaching and was waiting patiently for his visitor with a pointed gun. Elvis expected as much, though, and announced himself loudly before pulling himself into the conductor's room.

With a look of relief on his wrinkled face, Hank put the gun down, looked ahead for a moment to make sure that all was clear on the tracks and then turned back to Elvis. He spoke loudly, attempting to overcome the deafening engine noise, "WELL, IF THIS ISN'T A SURPRISE. WHAT BRINGS YOU UP HERE, MY BOY?" Elvis put his foreleg around Hank's shoulders and hollered, "GOT A QUESTION TO ASK, IF YOU DON'T MIND."

Hank yelled back, "OF COURSE. WHAT'S UP, ELVIS?" Elvis took the next turn in the screaming match, "DO YOU KNOW ANYTHING ABOUT A COUPLE OF GUYS FROM THE STATION GETTING ON HERE TO LOOK FOR A PASSENGER AT THE LAST STOP?"

Hank replied, "YOU BETCHA. ONE OF THE NEW PORTERS CAME UP HERE AROUND NINE-THIRTY TO ASK ME IF IT WAS ALL RIGHT TO LET 'EM ON TO CHECK ON

SOMEBODY. STATIONMASTER GOT A MESSAGE FROM SOME FOLKS WHO SAID THEY WERE WAITING ON A WIRE FROM A PASSENGER. THEY HADN'T HEARD FROM THE GUY AND WANTED THE STATIONMASTER TO CHECK AND SEE IF HE WAS ON THE TRAIN. NAME WAS TONY SOMETHING OR ANOTHER. HE WAS REGISTERED, BUT APPARENTLY HE WASN'T IN HIS ROOM. I DON'T THINK THEY EVER FOUND HIM. WHY, YOU KNOW ANYTHING ABOUT HIM?"

Elvis shouted back, "NO. WE JUST SAW SOME GUYS BANGING ON A DOOR LOOKING FOR SOMEONE AND WANTED TO MAKE SURE THERE WASN'T ANY TROUBLE. THOUGHT YOU MIGHT NEED SOME HELP. YOU DON'T KNOW WHO IT WAS ASKING ABOUT THIS GUY BY ANY CHANCE, DO YOU, HANK?"

Hank began to slow the train for an approaching curve and the sound of the engine gradually retreated enough for him to speak at relatively normal volume. He said, "Nah. The porter said he asked, but the stationmaster said he didn't know who it was. I think everything's okay, though. I mean, I don't think we need to bother you with it, Elvis. I'll send somebody back to let you know if I hear anything else."

Elvis said, "Thanks, Hank. Just let me know if I can help. I'll see you soon. Keep up the good work up here, all right?" Hank nodded as Elvis climbed out the side of the locomotive, worked his way back over the coal car, hustled through the kitchen and the dining car, and slipped back inside the cabin to wait for Frank.

CHAPTER FIFTEEN

SCUZZY RENDEZVOUS

It was a bright, clear morning high atop Aracat. Eleven o'clock was approaching and the hot mountain sun beat down unfettered on the eastern side of the peaks. Fatscat emerged from his office, slobbering on a cigar and grumbling to himself about not getting the respect that he deserved. He went bouncing down the hill and Heinrich, who had been standing guard outside of the office, took off after Fatscat, doing his best to maintain a reasonable distance.

Fatscat didn't bother to stop by the mess hall or any of the other buildings, and was going straight for the stable area. Heinrich was ten or fifteen yards behind, zig-zagging to dodge the smell that followed the head honcho. As Fatscat approached the barn, he began yelling progressively louder, "Felaine. FELAINE. FELAINE!" Then he said under his breath, "I told her that I'd be down here at eleven. Where the hell is she? And where is my dog? I swear that girl is next on my list!"

Just as Fatscat was about to start into a new tirade, Felaine came walking out of the barn leading a large black German Shepherd named Louie, who was saddled and bridled. There was a time when Louie was as dirty, nasty and flea-ridden as his master, but after Felaine arrived and took charge of the canines, Louie was transformed into a neat, well-behaved, happy dog. Not particularly suited for Fatscat anymore, but like most of the help at the compound, Louie didn't have much choice in the matter. So, he continued to go about his job as good dogs do.

"There he is," Fatscat said as he flicked his chewed up cigar butt to the ground and hopped up into the saddle. Then he said to Felaine, "Do you have anything back there big enough for Hemlock here to ride?" Heinrich said, "That's Heinrich, Mr. Fatscat." Fatscat sneered down at him and said, "Hemlock, Heinrich, whatever." Fatscat reached down to adjust his stirrup and said, "Well, Miss Felaine, can you help us out here?"

Ever efficient, Felaine already had gone back into the barn and now was coming out with a large, shiny Rottweiler. She looked at Heinrich and said, "This is Ben. He should be able to handle you, but don't ride him too hard. He's Chucky T's dog and Chucky's going back to the Coast later this afternoon. If I know Chucky, he's probably hungover and won't leave until late, but once he does, he'll be riding hard all the way, trying to make it as far as he can before sunset."

Fatscat barked out, "OKAY, OKAY. Enough with the chit-chat. Just get that mutt saddled up, so we can get out of here. And don't worry about riding him hard. Nobody's headed to the Coast or anywhere else this afternoon. Not Chucky T. Not nobody. This place is in lockdown until those kids are out of here. You got that, Felaine? I'll be right back, Hemlock, and you best be up on that dog and ready to go when I get here."

With that, Fatscat rode Louie down along the side of the barn to the very end, hopped off and bounced over to a guard standing beside a padlocked door. The guard relinquished the key to Fatscat without a word and quickly slipped back a few steps, keeping his nose pointed upwind. Fatscat unlocked the door, stepped inside and snickered, "So, how are my little friends doing this morning? Feeling frisky? Who knows? If you're good little prisoners today, we might even let you out for a walk. Don't count on it, though."

Clevin Pusserschmott sat on the dirty wooden floor tied to his wife, Melba, in the back corner of the small, dingy room. He looked up at Fatscat and said, "You'll never get away with this, Fatscat! You better let us go while you've got the chance."

Fatscat smiled and said, "Well, I wouldn't be so sure of that, chump. I've got a telegram on my desk from Daddy. Says he's working on getting the cash together and he's gonna pay it, too. Maybe I'll show it to you if I remember to bring it down on my next visit. If not, you can just take my word for it. Looks like they want to have you back. I don't know why. Especially your idiot lady friend here. If she wasn't so pig-headed, you wouldn't have sent your stupid guards and servants packing for the weekend, and none of this ever would have happened. You've got only yourselves to blame. I'm just the beneficiary."

Fatscat turned and hopped back through the door. He stuck his head inside as he was about to close it, flashed a nasty grin at them and said patronizingly, "Don't run off now, okay?" He cackled as he slammed the door shut and locked it. Then he flipped the key back to the guard and said, "I assume you do know what will become of you if something happens to them on your watch." Fatscat hopped out of the barn, pulled himself up onto Louie's back with his foreleg and began riding around to see if Heinrich was situated with Ben.

Felaine was tightening the cinch on Ben's saddle one last time when Fatscat came around the corner shouting, "WELL, ARE WE READY YET?" Felaine tried not to let her distaste show as Heinrich jumped into the saddle and slid his rifle into a long holster. Without a word, Fatscat gave Louie a good kick and they took off up the hill, past the other buildings and toward the top. Ben took off as well, as Heinrich struggled to keep his balance, still bent over trying to adjust his stirrups. Fatscat started for the telegraph room to check on Treeclimb and Tomboy, but decided against it at the last minute and went straight over the mountaintop and down the other side.

Ben was strong and was starting to catch up to Louie, although Heinrich was leaning back hard on the reins, trying his best to keep a safe distance from Fatscat's pungency. As they descended the south side of the mountain, the oaks and pines of the Longtails began to get thicker and thicker, and Heinrich was forced to stay a bit closer for fear of getting lost on the broken trail. They rode for nearly forty minutes without an utterance, save the occasional cussing and spitting from Fatscat when he'd catch a twig in the eye or a spider web in the face.

The sun was nearing its peak and the temperature was soaring quickly, even in the thick shade of the forest. Before long, Fatscat let out a loud "Whoa" and they came to a stop. Just ahead was a small creek and on the other side was an Irish Setter, saddled and drinking from it. Over to the right, standing under a big, shady oak tree, was a chubby, light brown cat smoking a cigarette. He had a dirty face and an even dirtier hat that appeared to have been red in earlier days, and he wore a beat-up leather vest and a crusty gun belt.

Fatscat nudged Louie over to the creek and Louie put his head down to take a drink. Ben followed suit, but neither Fatscat nor Heinrich bothered to dismount. Fatscat pulled a cigar from his saddlebag, stuck it in his mouth and reached back in for a pack of matches. He bit off the end of his cigar and spat it to the ground, stuck a match between his teeth and ripped a claw across the tip to ignite it. He pulled the lit match from his mouth, replaced it with the cigar and began puffing away as the flame grew from his match. He flicked the match into the water, looked over at the treeside cat and said, "Well, Hardcrass, you're sure you've got that boat squared away? And all of your boys, they'll be ready when I need 'em?"

Albert Hardcrass took a step forward, looked up at Fatscat and spoke slowly, "I said they'll be ready. The boat, the guys. They'll be ready. You just better show up with that ransom. I didn't ride three hours up here for nothing." Fatscat sneered and said, "I'll be there with it. What do you care? I already paid you more than you deserve to line it all up. And this crew you're sending, they'd better be everything you say they are. I ain't payin' a thousand a head for bartenders and sales clerks, and you damn sure won't see another dime unless they turn out to be worth it. They better be tough and they better know how to handle themselves."

With his graying belly protruding from the bottom of his vest, Hardcrass said, "Don't worry about those boys. All I know is that you'd better be there with that money, Fatscat. I ain't seen nothin' since the fifty grand you gave me last week, and most of that's been spent lining all of this up." Fatscat said, "I'll have the rest of the money. You just make sure that you and the rest of your gang keep your mouths shut about this. I need you running your big, fangy trap all over who knows where like I need another hole in the side of my head."

Fatscat spat and continued, "By the way, sounds like your stupid arson idea fell on its face. Nice. Very nice. I told you that was a bad idea. I don't know why I listened to you to begin with." Hardcrass replied, "Well, the way I hear it from my boys, your hot shot hit man panicked and then got hit making a run for it. And then he disappeared. My boys still are out there and they don't know what happened to him. Probably ran off to die somewhere."

Fatscat glared at Hardcrass, took another puff from his cigar and said, "Well, never mind that now. Here's the deal. That crew needs to be up where I need them by sundown Wednesday. Nobody comes the day before. I MEAN NOBODY! I don't need any cops getting suspicious. I'll send somebody down Monday night to meet you with some maps. You just make sure that they get into the right paws. I'll see you at that boat sunrise Thursday. Any slip ups and your ass will be fried before the week is out."

Hardcrass, who had been alternating his stare between the ground and the sky as he listened to Fatscat spout off, looked at Fatscat and said, "My crew will be up there and they'll take the rest of their pay when they finish the job. Yeah, I'll be at that boat sun-up Thursday. It's the fastest one in the marina. They've been moving things around a lot down there. I'll send word with the dock number Wednesday afternoon, after all of the boats are back in. Be on the lookout for it."

Fatscat turned Louie around and started trotting back up the hill with Heinrich and Ben not far behind. Fatscat looked back over his shoulder at Heinrich and said, "Keep an eye out and make sure he doesn't try to follow us. I don't like the idea of meeting him this close to the place to begin with, but the way things have been going lately, I can't afford to leave for more than a few hours at a time. I don't need him or any of his bums finding out where we're holed up until they have to. That sort of stuff gets into the wrong paws and we've got big trouble. And you don't say a word about this to anyone. YOU HEAR ME?" Fatscat farted and Heinrich just nodded, keeping his breath held and hoping for a quick breeze to clear the air.

CHAPTER SIXTEEN

BACK TO THE COMPOUND

Heinrich never did get any help from the breeze. About to pass out, he was left with no choice but to chance a deep breath and he paid the price. His eyes began to burn and he wanted to cry. The return trip uphill consumed a good bit more time than the romp down had taken, but Fatscat was glad to have some peace and quiet to think things over for a little while.

Fatscat trusted Hardcrass about as far as he could throw him. With that one foreleg, mind you. Accordingly, Fatscat kept Hardcrass completely in the dark about the ransom details – where and when the exchange would take place, who would be involved, even the amount for that matter. As far as Hardcrass knew, they had demanded only two million dollars, and Hardcrass was more than happy to be getting half of that, less the cash that he already had pocketed.

It was almost two o'clock when they returned to the top of Mount Aracat. Fatscat didn't bother to trek back down to the stable. He ordered Heinrich to take Louie and Ben back to Felaine, and to return right away to resume guard duty at Fatscat's office. Tomboy came running into the office with a concerned look on her face just as Fatscat landed in his desk chair.

"What's the problem now," Fatscat growled. Tomboy was trying to catch her breath and uttered, "I don't know if it's a problem or not, sir, but Nickels down in Catalina says he hasn't heard a thing all day from Tony the Tiger. He said Tony was supposed to send a message from Fallston Station this morning to let us know how things were going. I checked and his train's on schedule. Do you think something happened to Tony? He was on a job, wasn't he?" Fatscat sneered and said, "I know what he was doing. Who do you think sent him out there to begin with? It might not be a problem. We'll just have to wait a little longer and see if he checks in."

As Tomboy was running out, Treeclimb stepped through the doorway, politely removed his hat and said, "I wouldn't be too sure, Harold." Fatscat looked up at Treeclimb and mimicked him with a nasal, sarcastic whine, "Oh, I wouldn't be too sure, Harold." Then he looked down, shook his head in disgust, looked back up and said, "Mr. Treeclimb, I wasn't aware that clairvoyance was one of your talents. How is it that you're so certain something has gone awry? One lousy missed check-in and you've got it all figured out?"

Treeclimb replied, "If I may, Harold. Tony by far has been our best hitter for over a year now. It's not open to debate. I know he may be tardy to meetings up here on occasion, but he *always* checks in from the road when he says he will. I took the liberty of wiring the stationmaster at Beaumont, the mid-morning stop for that train, and asked them to send a porter to Tony's cabin during the stop.

"The stationmaster wired back and said that Tony definitely is registered on the train, but there was no response when his men knocked at Tony's door, and no one was inside when they unlocked the door to look in. They said there didn't look to be any signs of trouble. I understand that nothing is certain, Harold. You and I both know that Tony easily could have spent the night elsewhere on that train, and he is a late sleeper as well. I considered requesting that the staff undertake a full-blown search, but I didn't want to make a big affair out of it and arouse any suspicion."

Fatscat said, "Thank goodness for that. At least you aren't the total idiot I sometimes take you for. Let's not jump to any conclusions until Tony has another chance to make contact." As Treeclimb started for the door, Fatscat yelled, "AND LET'S SEE IF THERE'S ANY WAY TO FIND OUT WHETHER ELVIS AND THAT SKINNY SIDEKICK OF HIS ARE ON THAT TRAIN."

Heinrich appeared at the door and Fatscat, still seated behind his desk, hollered, "It's about time you got that lazy tail of yours back up here. Let's get down there and get some grub before it's too late. You know how fast lunch goes when all of those pigs are here eating for free. We've got eight of them in camp right now and that's not counting you full-time freeloaders. I told Cal to wait for me to get down there before he serves it up today, but he can't put it off too much longer. Let's go. I'm starving!"

- - -

Because he was doing such a thorough job of looking and being angry, you couldn't tell (not that anyone cared) that Fatscat was deeply worried as he skipped down the hill toward the mess hall. Although he might not admit it, he knew that Treeclimb probably was right about Tony. Tony was expensive, but he was one of the few cats in the enterprise whom Fatscat felt was worth the money he got paid.

Whenever Fatscat really needed to put serious pressure on anyone, or even have someone scratched out, Tony always came through with exemplary speed and efficiency. And, just as Treeclimb noted, Fatscat couldn't remember Tony ever missing a check-in when he was on an important job. Something probably did happen to him, and there weren't too many cats out there sharp enough or tough enough to pull that off. Only one that Fatscat knew of for sure.

Fatscat wasn't so out of touch with reality to have thought that derailing Elvis before he could get to the East Coast was a plan that couldn't miss. In a way, he almost expected it to go up in smoke, and he had planned fully for that contingency. Until now, though, Fatscat hadn't given much thought to the possibility of Elvis completely turning the tables on Tony.

Did Tony get fingered? And if so, would they have been able to overtake him? Would Tony talk if they got the best of him? What was he carrying with him? Tony didn't know everything, but he knew a lot more than most. Fatscat tried his best to put all of it out of his mind and not worry. What he needed to do most was concentrate on the tasks at paw.

First and foremost, he needed to get his cruddy paws on the Pusserschmott money and, until he did, keep his rag-tag gang under control and in the dark about the details. Time was going to be tight, though, and he didn't need a wild card like Elvis floating around in the deck. Fatscat would miss his opportunity completely if everything didn't stay on schedule. He never would be able to live with himself if the whole thing fell to pieces and Hardcrass ended up walking away scot-free with a fat chunk of unspent advance money. Fatscat also knew that he'd need to let Treeclimb in on some of the details sooner rather than later. There was too much to be done and too little time left, and Fatscat wouldn't be able to deal with all of it by himself much longer.

- - -

By his own shrewd design, Treeclimb always made it to the mess hall door about ten paces ahead of Fatscat, and today they were just in the nick of time for lunch. The smell of two large trays of chicken catciatore filled the air and a small crowd hovered around the serving table in a near frenzy, each trying to fill his plate before the next. Calvatore, who always had the sense to eat in the kitchen before the mongrels came wafting in, was in the far corner of the room, cleaning up a table and grumbling to himself about the slovenly group that had been in the hall late the night before. Treeclimb and Heinrich quickly got plates of their own and joined in the fracas while Fatscat stood at the door and yelled, "YOU MAGGOTS CAN BEAT YOURSELVES UP ALL YOU WANT, BUT THERE BETTER BE SOME LEFT WHEN I GET OVER THERE." As he entered, he said, "Cal, quit your damn cleaning and get me some water."

Though it was the social center of the compound, there was nothing luxurious or enticing about the mess hall. A bunch of large, round wooden tables with scratchy metal chairs scattered about, and some small lanterns tucked away in crevices in the walls. Fatscat liked to keep it as dark and bare bones as possible, so that no one would get too comfortable. It was trouble enough keeping the work force focused on their responsibilities without any real distractions, and Fatscat was convinced that most visitors loitered in the compound longer than they needed to.

If the place were any more resort-like, Fatscat often said, no one would get anything done. Fatscat routinely had nightmares about girls dancing on top of a bar, serving drinks, and a billiards table having been installed in the back of the room. Despite his successful efforts to keep things rudimentary, a group still could be found in the hall most every evening, drinking cheap whiskey, smoking cigarettes and playing cards.

Fatscat was the last to make it to the serving table, and as much as the others would have loved to leave him in the lurch, he did pay the bills (including their salaries), so there was more than enough food remaining for him. Calvatore, conscious as the others about the dreaded scent, brought the water to the front table just when Fatscat was at the serving table grabbing the last of the chicken.

Not that you should feel sorry for Fatscat, but he usually ate alone at the front table, near the door of the hall, while everyone else typically could be found distributed evenly around the remaining tables. Occasionally, he would order one or more of the others to join him, so that he could dole out some instructions or administer a tongue lashing. But, he mostly kept to himself at chow time, reserving those other joyous activities for meetings in his office up the hill.

Except for the hubbub around the serving table at the outset of each repast, it ordinarily was very quiet during meals. Everyone focused intently on not much more than chewing, swallowing and picking out the next bite of sustenance. This week was different and the air was filled with the murmur of conversation. Theories abounded about what Fatscat really had in mind for the Pusserschmott kids, and everyone wondered why no one had been allowed to leave the compound for almost a week.

Only Tomboy and Treeclimb had any clue about the size of the ransom demand. During each meal, Fatscat kept constant watch through the corner of his eye over Heinrich, making sure that he didn't leak a word about the recent meetings with Hardcrass. Like most of the gang, Heinrich wasn't particularly fond of Fatscat and he was anxious to tell what he knew, but he understood that, if he cared to live another day, he'd do better to keep quiet about this for now.

The Tin Roof Gang had done some nasty things during their run, many much worse than simple catnapping, but this was a new venture. Prisoners on site? No one from the outside ever had been to the compound, voluntarily or involuntarily. Not without being shot on sight. Beyond that, business seemingly was good. They all understood that every little bit helps, but it didn't appear to any of the rank and file that something along the order of a big ransom windfall was needed to maintain positive cash flow.

No one dared to say it in Fatscat's company, but they all were thinking the same thing. Catnapping a Pusserschmott and demanding what they all assumed must be big money? Why not just write a letter and ask the feds to come overrun the place? It all was too risky with the way things were going. Something big must have been up and everyone wanted to know what it was.

Fatscat finished the last of his meal, got up from his chair and hopped toward the door. Just before he slammed it behind him, he yelled across the room, "TREECLIMB, I NEED TO SEE YOU IN MY OFFICE RIGHT AWAY." Treeclimb waited a moment and then began mimicking Fatscat. He growled, "Treeclimb, I need to see you in my office right away." A loud roar bellowed out from around the room as the other cats slammed their paws on their tables with laughter. Suddenly, the door swung back open and an uneasy hush quickly overtook the room. Treeclimb's jaw dropped open and his eyes bulged from his head.

Fatscat stood in the doorway, looked at Heinrich and said, "Let's go, Hemlock. Do you think I've got all day?" Treeclimb felt relieved as Fatscat started to close the door, but that changed quickly when Fatscat stuck his head back inside and yelled across the room, "AND TREECLIMB, ONE MORE SMART ALECK CRACK LIKE THAT AND YOU'LL BE TIED UP BACK THERE WITH THOSE

PUSSERSCHMOTT KIDS. I don't see any good reason not to turn you over along with them for that ransom." He stared silently at Treeclimb for a few seconds and said, "And if you think I'm joking, pal, why don't you just try me?"

Fatscat turned and started up the hill, and Heinrich jumped up from his table, grabbed his rifle and began chasing after him. No one in the hall said another word until Calvatore, looking out the window, turned back and said, "Okay, I think he's gone now."

Treeclimb decided that, after that little episode, it might behoove him to finish his lunch and get right up to Fatscat's office without delay. Despite his uppity tone, Treeclimb was well-liked and a popular lunch companion for most everyone who came through the compound. Not only was he somewhat humorous, but he also was the only one willing to stand up to Fatscat when push came to shove, a trait that brought with it the respect of every member of the gang. Treeclimb was the glue that held things together whenever Fatscat became entirely unreasonable and important spokes in the Tin Roof wheel threatened to break – an occurrence that was becoming more and more common. After a few more words, he dashed out of the hall and up the hill, prancing as if he were a show cat of sorts.

Fatscat looked up at his office door as Treeclimb entered and said, "I was wondering where you were. Do you think I've got nothing to do beside sit around here and wait for you?" Treeclimb replied, "Just calm yourself, Harold. You've been up here barely two minutes. Somebody's got to keep that crowd together or this whole operation is going to come crashing to the ground and you know it. You're certainly not helping."

Fatscat sat silently for a moment while Treeclimb readied himself for another verbal explosion. Surprisingly, Fatscat just nodded and said, "I guess you're right, but it grates on my nerves to talk to some of those imbeciles. If they just weren't so damn dumb." Fatscat paused for a moment and continued, "Anyway, that isn't what I need to talk with you about right now.

"I know you like to stand way back there for some reason, but you need to pull up one of those chairs. This is going to take a little while and I can't afford to have anybody listening in on us." Then he looked toward the door and said, "Hemlock, get outside, close that door, and shut your ears until I tell you to open them. I don't care who it is. Nobody comes near this place until me and Treeclimb are through. YOU HEAR ME?"

Treeclimb interjected, "That's Treeclimb *and I*, Harold. And his name is Heinrich, not Hemlock." Fatscat looked back across his desk at Treeclimb with an evil eye, but didn't say a word, as Heinrich turned away with a smirk and slammed the office door shut behind him.

CHAPTER SEVENTEEN

WORKING HARD, PLAYING HARD

As Frank entered the cabin, Elvis was setting Tony's trail map back up on the easel. They sat together on the couch and began to ponder. There wasn't much reason to be distracted by the scenery at this point. The current landscape was dominated by broad plains and their tall grasses, lightly peppered with a few livestock ranches and the occasional fish farm. Peaceful in its serenity, but not nearly as impressive as the breathtaking mountains and plunging rivers that had characterized the preceding leg of the ride when they were passing through the Catzarks.

Before long, they could feel the big train slowing, and the plains temporarily gave way to the trappings of a small country town. It was here at Yarnhood Station where the north/south line intersected with the transcontinental, where Melissa and Kelly would switch trains and head for the beaches. Elvis and Frank each thought to himself for a coincidental moment about how hopping onto the southbound to spend a week of fun in the sun with two hotties would have rated far better than dealing with the whole Pusserschmott affair.

As the train began to roll again, Alley appeared out of nowhere with refreshments to help alleviate their disappointment. They asked her what she knew about the search party hunting for Tony the Tiger a few hours before, but all she could do was confirm that it wasn't the rail line's idea, and that someone on the outside had indeed inquired about the chap. They chatted for a few minutes and then she left them in solitude.

The hours drifted past until their heads were saturated to the maximum degree. It was indeed official – more information was bouncing off of them than was sinking in. It is times like these when the bar is your clear option, and it would have been under almost any other circumstances, but tonight was poker night and it was way too early to start dulling their senses. With no viable alternative, they cleaned up the cabin and seized upon what they knew would be their last chance at a nap anytime in the foreseeable future.

Frank and Elvis surely would have slept through dinner, and quite possibly the games as well, if Alley hadn't pulled them from the ditch with some loud banging on their door circa nine-thirty. They never would have forgiven her if she hadn't. They jumped up, went straight to the dining car, tore through a delectable roast pheasant and sat at their table warming up with a few hands of gin rummy.

After the last of the dinner crowd cleared out, everyone left in the room was there for a singular purpose, and the dining car suddenly transformed into a multi-table poker extravaganza. Frank and Elvis went their separate ways to different games, in order to avoid the prospect of trading money between themselves. In just a few short hours, each had built himself a nice little pile of chips.

It was almost two o'clock when Annie finally broke the bad news to everyone. It had to stop sometime. Left to their own devices, they probably would have played through sunrise, but they all were good sports about it. No one was happier than Willis, who was worn out by now and was finishing off the last of the orders. The help always tolerated the games on the final night of the trip and, truth be told, Willis and Annie looked forward to the heavy tips that the winners tended to parse out, especially after the drinks began to flow. Despite the extra cash, it still made for a long shift.

Fortunately for the staff, Monday was brunch day and no one would have to deal with the early breakfast routine. The only thing east of Littermark Station was the Catlantic Ocean, so that signaled the end of the train ride. In lieu of the staff having to scramble and clean up an entire breakfast mess for an abbreviated lunch hour, a buffet was served on the last day of the transcontinental from ten until one. It always was impressive. A colorful array of fish, fowl and catnip, and all of the milk, wine and other beverages that hadn't been consumed since the departure from Albemarle. And, all for the low price of forty cents.

Elvis and Frank returned to their cabin, and just as Frank stepped into his bedroom, Calli appeared at the cabin door with a bottle tucked under her foreleg. As Elvis slid the door open, he thought to himself how much things had improved in just one short day. Pouring a smelly thug off of a train one night, playing poker and then pouring Champagne with Calli the next.

It was after ten when Elvis finally awoke. Calli was long gone and Elvis could hear Frank rummaging through his papers and bags. The train wasn't due to arrive at Littermark Station until after two, but Frank always packed his bags as soon as he woke up on departure day, even if his destination still was hours away. Elvis never quite understood how the advance packing habit jibed with arriving at train stations and ferry terminals only seconds before departure time. Full comprehension of the inner workings of nervous Frank's brain was a goal that Elvis had abandoned long ago.

As they were returning to the cabin from brunch, Frank said, "I sure hope I'm wrong about your new lady friend, partner. That might be the best brunch I've ever had on this train." Elvis said, "Just thinking the same thing myself. If we *do* find out that she's in cathoots with Fatscat or one of his crew, you're going to have to be the one to knock her off, my friend. I don't think I could bring myself to do it." Frank looked back to see if anyone was listening in and said, "Like I said, let's just hope it doesn't come to that."

CHAPTER EIGHTEEN

SURVEILLANCE: A DANGEROUS OCCUPATION

As Frank and Elvis walked through the aisles on their way back from the stable car, they could see the northern tip of the majestic Longtails rising out of the ground. The sometimes mighty Sebastian River was running at its not-so-furious summertime pace, down the eastern side of the range and toward the coast ahead.

The station wasn't far off in the distance and the train's whistle suddenly broke the quiet that hung in the air. Frank went into the cabin to empty the Sabertooth and get the last of their things together, while Elvis made one final trip to the kitchen to say goodbye to Calli. If only he had twenty minutes instead of two, he thought to himself as he entered and saw the outline of her body next to the staff table in the back of the room.

Disembarking the train was significantly less adventuresome than the boarding process had been, and before they could take more than a few steps, old man Pusserschmott was standing right in front of them. Gray all over, wearing a sharp-looking blue jacket and tie, and bearing a wide grin, Elvis and Frank were surprised to see him. The old man almost never left the house these days, other than to vacation or to attend a charity event or gala of some sort. Picking up visitors at the train station, even if one of them was Elvis the Gunslinger, was not part of the old man's ordinary routine.

He really must have been glad to see them this time, Elvis thought. Frank said that they'd need to break for a moment to get the dogs from the stable car, but the old man assured them that it was being taken care of. Sure enough, as they walked out of the front doors of Littermark Station, Daisy, Stella and Amos were coming around the building. They were under the careful tutelage of Eddie Arcato, a first-class rider and dogsman who had been in charge of the Pusserschmott stable operation for over two years now.

They went over to the hitching post where one of the old man's entourage helped him onto his dog, a wonderfully fit Catapeake Bay Retriever named Lucky. Meanwhile, Elvis and Frank tightened their gun belts, secured their saddlebags and hopped aboard their mounts. There were nine dogs altogether and the convoy started southward along East Station Road. Once they had put some distance between themselves and the crowd greeting the arrivals at the station, old man Pusserschmott rode up next to Elvis.

He spoke quietly, "I really appreciate you two coming out here just for us, Elvis. Once we get back to the place, we can have a drink or two and sit down for a real dinner. A couple of our ranch workers are down at the river right now pulling in some of that rainbow trout you love so much. You boys don't have time to get anything done before dark anyway, so you may as well wait until tomorrow before you start doing any real work."

The city limits of South Sebastian reached far and wide, almost to the coast on the eastern side, but downtown proper was situated farther west, where the northern edge of the foothills gave way to the valley. The Pusserschmott estate was not too far beyond the western end of downtown. It would have been just over half an hour's ride breezing straight through town, but the old man didn't want to raise any eyebrows. They had come to the station by way of a little used trail that wended through the northern edge of the foothills and they were returning home along the same route. It made for a longer ride, but the views into the valley were magnificent. Almost as spectacular as the looks out over the ocean, which was visible from the higher switchbacks after the trail began to climb.

They had been riding for nearly thirty minutes when Elvis looked at Frank, nodded toward a peak ahead on the left, nearly one hundred yards high, and dropped back toward the rear of the convoy with Daisy. Old man Pusserschmott's entourage were a loyal bunch that meant well and did a respectable job, but most of them fantasized that they were more formidable than reality might suggest. Warren was a significant exception.

He was a big, quiet, dark brown cat who was in charge of security at Pusserschmott Farms and at the Pusserschmott residences. During four action-packed years in the catvalry, he had amassed a long list of well-deserved awards and honors, before tiring of the military grind and settling into catvilian life. When Daisy had fallen back to the rear, next to Warren's dog, there was no need for words. Elvis motioned his head up at the peak and Warren instantly spotted three cats on their dogs watching over the caravan.

Elvis spoke so that only Warren could hear, "When we get past this next bend and out of their sight, is there a quick way up?" Warren replied in his deep voice, "Two trails, Elvis, but the back one's probably best if you want to sneak up on them." Warren looked back up at the peak for a moment, then ahead at the rest of the group and continued quietly, "They were up there watching when we were coming down from the ranch to get you, but I didn't say anything. Didn't want to scare the old man unless something was going to pop, and we had numbers on them, so I didn't think they'd try anything. If it's okay with you, I'm gonna stay down here in case trouble starts. You want to take any of the boys up there with you, just in case?"

Elvis watched the overhead trio out of the corner of his eye as he said, "No, I'm sure Frankie and I can handle them. You know how loud these guys can be. I don't want to take a chance on anyone up there hearing us coming." Elvis smiled as he continued, "We've been off for a while anyway, and we could use a little warmup if this trip is going to go like I think it might." He looked over at Warren and said, "You're right, you need to stay here, but make sure you let everybody know what's up as soon as we take off up the hill."

Warren paused for a moment and then said, "We're coming up on that trail, right after this line of bushes. You better get up there and get Frankie." Elvis nudged Daisy and she trotted quickly to the front of the pack, and Elvis began to speak to the old man, "We've got some visitors on top of this cliff coming up. I don't want to make a big scene out of it if we can help it, Boss. Can you or one of your boys keep hold of Amos for a little bit while Frankie and I go check it out? He won't slow you down if you have to run."

To Elvis' surprise, the old man said, "Probably the same bunch that was hanging around up there a while ago when we were coming down from the house. I saw only three, so I didn't think Warren was too concerned with as big a group as we've got. Amos? No, no, he's not a problem. Barry here can take him for a bit. You need us to do anything?"

Elvis shook his head "no" as Frank passed Amos' lead line to Barry, who was riding just behind the old man. Elvis and Daisy vanished into the bushes with Frank and Stella close behind. The trail was clear, but very steep. Even so, Daisy and Stella ascended it in a pinch, fresh off of two day's rest on the train. All that could be seen from below was a little bit of dust and a few pebbles being kicked up in their wake. Just before they emerged from the thick trees and bushes at the top of the trail, Elvis drew back his reins and Daisy ground to a halt, and Frank pulled Stella up alongside of them.

They could see the three sentries peering down over the cliff from the backs of their dogs, and Elvis and Frank quietly dismounted and began to sneak up on them, leaving Daisy and Stella behind in the brush. The wind was blowing in from the coast, enough to prevent any detection of their scent, and rustling just enough leaves in the trees to mask any noise that Elvis and Frank might make in the unlikely event of a misstep.

Frank and Elvis took advantage of the unexpected opportunity to gaze for a minute at the blue waters of the Catlantic that filled the background all the way to the horizon's edge. After a brief moment to enjoy the scenery, they approached slowly until they were just less than ten yards from the trio. Elvis went slightly to the left and Frank to the right, where they stood quietly. Frank held a pistol in his right forepaw and Elvis had one in each.

The riders began talking. "Hey, I think there's a couple missing," said the cat on the left. The one in the middle replied,

"Yeah, I think you're right. I count six. No, seven. It looks like a couple of the new ones are gone. You know, the ones we didn't see coming on the way in." The cat on the left spoke again, "Just keep your eyes peeled. They've gotta be down there somewhere. They couldn't just disappear into thin air. If we lose track of those two, Fatscat ain't gonna like it. Those are the ones that he said we need to keep an eye on."

Elvis spoke loudly, "Don't get yourselves all worried about us. We'll be back down there in a few minutes." All of them jerked their heads around to the left toward Elvis. The one on the right began to reach for his gun when Frank said, "I wouldn't try that." They all quickly swung their heads in the other direction, toward Frank, and the one on the left pulled his gun from his holster.

BOOM!

Poor kitty's gun barely had cleared leather when Elvis fired off a shot. The cat threw his forepaw into the air, squealing in pain as his gun fell and blood began to run down his foreleg. Elvis said, "Are you kids having trouble hearing or something? My partner over there said." Elvis paused for a moment and said, "What was it that you said again, Frankie? I don't know that I heard you."

Frank kept his gun pointed at the one on the right and started walking directly toward him as he said, "I think what I said was, 'I wouldn't try that.' Something like that. I can't remember exactly myself." When he was just a couple of steps from the dog on the right, Frank looked up at its rider and continued, "Can you remember, fat boy?" The cat looked down at Frank with a sneer and didn't respond.

Frank spoke again, "Well, while you're thinking about it, you can throw down that little gun of yours and get off of that dog before I pull you off by your ugly head. Either way is fine with me, but if I have to do it myself, there's a good chance that I might slip and send you flying off this cliff. I don't know how many lives you've got left in that dumpy body of yours, but I think you're gonna be short a couple when your fat ass hits those rocks down there."

The cat looked down at Frank and was about to speak.

BOOM!

Elvis fired a shot from his other pistol, and the hat of the cat in the middle went flying into the air and over the cliff. Elvis yelled, "YOU HEARD HIM. NOW, MOVE!" The three looked back and forth at each other, but not for long, and the two who weren't bleeding grudgingly threw their guns to the ground. They dismounted as the other cat moved slowly, complaining of pain in his paw. Suddenly, he threw his leg back over the saddle, kicked his dog hard in the sides and urged him straight at Elvis, who was slightly off his guard and taken a bit by surprise.

As the dog was about to land on him, Elvis sprang into the air, over its head, and tore the claws of his left forepaw across the face of the rider. The cat flew sideways off of his saddle and crashed to the ground. He was screeching in pain and holding his face in the crick of his foreleg, and his dog dashed into the woods.

Elvis landed squarely on all fours, straightened his hat, looked down at him and said, "Don't you think you were ugly enough without your face all torn up? Just look at your hideous mug." Elvis walked over to the edge of the cliff to signal to Warren that everything was under control, and then turned back at the writhing cat and said, "You would think that a gunshot through your paw is damage enough for one day. Don't you, sweetheart?"

Elvis stepped back from the cliff a few paces and picked the guns up from the ground. Frank coaxed the other two cats over to the spot where their colleague was busy bleeding, moaning and groaning, and shoved them down to the ground with him. Frank looked back at Elvis and said, "What do you think we ought to do with them, Chief?"

Elvis took a few steps toward Frank and their new prisoners, and said, "If they weren't so dumb, we could take them over to East Coast HQ and see if there's any information to be gotten out of them. But, anybody out here on recon duty probably is too much of a peon to know anything worth hearing." Then he looked down at them and said, "Isn't that right, pinheads?"

Elvis paused and then said to Frank, "You know, from what I understand, they've been up here for at least a couple of hours now." Elvis looked over at them and said, "You guys must really like it up here, eh?" Elvis walked over to the two dogs by the cliff, pulled the ropes off of their saddles, threw them to Frank and said, "I don't see any reason to spoil it now. Why don't we just let them stay here for a while?"

Frank started chuckling and said, "That's a wonderful idea, E." He looked down, back and forth between the grimacing cat and his two cohorts, and continued, "What do you kids think about that? I mean, you can't beat the scenery. This is prime real estate. Rugged cliffs. It's ocean view for cat's sake. And there's not a cloud in the sky. It should be a beautiful night. If we had the time, we'd probably camp out right here with you and try to keep you cheered up. You know how it is, though. Busy, busy."

Elvis held his guns on them while Frank pushed them closer together and began circling, kicking them seriatim as he went round, into what he felt was the optimal arrangement. Frank rapidly exhausted both ropes with a masterfully complex weave. He over-undered and he under-overed. He criss-crossed and he cross-crissed. He yanked firmly every time he caught the majority of the lot in an exhale, squeezing them down to create more slack for the next wave of restraint.

Rears to fores, necks to torsos and various other uncomfortable permutations, all conducted with a steady murmur of grunts, grumbles and whines in the background. When he finally outran his supply, his creation was nothing less than a Gordianic morass of fur and twine, with just a smidge of blood smeared in for good measure. Even an ordinary passerby, much less someone caught within it, would have been hard-pressed to undo the mess with anything less than a sharp set of cutting tools.

After Frank wiped off his paws in the sand and Elvis finished laughing, they dragged the clump of scummy felinity over to nearly the edge of the cliff, about one foot away from what would have been the start of a precipitous drop. As Elvis and Frank began walking away, Elvis whistled loudly. Daisy and Stella came running out from behind the shrubbery and, upon their arrival, their masters jumped into their saddles. Frank turned back and said, "Now you boys don't do anything that we wouldn't do."

Elvis looked back and chimed in, "And don't worry about Fatscat. We'll make sure he knows where you are and how much fun you're having up here, and we'll definitely tell him what great work you guys are doing. Keep your claws crossed and you might even get a raise. Assuming he doesn't kill you, that is." Elvis and Frank giggled for a moment and Elvis continued, "Don't let that get you down now. You've probably got more important critters than Fatscat to worry about for the time being, don't you think? Make sure you stay away from the edge of that cliff, you hear? It's dangerous." Then he smiled and blew them a kiss, as Daisy and Stella turned the corner and went back down the trail.

The steep grade made the trip down slow going, but once they reached bottom, Daisy and Stella smiled at the sight of the open road ahead, and blasted full tilt toward their traveling companions. Other than canines who were racers by occupation, and even then only the good ones, Stella was one of the few dogs around who could stay close to Daisy on a dead run. Their red and golden fur blew in the breeze as their riders glanced back and forth at each other with huge grins, doing their best jockey impressions and taking short peeks toward the ocean for glimpses of the whales that were spouting and breaching off in the distance. Daisy had started to open up a bit of a lead as the Pusserschmott crew came into view, and they slowed to a casual canter for their approach to avoid startling the dogs ahead.

When they reached the group, Warren turned in his saddle to look back and said, "Were you just getting their attention with those shots, or do we need to send a crew up there with a couple of shovels?" Elvis said, "Nah, no need for anything like that. Everybody's breathing for now. We'll tell the gang at HQ about them tomorrow. They can check on them and do whatever it is that they do. The only things I'm really concerned with now are that trout the old man was talking about and the awesome bourbon he keeps behind that bar of his."

Warren shook his head with a slight look of disappointment and said, "I know. Ever since I gave it all up, that's probably the one I miss the most. With the way I used to hit the bottle during all those years in the service, though, I just had to put a stop to it. Doc said my liver might not be able to handle much more." Then he smiled and said, "But, at least we've got those catnip fruit trees growing all over the place up at the farm." Elvis smiled back and said, "Yeah, I'm looking forward to getting this job done, so we can come back and hang out with you guys for a few days up there. Gives me something to look forward to."

Elvis squeezed Daisy's sides and she trotted up to the front of the pack, where Frank already had gone to resume the responsibility of leading Amos. The old man turned when he heard Daisy approaching and said, "Frankie here tells me that things up on the cliff have gotten a little more intimate for our friends." Elvis replied, "Yeah, they're a real close bunch these days," and all three of them broke out in laughter.

The ride down into the valley was splendid, with a soft breeze blowing in from the coast and temperatures well below the scorch level that Frank and Elvis had left behind in Woodville. Elvis, Frank and the old man reminisced about some old times and caught up on a few things anew, and in what seemingly was no time at all, they were coming up the long, wide drive of the Pusserschmott estate. The green trees of the farm stretched behind the house for as far as the eye could see. Elvis thought to himself that almost nothing could make the setting more beautiful. The sight of the Pusserschmott sisters coming out of the front door to greet everyone was just the thing to do the trick.

CHAPTER NINETEEN

FULL-SERVICE ACCOMMODATIONS

Left on its own, the word "large" would not aptly describe Chez Pusserschmott. Behemoth would not be inappropriate, but beyond its sheer size, pretentious it was not. Along the order of a way, *way* oversized country home, save that the exterior walls were fashioned of finer hardwoods and the landscaping was more kept up with. They were a family of tree-growing farmers after all. Two stories of roughly six feet each (very high by cat standards), almost one hundred feet from end to end, and nearly half that from front to back. Most of it was painted a deep brown, although the many windows were trimmed in white, and a covered, tan porch spanned nearly half of the front of the house.

Almost before Elvis and Frank had landed their dismounts, Barry and two farm workers were leading Daisy, Stella and Amos away toward the huge barn behind the house. A large gray cat was happily walking up the porch steps and then into the house with Elvis' and Frank's saddlebags over his shoulders. Sarena and Jeanine, the old man's lovely daughters, greeted Elvis and Frank with warm hugs, not having seen them for nearly a year. Their usually grouchy mother, Carla Baines Pusserschmott, stood in the front doorway waiting to bestow welcome.

Carla's hugs were contrived, and thus much shorter and less enthusiastic than those of her daughters. Perfectly fine with the boys, who, if they had their druthers, would have preferred a simple paw rub to avoid the lethal mix of her gaudy perfume and stale breath. Frank always joked that if a rogue spark were to land near her, the gaseous concoction could ignite her ridiculous hairdo into a raging inferno. She flashed her trademark phony smile and blurted out in an even phonier voice, "Elvis, Frankie, don't you two look handsome? It's so good to see you."

The old man came up the porch steps behind them and said, "You two come on in. Charles here can show you to your rooms. Then you can get back out here, have a drink on the porch and catch up with the family while we wait on supper."

Elvis and Frank followed the portly butler through the front door, across the foyer and into a large, airy living room. A huge stone fireplace stood across from them in the back of the room. To the left was a bar with eight stools in front and far too many bottles to count on the shelves behind. Facing the fireplace in somewhat of a semicircle was a slew of leather furniture. Two massive couches, three chairs and two love seats, in no particular order, with a few wooden coffee and side tables smattered about.

To the right of the fireplace was a large, straight stairwell that ascended to a landing halfway up and then turned 180 degrees before leading the rest of the way to the second floor. Charles moved quickly up the steps, turned right and started down the hall, with Elvis and Frank close behind. The corridor was lined on both sides with several doorways, antique wall lanterns that were not yet lit for the evening, and oil portraits of nearly every Pusserschmott gone by, families and individuals alike. Charles showed them to their rooms and went zipping back down the hall.

As Elvis and Frank started to unpack their bags, a stern voice rang out from the hall: "We haven't seen either of you for almost a year, and you two want to unpack those little bags? For one night?" Sarena walked into Elvis' room, unbuckled his gun belt and let it drop to the floor. Then she went back into the hall, looked into Frank's room and said, "Francis, do I need to come in there and take yours off, too?"

Frank just stood there with a look of surprise on his face and then shook his head from side to side as she continued. "Both of you come downstairs right now and visit with us before I bring Jeanine up here and we drag you down by your tails, okay?" She peeked over at Elvis, smiled and flashed a quick wink as she started back down the hall.

By the time Elvis and Frank had stepped out of the front door, Charles was on their heels with an array of filled glasses, and Jeanine looked up from her chair to say, "It's about time you gentlemen got down here. You know how we hate to drink alone." Scattered all around the porch were beautiful maple rocking chairs that the old man's grandfather had purchased years ago during a summer excursion to Catada. Eight of them surrounded a large rectangular iron table that was situated on the right side of the porch as one looked out of the front door.

Carla was seated at the far end, looking back toward the door. Eddie sat to her immediate right, he being the best at breath tolerance, thanks to his olfactory senses having been pummeled by a lifetime of barn activity. Continuing around, counter clockwise, were Sarena and then Jeanine. Warren was at the closer end of the table facing directly across at Carla, whether he liked it or not. Elvis quickly jumped into the adjoining seat across from Jeanine and facing out into the front yard. Frank sat down next to his pal, across from Sarena, and declared that he'd leave the seat to Carla's immediate left open for her spouse.

The old man himself came through the door moments later and made way to his seat, as Charles finished passing out the glasses. Knowing what the near future likely held in store for them, Frank and Elvis were determined to enjoy the evening to its fullest. They thought the world of the Pusserschmott sisters, and for more than just the obvious reasons. They were exceptionally bright, having taken over entirely the complex operation of the remaining array of Pusserschmott businesses (an assignment well beyond the ken of their brother), extremely witty and insatiable in conversation. The old man was a riot once he got going, and Warren and Eddie were among the finest that the country had to offer in their respective fields, each exceptionally talented and interesting. The only weak link in the entire chain of chatter was . . . .

Charles didn't wait long before returning to the porch in search of anyone needing a refill. A few minutes later, two riders could be seen coming toward the house, with rods and nets slung over their shoulders, and creels overflowing with hefty specimens from the river. They smiled and waved at the porch sitters, and rode around to the back of the house. As much fun as everyone was having just chatting away the afternoon, no one was disappointed when the dinner bell rang roughly an hour later. Just in time to keep everyone from tying on too big of a load.

The Pusserschmott dining room was much like the rest of the house; understated in décor, but big. The long oak table seated up to sixteen had there been the need, but the eight who had emigrated from the porch congregated at one end, with the old man seated at the head. Charles arrived momentarily with a magnum of Champagne from the cellar and Pepé made his appearance, wheeling a large serving cart in from the kitchen.

Pepé had sneaked across the Mexicat border when he was just a kitten, and had spent his entire life in and around kitchens. Only the world's best chefs could match Pepé in most respects, and likely only a few of those could hold his or her own with Pepé when it came to seafood. The cream of chicken soup he served for an appetizer was thick and rich, and loaded with chunks of white meat, but the trout was the shining star of the evening, sautéed in a peppery, light brown roux and served with a tangy sauce on the side. It was all that he could do to hold the cats at bay for the few minutes it took him to circle the table and flawlessly de-bone each fish before their eyes.

Most everyone was full by the time fresh catnip fruit pie arrived for dessert, but each of them managed to eat nearly every bit. For those who couldn't finish entirely, Frank was all too happy to help out. Warren and Eddie left to tend to their evening duties and retire to their quarters, while Elvis, Frank and the Pusserschmotts relocated to the warmth of a roaring fire in the living room. There, they could digest their meals properly, and discuss how Clevin and Melba had gotten themselves into their unfortunate situation.

It had been barely over a week since they left South Sebastian by coach with plans to spend a romantic long weekend at the lake house. Melba for some reason was adamant about not having any of the help on the premises. The old man had sent word that at least a small contingent should stay on, just in case of emergency. Unfortunately, they all returned to South Sebastian on the coach, having been ordered by Melba to depart upon her arrival. The old man sent them back a couple of days later with orders to not return home again, but instead of finding Clevin and Melba, they found the following note that the old man produced:

Deer Marris Pusersmot

By the time you reed this your sun and hiz lady will be under my soupervizon. If you do as I say thay will not be harned. But I dont think their new quarterz is as cumfterbul as what thay are use to. If you hope to see them again you will asembal five millon dollarz in cash and send it to me. We will contack you with more detales. If you try anything fansee we will not hezitayt to kill them.

X

The old man went over to Elvis, took back the note and said, "I took it to East Coast HQ as soon as we got it, Elvis. Kathy Barncat recognized the pawwriting and spelling right away. She said she'd seen more than enough notes from Harold Fatscat when she was helping put evidence together for his trial a few years back. I guess something like this always was possible. That sort of gang is capable of anything if there's enough money in it, but everything that they're into is on the other side of those hills. No one ever expected him to try something like this. Not all the way over here. It's not like he has some kind of grudge against us. Nothing that I know of, anyway."

He walked over to the bar and continued as he poured himself another drink, "We got a telegram a few days later saying that we had three days to put the money together. Barncat wanted to take a bunch of troops and go hunt down Fatscat and some of his crew, but I was nervous. I mean, I know they want to stop that gang of his, and I do want to help, Elvis. Sure, five million is a lot of money to most cats, but we've got it. I just don't want my boy getting hurt, and I know they'll kill him if they get wind that there's a crowd coming after them. I didn't know what to do, so I sent a wire to Leo and asked if he could do anything to help."

The old man came back from the bar, sat in his chair, began swirling his drink and continued, "Next thing I know, Barncat's here at the house saying that there's a new plan. She said she didn't know how, and I didn't have the heart to tell her, but that the President found out about the whole thing. She said that Central's gonna send Elvis and Frank out here to help make sure that we get the kids back safe, and then maybe they can take a run at Fatscat.

"She said that we'd need to buy a little time and asked me if I would mind sending a wire saying that we'll pay the ransom, but that we need a few more days to round up that kind of cash. So, that's what I did, just a couple of days ago, and we've been waiting for you ever since. We know nothing's for sure on something like this, Elvis, but Leo figured that if anybody's got a chance, it's you two, and all of us feel the same way. If there's anything that we can do to help, *anything*, you and Frankie just say the word."

Elvis took a big swig of bourbon and said, "Well, since you're offering, I think we could use a little help. Barncat's got some good riders and good shooters, and we'll take what she can give us, but nobody in her outfit is as sharp as Warren. Do you think we could take him along and maybe another one of your security patrol who he thinks is good? We also could use Eddie and the quickest dog he's got, if that's not asking too much. We'll do everything we can to keep him out of danger, and I know I can't promise anything, but we could be up in those woods for a little while. If we need to get a message in or out of there quick, nobody could do it faster than him."

The old man looked excited as he replied, "Well, Warren didn't want to say anything. He didn't want to impose unless you asked first, but he's dying to help out on this. He does such a fantastic job for us, Elvis. We do pay him well for it, but even as big as we've gotten over the years, running security for us isn't all that exciting for someone who's been where Warren has.

I know he'll be happy as a lark, Elvis, and I'm sure he's got another boy or two who can help. We never thought about Eddie, but like I said, whatever we can do. So long as it's all right with him, I certainly have no problem with it. He's got a couple of dogs he's been training for endurance runs and he's all excited about them, so he'll probably jump at the chance."

Elvis tipped the bottom of his glass toward the ceiling, set it on the bar and said, "That's great news, Morris. Those guys would be a huge help." Elvis pulled out his pocket watch, peeked down at it and said, "Speaking of which, one thing that probably will help more than anything would be a good night's sleep." Elvis nodded toward Frank and said, "Frankie here says we're getting off to a really early start tomorrow, so we can spend a little time at HQ before we get on the road."

Elvis got up and said, "Good night, everyone, and thanks again for the wonderful hospitality, as usual." Then he walked up the steps and went on toward his room. Frank was only a few steps behind and, within minutes, everyone had drifted upstairs while Charles was busily about the living room, picking up glasses and extinguishing lanterns.

Out of his bedroom window, Elvis gazed at the flickering lights of South Sebastian. They were brilliant in the distance, with stars twinkling behind and one-third of a moon lit high in the sky, peeking in and out of scattered, thin clouds. He darkened the lantern above his bed and slid under the covers, as the light from the evening sky beamed through his window. The last of the pawsteps seemed to have gone down the hall and it was very, very quiet.

Elvis was nearly dead to the world when he heard the sound of his doorknob slowly turning. He grabbed one of his pistols and quickly rolled off of the side of his bed, away from the door, without a sound. He reached his forelegs and peeked his eyes over the bed, and pointed at the widening crack in the door. He couldn't help but wonder how anyone could have gotten within two hundred yards of the place, much less into the house and up to his room.

A tall silhouette began to emerge through the doorway, and as Elvis slowly began to squeeze the trigger, the remainder of the silhouette moved fully into the window's light. Suddenly, a familiar voice broke the silence and whispered across the room, "Elvis, you aren't going to shoot me, are you?" With a sigh of relief, he began to stand, realizing that the only thing truly in danger was some of the sleep that he had been so looking forward to. Elvis whispered back, "Of course not." Then he paused for a moment, held his gun out and smiled as he said to Jeanine, "Well, not with this anyway."

CHAPTER TWENTY

DROPPING IN ON THE QUEEN

It was well before dawn had cracked when a loud knock hit his bedroom door, and Elvis jumped up quickly and began to rub his eyes. Frank's voice muffled its way through the thick wooden door, "Let's get a move on, tiger. Breakfast is ready when you are."

Elvis strapped on his gun belt and threw on his vest, and made sure that the things in his saddlebags were in order. He grabbed his hat from the hook on the wall as he hurried out the door and down the hall with his stuff. Pepé had prepared fresh lox and homemade bagels, and served up some of the unmistakable Pusserschmott milk, fresh from the ranch up the road that produced all of the meat and dairy products (well, all of the domestic ones) for the Pusserschmott family and staff. Elvis and Frank sat at a large, round table by the kitchen window and whipped through their portions without speaking a word, while Pepé cleaned up and readied for the day's prep work.

They thanked Pepé for breakfast and for the fabulous dinner the night before. He flashed a wide grin and rubbed paws with them enthusiastically as they went out the back door and began walking toward the barn. The top of the sun had just breached the horizon, and its light was starting to gleam off of the dew on the bright white, wooden gutters that edged the roof of the big red structure. Eddie was carrying a saddle toward the last of the dogs, and his muscles rippled across his small, slender, gray frame. A sharp contrast to the husky, dark brown body of Warren, who was standing nearby and talking with a tall, young, stocky cat with jet black fur.

As he and Frank approached the barn, Elvis said, "Who you got there, Eddie? I don't think I've seen that one before." Eddie smiled and said, "Nope, I doubt you have. Not since he was just a pup anyway. This is Catation. He's part rotty and part setter. I never really thought he'd be anything special, but I've been working him hard for the last six months and he's my new star. Might be the fastest I've ever had for an endurance runner."

Eddie reached under for the saddle cinch and continued, "Agile, too. Only things he can't catch are our best greyhounds, but they wouldn't do us much good where we're going. If we get a little open road this morning, maybe you and Frankie can bust it open with me for a stretch and I'll show you what I'm talking about. Those two of yours look like they're still fast as ever."

Elvis smiled and said, "I know they'd love to get out and run with a new playmate." Then Elvis looked back over his shoulder and said, "Who's the big kid over there standing by Warren?" As Eddie jumped into his saddle, he replied, "That's Benji, one of Warren's young boys. A little quiet, but a he's great rider, and strong as a dog. Warren says he's a pretty hot shot with the rifle, too."

Frank already had started walking toward Warren and Benji, and Elvis came following after. As they introduced themselves to Benji, Elvis could see from the look on Warren's face how excited he was to be coming along. Warren and Benji hopped onto their big Chocolate Labradors, and Eddie was leading Daisy and Stella out from the barn, saddled and ready to go. Amos was close behind, tied to Frank's saddle and prancing away, excited as usual to be going anywhere. Daisy, Stella and Amos all were smiling as they licked their chops, having spent the night in the luxurious stalls of the Pusserschmott barn, eating fresh meat from the ranch up the road and drinking icy cold spring water.

Elvis and Frank threw their saddlebags on and tied them down, and hopped up for the ride. Warren took the lead alongside of Benji, with Elvis, Frank and Eddie side by side behind them, and Amos trailing behind happily, ignoring the weight of his load. They headed around the house and down the pathway toward the road. The sun had risen fully and was beaming straight at them through the cool sky, as the dew glistened on the thick, green grass of the front lawn. They turned left at the end of the path and started toward the city, and Frank and Elvis began briefing the others on some of what they knew.

Although it still was extremely early, they rode along the edge of the hills, hoping not to attract attention. Even so, they reached the outskirts in less than half an hour, and marveled at the views as they rode down into the south side of downtown. South Sebastian had been undergoing somewhat of a growth spurt in recent years, but still was considered one of the most charming towns in the East. Wide streets and well kept, brightly colored buildings, and homes that owners obviously took pride in. Midway through town on the south side stood a somewhat less colorful, nondescript gray building that housed East Coast Headquarters. Though it paled in charm compared to the surrounding structures, it wasn't bad for government work.

It was an earlier hour than that ordinarily kept by those maintaining the bureaucracy, but Frank had made plans in advance and several workers surprisingly were up and about. The visitors all tied their dogs to a hitching post in the back and entered the building. Before they could look around for more than a few seconds, a deep voice came bellowing out from the top of the stairwell straight ahead: "Well, well. If it isn't Elvis the Gunslinger and his trusty pal. And Mr. Warren, I see you let these scoundrels drag you along this time. So, who's the rest of this motley crew?"

Kathy Barncat was taller and wider than most tomcats, and probably stronger, too. Light orange in color, with white markings on her head, and wearing her usual faded, brown leather vest. She was one of the first women ever to serve in battle in the military, and she had continued along in the public service. Moving rapidly up the ladder from her beginnings as a munitions specialist, all the way to Director of East Coast Operations. She was tough as masonry nails and a lot smarter than your average, well, barn cat.

Had she been a little less gruff and a little more sophisticated, she probably would have been next in line to be chief of Central's entire operation. It was all just as well with her. Being away from the Capitol and all of its politics gave her freedom to do things as she liked, and allowed her to get her paws dirty in the field every once in a while if she wanted. Opportunities that surely would have disappeared with any further ascension through the ranks.

She lumbered down the steps as Elvis put his foreleg around Eddie's shoulders and said, "Kathy Barncat, this is Eddie Arcato, whom you've probably heard of unless you've had your eyes and ears wired shut for the last few years, and this is Benji, one of Warren's best young men. They're going to help us out on this one, with a couple of yours if you can spare them."

Kathy motioned for them to follow her up the steps and she replied as they approached, "I do think I recognize you, Mr. Arcato. It's just that the big E here doesn't usually come strolling in at six-thirty a.m. Much less with a big-time jockey star. Nervous Frankie, now he might be up at this hour, but not the man himself. Usually shacked up with some bombshell at this time of day. Anyway, it sure is a pleasure to meet you."

She continued, "The other thing, Elvis, is that we do have a lot going on right now. That gang out there is trying to squeeze into every last place that they haven't gotten to yet, and we're doing everything we can to at least keep tabs on them. But, the boss says to give you however many you need, so that's what we'll do. If you could keep it to just a couple, I'd damn sure appreciate it, slick. We've got only so many really good ones to go around and we're already stretched about as thin as we can go."

Elvis put his right forepaw on her shoulder and said, "Two will do just fine, my dear. By the way, Frankie and I have some stuff that you and your crew might want to take a look at, and we'd love to see anything new that you've got before we hit the trail."

She turned at the top of the steps and started down the hall, motioning for Elvis, Frank and the rest to follow along. She waddled as she walked, and she stopped for a moment to look back over her shoulder and yell at the guard sitting at the top of the steps. She said, "Herb, pull yourself out of that chair for a minute before you fall back asleep and tell those boys on the Tin Roof team that I need them up here in the briefing room. PRONTO, ya hear? These highfalutin visitors of mine don't have much time to burn."

She led them halfway down the hall and into a room. Kathy told Warren, Benji and Eddie to sit tight for a moment, and she motioned with her head for Elvis and Frank to step outside. They followed her out of the room and down to the end of the hall. Kathy opened the last door on the right, pointed inside and said, "Since the local police, if that's what you want to call them, really aren't capable of anything this nifty, I can only assume that this is your work?"

Frank peeked in first and, to his surprise, there sat the three cats that had been spying from the cliff the previous afternoon, each tied to his own chair. Frank smiled and began to chuckle, and then declared, "Well, look who it is! Fancy seeing you here." Then he turned to Kathy and said, "How did you come across these little rats so fast? Don't tell me they got out of that pickle all by themselves." Elvis was curious as to what was going on and he hurried to peek in behind Frank. Then he broke out laughing himself and said, "Hey, kids. Everything comfy cozy in there? You've got your own chairs and everything."

Kathy slammed the door, started back down the hall and said, "One of our men who was out on patrol late yesterday afternoon came across a dog running along the trail, all saddled up without a rider. He followed the tracks and ended up running into those three, tied up on top of a cliff, next to a pair of dogs. We didn't have anyone assigned to that area yesterday, so I figured it had to be you two. Looked like your work anyway, leaving them out there with no guns, all tied up and bloody. They're lucky we ran into them before nightfall. Who knows what might have gotten to them?"

Elvis said, "We were going to tell you about them this morning, Boss. Really, we were. We thought that a night out in the cool air with some bobcats and raccoons might teach them a little lesson about minding their own business." Kathy snapped back, "A little lesson? Don't you know how hard it is for us to bring in anyone who might know a little something about what's going on with that gang out there, E? I know they probably deserved whatever was coming to them, but please do me a favor and at least let me know when you find anyone around here who might have some useful information. It sure would make my life easier if I could get my paws on some snitches with something good to tell before they get sent to the undertaker."

CHAPTER TWENTY-ONE

READYING FOR A RIDE

As they started back down the hall, four more cats had cleared the steps and were going toward the briefing room. They were carrying papers and chatting amongst themselves, and one of them obviously was perturbed about the early hour. In the room were three rectangular wooden tables, configured in the shape of a U. Eddie, Benji and Warren already were seated at the table nearest the door, facing out at the exterior window. The staffers found their way to some seats at the table directly across. Elvis and Frank took seats at the table on the right, facing a board on the opposite wall, upon which Kathy was beginning to scribble some gibberish in yellow chalk.

She was facing the board while she wrote, and said in a firm tone, "Wilson, you can quit your damn whining now. You think it's early, do you? Care to take a wild guess as to who was here at five-thirty firing up lanterns and opening windows while your lazy ass still was home tucked away in bed? I've said it more than once. If it's all too much for you to handle, then you're more than welcome to go out and get yourself a job where you might have to work for a living."

Still facing away as she wrote, she continued, "I told you before that Elvis and the rest of these gentlemen have a lot to do and that they need to get an early start. How about you wipe that little pout off of your face and see if you can't act like a man for a few minutes, and we'll all try to get out of here as soon as we can." Eddie and Benji sat wide-eyed as Wilson, who was medium-sized with brown and black stripes, squirmed behind his round spectacles. Warren, Elvis and Frank each looked down and snickered, trying their best not to laugh out loud, but Wilson's own colleagues were completely unsuccessful in restraining themselves.

"Okay, enough giggling," Kathy said as she finished writing and turned to face everyone. She pointed up at the board and said, "The only communications that we have so far from Fatscat are the note that was left at the lake house when the Pusserschmott couple were taken and a telegram that came a few days later. There hasn't been any response to the old man's wire back saying that he needs a little more time to get the money together, or to the message that we sent, but you know Harold. If that mangy runt thinks there's even a slight chance that he'll collect this ransom, he'll wait a little longer, but we don't want to push it too much and take any chances.

"If we're correct about where he is, any way up into those peaks has to be well-guarded near the top, and we haven't had the manpower on this shoestring budget of mine to go up there and start hunting all over for him. Not without some real help from the military anyway, and they've made it clear that they aren't going to mobilize a force as big as I've asked for to let me take them on some wild mouse chase. So, unless I can get my paws on some solid proof about his exact whereabouts, Fatscat and his cronies are pretty safe up there for the time being."

Frank started reaching into his bag for the trail map that they had swiped from Tony, but Elvis reached under the table, grabbed Frank's foreleg and said under his breath, "Not now." Frank looked back up at Elvis a bit puzzled, but figured that there must be some justification for holding it back, so he pushed the papers back into his bag, straightened up, and continued watching and listening to Kathy.

The Barncat sat down in a large, padded chair next to the board. Leaning back with a big yawn, she said, "It's been over half a year since we've even had a reported sighting of old Harold. With all of the activity that we're seeing from that gang of his lately, we've got to believe that, wherever he's hiding, it has to be a pretty substantial operation and there must be at least a few others up there helping him run it. He's just getting too much done to be working all alone out of some little hole in the ground.

"And one other thing really is curious. We've heard from some pretty reliable sources that Albert Hardcrass has been trying to round up a bunch of guys for some sort of project. All we've got is a lot of talk at this point, but he supposedly is offering up a fat chunk of cash to anyone who will get on board with him. I know that little SOB and his crew have been pretty much broke since he got out of jail last year, so I don't see how he could be doing it all alone.

"Something tells me that Fatscat has to be behind it, but I have no idea what the connection could be. What doesn't make sense is that Albert and Harold can't stand each other. Fatscat tried to kill him when they were in prison together a few years back, and Hardcrass has a cruddy little gang of his own. They're arch rivals. Fatscat's been moving in on some of Hardcrass' territory lately, but Hardcrass still has a lot of weight in a few little coastal towns that those Tin Roofers haven't gotten to yet. I don't know what to think for sure."

Elvis looked at Kathy, nodded sideways toward the staffers and asked, "Are any of these gentlemen coming with us or are they just taking notes?" She replied, "Unless you just can't get by without more, I was going to let Burt and Timmy here ride with you. They know their way around up there as well as anyone. Anyone we have, that is, and they're our most experienced trackers. Does that sound okay to you boys?"

Elvis and Frank looked across the room at them and then turned toward Warren, who gave a half-hearted nod. Elvis looked back at Kathy and said, "Okay, Boss, you've got a deal." Then he continued, "What about the money? Are we really going to take it or are we supposed to make a run at it empty-pawed?"

CHAPTER TWENTY-TWO

MAPS AND MONEY

Kathy smiled at Elvis and said, "Yeah, the money. We're going straight to the bank in about half an hour to load all of you up with the cash. As much as I don't agree with it, the plan is to show up with the money and give it up, and we'll just have to chase it down after we get our paws on those Pusserschmotts. We're under strict orders from the top, and I mean ALL THE WAY from the top, that we don't pull any tricks or make any kind of move to go after any punks or money until those kids are completely safe."

She continued, "The bank doesn't open for another two hours and we're going to get over there and square all of this away long before business starts. We sent a telegram to Fatscat saying we'd have the cash in our paws by the end of the day today, and that if he wants it, he'd better send drop-off instructions by three o'clock. We said we'd meet him with the cash twenty-four hours after we get the location, and you know that SOB will wait until the last minute to send those damn instructions.

"Something that's really been worrying me is that there's been a ton of cash moving into that bank over the last few nights and the cops have to be wondering what's going on. They're all buddy-buddy with those delivery crews. I can't believe they haven't been over here or to the bank asking about it already. I need to come up with some kind of story to divert their attention. None of them has any idea about this catnapping and it needs to stay that way.

"So, we've got a decoy pickup set up at the bank for just after the close of business today. Don't worry. I'll come up with something to tell the cops. No one not sitting in this room is going to know that this pickup later today isn't for real. EVERYBODY HEAR THAT? I'll send a few of my men off this afternoon in the wrong direction in a wagon with a safe on it. If I get it set up right, they'll have a bunch of cops trailing them who won't have any idea that my crew is just bouncing along on their merry way with a box full of who knows what. I can tell you one thing for sure. There ain't gonna be any money in it.

"Sorry about all of the hoopla, boys, but I can't trust these locals anymore. The last thing we need is a bunch of wannabe heroes getting wind of what actually is going on. Next thing you know, they'll be out there trailing the real money or trying to stakeout the actual exchange location. If Fatscat sniffs out anything like that, he'll call the whole thing off and who knows where we'll end up. That's why I want all of you out of here and long gone with the cash before anyone starts paying attention.

"We can't be sure that some of Fatscat's crew might not be watching the banks either. He's got a lot of crooks crawling around in those woods and in a lot of other places. Nothing but crooks. If any of them knows about this ransom demand, I wouldn't be surprised if a few get the bright idea to keep an eye out for a big payload, try to snatch it for themselves and make a run for it. That won't do us any good either. I don't like turning over that cash to begin with, but if we're going to do it, then it needs to get to the right place and we need to come back with those kids."

Elvis asked, "What about the location instructions?" Kathy said, "We'll send someone after you with the instructions as soon as we get them. Be sure that y'all make good time getting out of town and down the main trail into the Longtails, but don't be going so fast that someone can't catch up tonight. Elvis said, "If you don't mind, let Eddie bring the instructions. He says that little rotty-setter mix he's got out there on the hitching post is a real burner and can run all day. He'll be able to catch up a lot faster than anyone you've got. And he can lose anyone who tries to tail him, too."

Kathy replied, "I have no problem with that, E." Then she looked over at Eddie and said, "But you be careful out there, Mr. Arcato. I don't know who or what is going to be out on that trail this evening. I doubt that anyone out there is going to try to take on six riders, but anyone riding alone certainly is an easy target. I know you might have a quick mount, but unless he can outrun a rifle slug, you're not necessarily safe out there alone these days." Eddie nodded a few times and said, "Thank you ma'am. I'll keep my eyes open, but I don't think it'll be a problem."

Kathy got up and waddled to the door, where she turned and said, "I'll be in my office for a few minutes if anyone needs anything. We meet by the front door in fifteen and head over to the bank." Everyone else followed out behind her, each making his way down the hall and down the steps, except for Elvis and Frank, who followed Kathy past the steps and straight to her office in the front corner of the second floor. She walked in and sat down in her wide, high-back leather chair, which was behind her desk and up against the interior wall, facing across the room and out of a large window. Elvis and Frank came in behind and shut the door.

She said with a wink, "So, you two got something juicy to tell me, or did you just want to hang out in here for a few minutes and hope that a little of the ol' Barncat savoir faire rubs off on you before you get on the road?" Elvis walked over to the window and looked out onto South Street for a moment. Still facing away, he said, "Not that we couldn't use a little extra oomph to get us through this excursion, your majesty, but *we* actually have something for *you*."

Elvis turned back to look at Kathy and continued, "Frankie was going to bust it out at the meeting, but with the weekend we just had, we're starting to get a little skittish around almost anyone we haven't known for a while. Even here at HQ. Just too many signs that Fatscat might be getting wind of supposedly classified things as fast as we are." Kathy looked up with concern on her face and broke in, "What's going on, E? Sounds like something I need to know about." Elvis replied, "Well, a few bums tried to burn down my barn the night before Frankie and I left Woodville, and then we ran into somebody on the train who almost surely is one of them."

Frankie chimed in, "I didn't even find out about this trip until a half day before I came knocking on his door. It's like that SOB has somebody sitting right there on the telegraph line, and with the code to boot!"

Kathy looked down for a minute and said, "You know I do my best around here, but with the kind of money that gang has been throwing around, I can't tell you for sure that even this place is watertight anymore. We screen everyone to the hilt like always, and nobody knows anything really important until he or she's been here for a good, long while, but nobody's immune these days. We haven't had anything really suspicious happen yet, but when you're paying government salaries, there's always a chance that somebody might get sucked in. That's why I wanted to meet so early today with you and just a few that I know I can trust. So, whaddya got, Francois?"

Frank walked over toward Kathy, pulled out the bag that he and Elvis had pilfered from Tony's train cabin and dumped it out on her desk. Then he said, "The guy that Elvis mentioned, the one on the train." Kathy nodded and Frank continued, "We wrapped him up good and sent him overboard for a little nighttime side trip, and afterward, we found this in his cabin.

"You'll have all sorts of fun with these notes and letters, but this is what really caught our eye. Looks like a map of trails way, way up in the upper Longtails, doesn't it? The man and I don't recall ever riding that far up in there and this ain't exactly our first time out to these parts. What do you make of it?" Kathy stared down intently for nearly half a minute, slowly raised up from her chair with her gaze still fixed on the map, turned and walked across the room, and opened the door.

"BURT! BURT!" Her voice all but shook the paintings off of her office walls as it thundered through the hall. "PRONTO, BABY. I NEED YOU NOW." Kathy came back to her desk and barely had gotten back into her seat when Burt came dashing through the door with a few papers jammed between his teeth. He dropped the papers on the floor and said, as he closed the door behind him,

"What's up, Chief?" Kathy, staring back at the map, replied, "Take a look at this little gem that our buddies got their paws on."

Kathy asked, "Who was this guy anyway? What did he look like?" Elvis said, "He was a big, loud, fluffy white guy who called himself Tony. Tony the Tiger, if you can believe that." As Frank snickered, Kathy and Burt looked quickly at one another with somewhat surprised facial expressions. Kathy turned back and said, "No, slick, we believe it. We never can seem to bring him in on any sort of federal charge, and the locals in most of these towns are so deep into Fatscat's pocket that they're absolutely zero help.

"If it's the guy we're thinking about, then you're talking about the top hit cat in the entire Tin Roof Gang. If Harold really needs to have somebody knocked off, or even just roughed up, and he wants to make sure it gets done right, Tony is the one he calls." Then she asked, "Is he a goner or did y'all just set him back a bit?"

Frank replied, "I really don't think he's finished. Not unless he landed perfectly on his noggin. Anything's possible with no way to break the fall, but he's probably just roughed up, and he shouldn't have ended up too far from the tracks. Then again, he was out there with no dog and we took his gun, so I guess anything *could* have happened to him. Assuming he didn't break anything, though, he should have been able to flag down a train or hitch some kind of a ride sooner or later. After he got his head cleared anyway."

Kathy leaned back in her chair, looked around at everyone in the room and said, "Not a word about this map or Tony to anyone." She whispered at the top of her lungs, "YOU HEAR ME? No one." Everyone quietly nodded at each other. She stood up and said with a smile, "Now let's get over to the bank and get you boys a little pin money, eh?" Frank scooped up the map and put it back into his bag, and he and Elvis followed out the door after Burt, who already was halfway down the hall. Kathy shut the door behind her, locked it and began waddling quickly to catch up.

CHAPTER TWENTY-THREE

GETTING THE SHOW ON THE ROAD

The South Sebastian branch of the Fourth Cational Bank was conveniently located just across South Street from East Coast HQ. After her first few knocks elicited no response, the Barncat began pounding progressively louder on the front doors with both forepaws, until everyone could feel the walls starting to tremble. Burt, Timmy, Frank and Elvis exchanged uneasy glances with one another, obviously thinking to themselves one and the same thing: "I thought no one was supposed to know about this!"

Fortunately, the sound of running pawsteps on the other side became audible and Kathy finally put an end to the banging. The doors swung open to the sight of a studious looking little gray cat wearing a tan blazer, a black bowler hat and a monocle that was attached to his shirt. He said excitedly, "Sorry, Mrs. Kathy. We're not used to getting started so early here."

Kathy said, "Boys, say hi to Oliver." She nodded toward Burt and Timmy, and said to Oliver, "You already know these two clowns." Then she pointed in the other direction and said, "Oliver, meet Elvis and his pal, Frankie." Oliver held out his forepaw, smiled and said, "Very nice to finally meet you gentlemen. I've heard so much about you." They both reached out to rub Oliver's paw and Elvis said, "The pleasure is ours." Oliver led them into the main room, around to the other side of the teller counter, pointed to a big, stuffed, brown canvas bag on the floor and said, "Well, here it is. You folks are more than welcome to count it, but unless somebody busted into our safe last night, it all should be there."

Burt knelt down, reached into the bag, and began pulling out stacks of crisp $100 bills and stuffing them into his saddlebags. Timmy, Frank and Elvis got down with him and did likewise. Kathy said, "You know that comes out to over eight hundred grand apiece after you divide it up with the other two. I hope I don't have to tell you what sort of fate is going to befall anyone who mysteriously gets lost up in those mountains or anywhere else with any of this loot." "No, ma'am," said Burt and Timmy in virtual unison. Elvis and Frank just looked at her and began shaking their heads as they chuckled.

Oliver went into an office with a "Manager" sign on it and sat down at his desk to start delving into his usual work, while Kathy escorted everyone else through the rear hall and out the back door. Daisy, Stella, Amos, and mounts for Burt and Timmy were there, all hitched to a post. Benji and Warren were sitting atop their rides in the back alley with their backs to each other, scanning intently for onlookers like security guys do. They rode over near the hitching post and started taking funds from those who had just exited the bank, until everyone had a relatively equal load in his saddlebags. Amos put his head down and appeared to look sad not to have been trusted with any of the currency, but he perked up after Frank reminded him that his load just might be the most important one in the entire group.

They rode out through the southern side of town, backtracking on the route that most of them had come in on barely an hour before. It was just after eight-thirty and the streets of the city still were mostly quiet as they crossed the edge of downtown and started making their way up a trail leading into the northern foothills. They appeared inconspicuous enough, looking like not much more than your average, everyday bunch of pleasure riders. If you didn't know who they were, you certainly wouldn't have suspected them to be toting five million bucks. There just wasn't enough ceremony associated with them. None at all, really. It was exactly the kind of look that the Barncat and the rest of them had hoped for.

It would be at least six hours before Eddie would be in a position to take off after them, and they could go only so far without the guidance that his instructions would bring, but they weren't completely hamstrung. The Barncat had a good hunch, and Elvis, Frank and Warren wholeheartedly agreed, that Fatscat had no intention of setting the exchange operation anywhere on or even near the eastern side of the range. He wouldn't take that sort of a chance. Too open, too accessible, too many eyes, even in the upper reaches. No, he'd surely aim to stay back on the dark side, near places that there was no good reason for anyone to go except maybe for sport. Someplace where, if anyone had a numbers advantage, it almost surely would be him.

They plodded along slow, but steady, stopping briefly at a few random streams to let the canines rest for a bit and get a cool drink. And once more when Frank just couldn't take it anymore and demanded that they break into some of the cans of tuna and salmon that he had picked up at Uncle Sam's store not long before he and Elvis had left Woodville.

It was almost four o'clock by Elvis' watch when he motioned that they call it quits for the day. Everyone knew that there was no telling for sure just when Eddie might have gotten off the mark. If he did get a late jump, then this would be more than plenty distance for him to cover in a short time. It quickly was unanimous and they stopped at the first decent clearing that they could find with a nearby stream. With just over fourteen miles behind them, it was a solid day's effort.

Each of them was off in short order, tending to his animal or dragging in some firewood from the outskirts. Except for Frank. He was fully occupied piecing together his fancy portable spit and laying rocks around it in a big circle, hoping that they might get lucky enough to find something to roast and not have to again resort to his canned supplies.

Everyone other than Elvis and Benji had made his way to the campfire that Frank had cranked up, and Elvis was coming through the trees carrying a bottle of bourbon in one foreleg. The old man apparently had arranged to have one sneaked into Elvis' bag for the trip. Elvis was carrying a stack of Frank's tin cups in the other foreleg and passed them out to everyone. Even Warren took one, deciding that it was appropriate for an exception to his longstanding abstinence. As Elvis began tilting the bottle into the first cup, a rifle shot rang out. It was loud and it had to be close.

Each of them went straight for the ground and reached for his gun; guns in Elvis' case. They all were looking around intently, wondering where it came from and making sure that no one had been hit. Almost as loud as the gunshot was the cry of "WOO-HOO!" followed by Benji jumping from high out of a tree holding a rifle. "He's mine, he's mine!" Benji yelled as he dashed over a ridge and began sprinting downhill. Warren knew better, but the rest of them instinctually took off after him. It had to have been nearly a hundred yards from where he fired his shot when Benji finally stopped and looked down upon a boar. It looked like it might weigh fifty pounds.

With a grin stretched from ear to ear, Frank immediately went skipping back up the hill, faster than a school kitten just released for recess. He had Amos, Daisy and Stella saddled in no time and was leading them back down the hill on his hind legs. He carried three lariats over one shoulder and a burlap bag with his other foreleg.

Benji was as quick with his knife as he was true with his shot, and by the time Frank arrived with the dogs, Benji had fully completed a masterful job of field dressing. They pushed aside a gooey pile of blood and guts, and used all of their strength to roll what remained of the animal into the bag. Though Frank couldn't match Benji's pure brawn, he made up for it with lightning quick moves, tying off the bag and hitching a line to each saddle in a blur. They were back up the hill almost as fast as they had made it down.

Elvis quickly was back to passing out the cups for his second attempt at shot pouring. They all held their cups high and Elvis said, "Shall we be as lucky in our endeavors tomorrow as we are to have Benji here with us tonight." The others chimed in with a "here, here," as they all looked smilingly toward Benji and quickly dispatched with their allotments.

Frank and Benji affixed the boar to the spit rod and, with the able assistance of Amos and Stella, they hoisted it upon the stand.

While Frank and Benji dashed off to the stream to clean themselves up, Burt began tending to the cooking operation. Except for a couple of brief shifts turning the spit, each of the crew was able to reorganize his load, tend to his animal, sit and chat, even clock in a brief snooze if he was so inclined.

By the time dusk began to set in, the smell that had been growing ever more enticing finally took its toll on Frank. He requested loudly that anyone so minded please explain why they shouldn't launch into consumption mode. There being no responders, cats and dogs alike tore into Benji's bounty with a vengeance. Unless you count grunts and burps, conversation was nonexistent for the next several minutes. Before long, no one was able to sit at anything approaching a ninety degree angle, and many had been relegated to lying on their backs or sides.

It was good that there still was more than enough food left, because Eddie and Catation blew in like the wind shortly thereafter. Not unexpectedly, Fatscat didn't cough up the exchange location until well after five o'clock. When the results were in, it had taken Eddie just over ninety minutes to cover the same fourteen miles that it had taken the others six hours to lumber across.

Eddie and Catation were even more stoked about the pig than the others had been. Well, with the possible exception of Frank. They grabbed a quick slurp at the stream, sat by the fire for a short blow, and then proceeded to chew and swallow for the better part of the ensuing half hour. After they finished, Catation joined the rest of the canines, most of which were in la la land about twenty yards away in a makeshift rope paddock. Each of the felines had assumed his position in the slumber circle.

No. No one expects you to know what a slumber circle is. It's certainly not a term of art as far as I know. But, even these guys don't traipse through the forest every day with five million clams. Frankly, they didn't know what to do much better than you or I would. After considerable debate, the consensus was that Timmy, who barely had spoken all day, had the best suggestion. They dug a shallow ditch and piled in the cash, covered it up with a load of branches and leaves, and proceeded to lie around it end-to-end, each with loaded weapons by his side.

Elvis took the first shift on watch, and he and Frank both were perplexed when Eddie, who they figured would be exhausted, volunteered for the second shift. Sure enough, just before Eddie went to lie down in his spot, he made a quick detour, sat down next to Elvis and began to whisper, "Boss, I know I was a little nervous coming out here, so it might just be my imagination, but I think somebody was on my tail. I don't know who possibly could have kept that sort of pace for that long, but I swear I was hearing something back there."

Eddie continued, "Catty was acting weird, too. Kept looking back over his shoulder. He never does that. Not even when we're racing and dogs are coming right up on him." Elvis said, "Thanks, bud. Let's keep this between us for now. I do feel really good about this crew, but there's no sense in taking any chances that we don't have to." Eddie said, "That's what I figured, E. Don't let me sleep too long. I just want to get a few quick winks in after that meal. I had a long nap at HQ waiting to get my orders. I can stay up all night if you need me."

CHAPTER TWENTY-FOUR

OH, WHAT A TANGLED WEB . . .

The bank closed for business that day at the usual time, three o'clock sharp. Kathy Barncat never actually expected Fatscat to be on time with his wire. Still, that didn't keep her from pacing around nervously in her office, anxiously awaiting the moment when her telegraph operator would come running in with the news. Most everyone else in the building likewise was on pins and needles, but maybe they just weren't as pointy as the ones digging into the Barncat.

Eddie was the lone exception. He had little difficulty sacking out on a couch in an empty office at the far end of the second floor, only steps away from the closet that still housed the prisoners that Frank and Elvis had disabled during yesterday's ride. As you know, the boss lady would be waiting around a while for those instructions, but it was just as well. The day had gotten away from her and she still had one more nagging, but important, item of business to take care of.

There was a knock at the door and she excitedly yelled, "COME IN." She clenched her teeth and looked back down at the floor disappointedly when through the doorway came not the wire she anticipated, but instead Will Greysome. Tall, stocky and with upper forelegs that bulged out of his shirt, big Will was full of brown fur and all dressed up in tight blue stuff. He wore a fancy silver badge on his shirt pocket, and an even fancier wide-brimmed, round brown hat that had a badge-ish looking gold patch emblazoned on the front.

Greysome was in fact the Chief of Police of South Sebastian, but he definitely was not the sharpest knife in the drawer. The Barncat did her best to avoid interacting with him as much as felinely possible, but today was one of those days where she'd just have to suck it up and take one for the team. It was a necessary evil this time around, even if it was just part of a big farce. She never would have had the patience to try to explain everything to him. No one would. Fortunately, she didn't have to.

"Greysome," she said, "thanks so much for coming by. Sorry for not telling you about this earlier today, but I've got strict orders from the top to keep this under wraps in this building until we can't wait any longer. Well, I can't wait any longer. I assume you and your crew know that there's been a few shipments of cash coming into that bank these last few days." Will nodded and she continued, "I'm sending four good agents across the street with a wagon in about half an hour to load up a safe with five million bucks."

Greysome stretched his eyes wide open with surprise and Kathy continued, "Yeah, I said five million. They're taking it through the northern foothills and over to either Collarsport or Leashing for delivery sometime tomorrow. They've got to stay off the beaten path. Can't take the regular roads, and it's all some sort of big secret. Don't ask me why, because I don't know. Who knows what they possibly could be doing with that kind of cash. And, there's one more catch. The money can't arrive before noon, so my men are going to have to spend the night somewhere out there on the trail with it.

"Unless somebody slipped up, *nobody* knows a thing about this. I mean NOBODY. Hell, I didn't even know about it myself until late last night. I know everyone over there at your shop is really busy." She looked away and tried not to laugh as she thought to herself how nothing could have been further from the truth, and then she continued, "But I don't know what might happen to my crew out there if they get ambushed by a big group, and I don't have the heart to tell them that. I know it's a long shot and I'm probably just worrying over nothing, but do you think you could send a group of your men to tail them from way back and keep an eye out? You know, in case something big does go wrong. I know it's a lot to ask, but I just don't want to take any chances with that kind of dough."

Greysome didn't want to make out like he was too excited, but boy was he! Elated, ecstatic, overjoyed. Any of those words would work. You might have a favorite of your own that you'd prefer to use. It was the most exciting news big Will had heard since . . . . Well, he couldn't remember exactly. This one could be a real barn-burner; the one he always dreamed of.

I'm not saying that you couldn't find real excitement in South Sebastian, but it was clean excitement. It was a gentrified place and good crime was hard to come by. Even the Tin Roof Gang had few dealings there. They had their fingers in a few small pies, but with what they had going on the other side of the range, Fatscat saw no reason to chance getting caught up in things right under the Barncat's nose, complete with a branch office in town to support her. There was nothing that good going on in town to get into anyway, even if he wasn't worried about the feds.

Like the trooper he was, Greysome outwardly held his excitement in check and said matter-of-factly, "Why sure, I think we probably can help out. Just let me run back over to the station for a few minutes and talk with some of my staff. You know, to make sure this won't interfere with anything they need to be working on. We've got some big investigations underway and I don't want any of them getting jeopardized." Kathy turned away for a moment to hide her smirk, and then turned back to reply with her best serious look and tone, "Oh, no, by all means. We don't want to get in the way of any important police work."

Kathy went on, "We can just take our chances if it's too much to ask. I know it's really short notice. I might even be able to get some help instead from the guys at." The big guy cut her off. "No, no," he said excitedly. "Don't bother anyone else. I think we can do it." He hurried to the door and said on his way out, "Just give me a few minutes. I'll be right back." Then he stuck his head back inside and said, "Mrs. Barncat, how many do you think we'll need? Fifteen? Twenty? More? Kathy held back another smile like a true champion and replied, "I think ten ought to do just fine, maybe even a couple less if that's all you can spare." "Yes ma'am," he said as he whipped the door shut. He had to hold onto his cool hat to keep from losing it as he took off. Down the hall, down the steps and out the front door.

- - -

She looked up at the ceiling and sighed as she shook her head. It had been a long day of well-intentioned deceit. That little episode you just witnessed wasn't the only law man rendezvous of recent vintage for the boss lady. She already had squandered most of her day going to and fro, and attending, a similar meeting with Dan Walker, the top cop in Collarsport. His wits weren't as dim as those of Will Greysome, but it still was an arduous task. As much as she would have liked to, it wasn't the sort of thing that she could delegate to a subordinate. Within any organization, some tasks are so miserable that you can't in good conscience ask another to do it, and so the boss ends up being stuck with it.

Did I mention that it was a hot day? Well, it was. It was at least hot for South Sebastian and the Barncat never did do all that well with hot. As she paced around in her office waiting on Fatscat's dilatory communication, she still was trying to decide what had been worse. Was it the two-hour ride each way in the scorching sun or the forty-five minutes she had suffered through having lunch with Captain Walker? She had given him the exact same schpiel that she just now dropped on big Will.

What was with the belt and suspenders routine? Keep in mind that, foremost, the Barncat wanted dearly to get her paws on anyone who tried to take a run at what he or she *thought* was a serious load of cash. She was all but certain that any crook far enough in the loop to have known that the ransom exchange was imminent must know at least some useful information. Quite possibly a lot of it.

Even if she couldn't land herself a prime stool pigeon, she still might get lucky and trap herself a scumbag or two that she'd been trying to get her paws on for a while. Kathy loved good bait and she was willing to go to great lengths to keep it from going to waste. But, she could put only so many men on the job and she needed to be sure that there would be enough firepower on hand to prevail, even if she had to resort to sub-par firepower.

A genuine difficulty she struggled with was that, if her hunch was correct and an ambush really was in the works, there was no telling exactly where it might take place. An ambush is one of those things that the prospective victim doesn't get to dictate the time and place for. Otherwise, it's not really an ambush, now is it? In the very unlikely event that you *are* trying to engineer an ambush upon yourself, you can do your best to appear vulnerable in a particular spot and hope that the perpetrators follow your lead. You certainly can't count on them, however.

What would happen if a group of local cops trailing her boys reached the limits of their official jurisdiction before trouble actually went down? Assuming that they even were paying enough attention to their whereabouts to notice, of course. Would they panic, throw their paws up and turn back, or would they bravely forge ahead? Because there was a legitimate risk that the former might occur, she had to be prepared with a solution that would work on either side of the municipal border. And thus, the Barncat got stuck spending the better part of the day lying her ass off about a "money shipment" in order to get her ducks in a row on two different ends. It was enough to wear down even her.

It isn't that there was no veracity at all to what she had been saying. In her defense, it was completely true that the four agents she was sending off into the hills, even if they were really good, might have difficulty adequately defending themselves in the face of a large group of adversaries. They'd almost surely need backup unless the stars just fell completely into line, or the marauders truly were an incompetent bunch in their own right. Let's not kid ourselves, though. She certainly hadn't been completely on the level. Not with everyone having been asked to protect what in actuality would be an empty box. But, what choice did she really have?

- - -

"Where in hell is that note from Harold?" she said under her breath as she waddled with four agents across the street, around to the back alley and up some steps to the back door of the bank. Oliver was expecting her and had left it unlocked, hoping to avoid another boisterous banging incident. She came through the door and there it was, sitting on the floor in the hall, a medium-height black safe.

As she had requested, Oliver already had stuffed the safe full of scrap paper, and he had thrown in a few pieces of metal to add some jingle. He came out of his office, gave a key to Kathy and announced, "Don't be alarmed about the noise. There's some coins in there. Not a lot. I just couldn't give up all of my bills. Need at least a few to get the tellers through tomorrow, so I had to throw in a few gold pieces to make up for it. It's all here, though. You can take a look yourself if you want, but I did count it three times before I locked her up."

Kathy said, "That won't be necessary, Oliver. If you say it's all there, it's all there. Thanks again, my friend. We sure do appreciate it." Then she turned to her crew and said, "Let's get this thing out of here and onto the back porch, so Oliver can lock up and get on his way. He didn't take this job because he likes being stuck late at the office. He's a banker and should have been on his way home already. Isn't that right, Oliver?" He replied, "Well, yes. Of course, Mrs. Kathy." With that, the four of them each took a corner, carried the safe down the hall, set it down just outside the back door and covered it with a small tarp. Two of them stayed behind to stand guard, and Kathy and the others started on their way back to HQ.

The two left behind on guard duty were the most recent additions to the staff at East Coast HQ. Neither of them had been in camp for a full year yet, and the Barncat had a hunch that, if there *was* a leak anywhere in organization, there was at least a decent chance that it might be one of them. The other two were Terry and Perry, whom she affectionately referred to as the "Erry Brothers."

The Erry Brothers really did look a lot alike, even though there was no blood relation as far as anyone knew. They had been her top field agents ever since she took over the East Coast branch almost two years ago. She said to them, "Remember, neither of those kids has any idea that this isn't the real thing. They think there's five million clams in that box and they better not find out any different, you hear?" She held out her forepaw and said, "Here's that key that Oliver just gave me." As Perry took it from her, she said, "Don't worry, it won't work."

She continued, "If anything really crazy does go down out there, I don't want you two putting yourselves in any real danger. You hear me? Not if you can help it anyway. I mean, I know you can't completely roll over. It has to look like you're trying to defend something, but if shots start getting fired all around, make sure that you're in a good spot and not exposed. Get down or even get out if you have to.

"I can guarantee you that, if it gets the least bit hairy out there, Greysome or Parker and his boneheads will be all over that shit like white on milk. Could be Greysome *and* Parker if it happens in the right spot. I already wrote out some phony instructions with your drop-off site, and I want you to stop and spend the night as soon as you cross into the Collarsport city limits.

"Most of these cops on both sides haven't had anything real to do since they joined up, and I've got a feeling that they'll come running out of the woodwork if there's the slightest hint of trouble. Remember, none of *them* knows that this ain't real either. AARRGGHH! I swear, if one of you lets that slip out somehow, there won't be a day before you retire that you don't regret it. You got that?" They both looked at her and nodded intently.

It was almost five-thirty when they walked back into the HQ building and a wire was coming across the line right then. Kathy snatched it before anyone else could so much as get a glimpse of it, and the Erry Brothers followed close behind her to the back corner of the lobby. She passed them the note that she'd already written, stuck the fresh script in her pocket and said, "You boys know what to do. Go hitch four dogs to the covered wagon, get back over to the alley across the street and you all hit the trail with that box." She winked at them as they started to turn away and said, "And make sure you look serious about it!"

She waddled up the steps as fast as she could, went to the end of the hall, stuck her head inside a door and said loudly, "Eduardo, no mas duerme." Eddie didn't say a word. He just jumped up from the couch, rubbed his eyes and took off down the hall to run out back to the HQ stable and saddle up Catation. As he zoomed past Kathy and down the steps, she said loudly, "Meet me in my office after you get saddled up."

Moments later, Greysome was coming up the steps as the boss lady was bearing down on her office door, and he followed her inside with major pep in his step. "I've got great news," he said. She replied, "That's good to hear, Will. Now get over here and take a look out this window with me." She continued, "You see that wagon crossing the street? That's my crew on their way over to the back of the bank. They'll be going out on the south side of town in just a few minutes, and then east on the North Trail. I assume your news is that you've got some boys who can be out there tonight?"

He said, "Yep, we're ready to roll out. There's me and I've got twelve more." Kathy replied, "That's great. I really owe you one. Just give my crew about fifteen minutes to clear town, so they don't know you're tailing them. Don't worry about losing them. I can tell you exactly where they're headed and where they're probably going to spend the night. Plus, there's four of them on that wagon and they're lugging a heavy safe, so they aren't going anywhere fast."

The big guy was so caught up in the excitement as he zipped back down the steps that he didn't even notice Eddie coming up. With little official work to be done on the average day – real work anyway, Greysome visited the Pusserschmott estate on a semi-regular basis with a few patrolmen. You know, to "check on" things and make sure that everything was "all right." Never mind that the family had its own private security outfit. The general consensus was that Will and his crew really went to see the Pusserschmott girls (yes, the girls were WAY out of their league) and eat free food. You don't have to take my word for it, but nine out of every ten visits, South

Sebastian's finest arrived during lunch. So long as they didn't abuse the privilege too often, Pepé was happy to oblige. But, I digress.

The upshot is that Greysome knew most of the Pusserschmott staff well and, if he hadn't been so utterly consumed with his exciting new classified assignment, he surely would have recognized Eddie in a heartbeat. Eddie looked over his shoulder as Greysome flew by, and just as Eddie was about to holler his name, Eddie saw the Barncat gesticulating wildly out of the corner of his eye. She was bouncing up and down, and motioning for a "shhh" with everything she had. Eddie just shrugged and whispered, "Okay," as he walked quickly toward her office.

"GET IN HERE," she yelled under her breath as she waved him toward and through the door. Eddie wondered to himself whether he had done something wrong. She said, "Damn, that was close. If big Will sees you in here this time of the day, who knows what he might start thinking?" She paused for a second and said, "Well, maybe it's not such a big deal. I mean, he is a little too dense to put all of this together just with what little he knows, but still."

She closed the door and said, "I've been busting my ass for the last two days to get this all lined up. I just don't need anything getting out of whack now. Let's you and I stay here and watch to make sure that my guys get off okay. After that, Greysome and a big troupe are going to follow along from behind to watch out for any trouble. Did you see him go down those steps? He didn't even notice *you*. This might be the highlight of his career so far. If something really does happen out there, he'll be talking about it for years."

Eddie said, "So, whaddya got for me, Boss?" As they stood staring out of the window, the wagon turned out from the alley behind the bank. It was about to cross the street and pass right by the east side of the HQ building. The Barncat held out a slip of paper in her paw and said, "Here, take this."

Eddie took the note from her and she said, "This is going to work out perfectly. Well, other than having to give up five million smackers to that SOB Fatscat. I never liked that idea. But, it ain't my call and I'd probably pay it for one of my kids, too, if I had that kind of money. Anyway, it should be an easy shot from where the crew probably will end up making camp tonight. If they made it as far as I think they did, you shouldn't have much more than a five-hour ride tomorrow, six tops. There shouldn't be any backtracking, no big passes or river crossings. About time we got some good news."

Eddie looked down at the paper and said, "Excellent. I wish it wasn't so late. No worries, though. I know that trail really well, and it gives me a reason to open it up out there with Catty. He's been stuck in the barn almost all week and he really could use a good stretch. He's got a big race coming up in a few weeks." Kathy said, "Yeah, it's just as well. The faster you have to go, the less chance there is of somebody following or anything else happening to you while you're out there."

They chatted for a few minutes as they continued looking out the window. Finally, a couple of blocks to the west, Greysome and his crew could be seen riding toward the trail. Eddie turned and started for the door, and Kathy said, "Good luck, Eddie. You be careful out there, baby." As he closed the door behind him, Eddie winked and said, "Will do, Boss."

CHAPTER TWENTY-FIVE

ARE YOU KIDDING ME?

It had been just over an hour since his shift had started, but it seemed like half the night to Elvis. His mind had been racing since the moment he took his post. Did anyone really tail Eddie all the way out there? Who could have kept up? Was someone actually going to try to steal the money? From them? They easily could handle ten, probably twice that unless they were professionals, and good ones at that. It just didn't seem to add up, and Elvis was anxious to fetch Daisy and get out for a good look around.

Elvis couldn't wait any longer and he started to get up and go roust Eddie. Suddenly, Eddie plopped down right next to him and whispered, "How ya doin', Chief?" Elvis looked up a bit startled and Eddie continued, "Hey, I didn't mean to worry you with that bit about being followed. I just thought." Elvis cut in with his own whispering, "No, no. If you think there's somebody out there, I need to know. You did the right thing." Eddie replied, "I know. I just hope it wasn't all my imagination getting the best of me."

Elvis said, "Eddie, you're the best rider I've ever seen. Ever! Dogs and their riders have been trying to catch you from behind almost since the day you were born. You know that ride of yours well enough by now, and you said it's not his first day at the circus either. You probably weren't imagining anything. Believe me, I hope it *is* your imagination, but I doubt it. I'm just wondering who? Why?" Eddie said, "Same here, Chief."

Elvis stood up and said, "There's only one way to find out for sure. If anyone wakes up and wonders where I am, just tell them I said I thought I dropped something back there on the trail and went to go take a look before I turned in. Unless it's Frankie. You can tell him what's up, but nobody else. I mean nobody! Not even Warren. Not yet anyway. I don't want anyone getting alarmed until we know for sure." Eddie said, "You got it," as Elvis got up and started for the paddock where the dogs had been sequestered.

Her eyelids were the only body parts that budged when Elvis patted Daisy on the head to wake her. She could tell right away from the look on Elvis' face that it was hush time, and they promptly exited the paddock without a sound. Not particularly impressive for a species routinely lauded for quietness, but it was pretty good work for a dog that weighed nearly sixty pounds.

Equipped well enough with a pair of pistols, a sharp knife and plenty of ammo in his belt, he slipped up onto her bareback to forego the noise that a saddling surely would create. They backtracked on the trail for a couple of minutes until their eyes had adjusted fully to the darkness, and then they turned around and began straying back and forth, into and then back out of the woods.

They were working both sides of the trail when Daisy suddenly picked up a scent and started nearly straight uphill. It was no guess. Elvis could tell that she definitely was onto something and he already was starting to have mixed feelings about it. It would be nice to make quick work of their search, but the preferable outcome by far would be a false alarm and finding nothing. It was appearing obvious that the latter alternative probably was unlikely, as Daisy lowered her head and continued ever more earnestly. Whatever was out there likely would stay put, too, because no one could have heard them coming. Even if Daisy hadn't been so stealthy, the local insects were making a huge racket and any silence that did remain was being filled by the sporadic howls of coyotes.

They were almost thirty yards above the trail now, coming up on a thick patch of brush. Elvis was peering downhill, looking for an easy way around it, and there they were. So much for some long-winded, crawl along the ground, messy expedition. Elvis could clearly make out the silhouette of what appeared to be a rather large dog lying next to a huge oak tree, and he could only assume that its rider had to be nearby. Daisy stayed behind as Elvis slid to the ground and crept all the way up to the tree. Elvis was only a few steps away from the dog, but it still hadn't budged. Might have had something to do with having run fourteen plus miles, mostly uphill, in ninety minutes, but that's admittedly just a guess.

Elvis reached down with his right forepaw and pulled out a pistol, cocking it as he raised it into the air. He crept around the tree counterclockwise with his back against it and his left eye was the first part of him to make it to the other side. He could see a figure lying under a blanket on the back side of the tree, and a touch of dark hair and a few whiskers protruded out of the far end. Daisy's eyes were fixed on the dog, and she was ready to pounce if she had to, as Elvis crawled slowly to the other end of the blanket. He knelt on his hind legs, put the end of his pistol barrel to the side of the cat's face and said firmly, but quietly, "One move and I'll splatter your head all over this dirt."

As you might expect, the sleeping came to an immediate halt on the heels of that declaration. The only movement that Elvis could discern was the slow opening of an eyelid, which was accompanied by the sound of some sort of half-hearted, close-mouthed yelp. The kind that you hear from someone whose mouth has been taped shut. The dog started to rustle and Daisy instantly was on top of it with her jaws around its throat. There was something vaguely familiar about the eye behind that lid, and the cat wasn't struggling. Elvis backed off just a few inches with his gun still trained on its head. As Elvis began to slowly stand himself up, his jaw began to slowly drop itself open. "Elvis, don't shoot," she said as she lifted her forepaws up by her head in a show of submission.

Elvis now was fully upright and his mouth was fully ajar. "What in hell are *you* doing here?" he said. She curled up into a ball and started to sob, "Please, Elvis, please. I'm so sorry. I can explain everything. Really, I can. Please don't kill me." Elvis took a moment to gather his thoughts, sat down next to her and said, "Don't worry. I'm not going to kill you. Well, I don't think I am. I guess that depends on what you've got to say." Elvis called Daisy off of the other dog, looked over and said, "Well, go ahead. I guess you may as well get on with it." She wiped back a few more tears, took a deep breath and started to speak.

She couldn't get a word out before Elvis interrupted, "And I need to know everything." He was staring right into her eyes and his nose couldn't have been two inches from hers as he began screaming about as loud as one can under his breath, "EVERYTHING! NO MORE GAMES, OKAY? DO YOU HAVE ANY IDEA WHAT'S GOING ON OUT HERE? DO YOU KNOW WHAT WE'RE DOING? WHO WE'RE DEALING WITH? CATS COULD GET KILLED OUT HERE. CATS I CARE ABOUT, BY THE WAY. THIS BETTER NOT BE SOME SORT OF A JOKE OR SOMETHING."

Still crying, she said, "I know, I know. I Promise. I can explain. Everything, Elvis. Everything." Elvis shook his head and said, "I sure hope so, and it better be good. You do know that I'm not the only one who's going to be wondering what you're doing out here? How did you keep up anyway? And whose dog is this? Did you steal him from some racetrack or something?" Then Elvis paused and said, "Okay, okay. I'm sorry. I'll shut up and let you talk. Like I said, this better be good or you're going to be in some deep, deep shit."

It turns out that there was more to Calli than most of us probably thought. She said, "Elvis, I don't even know where to start. If you have to kill me, well then just go ahead and do it, but this is the truth. I swear it's all true." Elvis nodded and she continued, "Well, I'm not from Albemarle. I grew up in a little town called Tribec. It's just north of Leashing. My mom died when I was just a kitten and I've lived there with my father all of my life. I mean, until I left for college.

"I don't know if you've ever heard of it, but there's a little fishing village over on the Coast, not far from school, called Catina Town. A few shops, a marina, a bunch of boat docks and not a whole lot more. There are a few small houses up in the outskirts where some of the fishermen live, but that's about it. Buyers show up at the docks every day, buy everything that they can, and take it back to their restaurants and stores. There's a place at the marina called the C-Town Tavern. I started working there over a year ago, right after I graduated. The money's actually pretty good with the fishermen raking in all that cash, and everything is super fresh. Right off the boats. It's where I really learned to cook seafood."

Elvis put his head in his paws and asked, "Does any of this matter? Do you have any idea what I'm doing out here?" Calli said, "Well, you said you wanted to know everything, so I figured I'd better tell you everything. You know, with you sitting there holding that gun and all." Elvis took a deep, exasperated breath and said, "I did. I did say everything, didn't I?"

Calli continued, "So there's this scruffy guy who comes into the tavern all the time. He hangs out there with the same bunch almost every night. They don't look like fishermen. I really don't know what they do. My boss says that this guy is just a thug, but I never had a problem with him. He's a good customer and he tips well. I don't think it's his first name, but they all call him Hardcrass." Elvis jerked his head up and looked right at her. She paused and said, "Yeah, I know, Hardcrass. What kind of a name is that?" Elvis figured he'd better not butt in just yet and he let her carry on.

"One Saturday night, a couple of weeks ago, he was the last one in the place, all by himself. I thought it was a little weird, because he doesn't usually hang out there alone, but I didn't care. It was pretty late and I still was cleaning up in the kitchen, getting ready to close for the night. I was hoping that he'd order another drink and bump my tip up a little before I had to cash out.

"Then I heard somebody come through the door. I figured that it had to be one of his buddies or maybe my boss, but then I heard a woman's voice. That *was* weird. I've seen Hardcrass in there with the usual guys and I've seen him with all sorts of other characters, but I don't remember ever seeing him there with a woman. Certainly not alone with one.

"I was peeking out through the crack between the kitchen doors and Hardcrass is sitting at the bar next to Melba Pusserschmott." Elvis said under his breath, "WHAT?" Calli said, "Yes, Melba Pusserschmott. Do you know who she is? She's married to Clevin. You know, *THE* Pusserschmotts." Elvis just nodded and asked, "Do you know them?"

Calli said, "I do, Elvis. I really do. I met Jeanine and Sarena when I was in college. I had gotten a catnastics scholarship and that's how I ended up there. They were on the team with me. They were just walk-ons and they were *so* nice to me. I practiced with them all of the time and I taught them everything I knew. We all hit it off right away and we became really good friends."

Elvis just sat there in a daze. Either it was completely true or she was the best liar, not to mention the hottest, that he'd ever met. Ever! He tried mightily to stay focused on the story, but one thing continually kept popping into his mind. Even if this was completely true, all of it, Frank probably wouldn't believe a word.

She went on, "I was just young and naïve. I had no idea who they were. All I ever did my whole life was go to school, practice in the gym and help Daddy take care of the house. So, the girls. They invited me to come stay with their family one weekend. I told them I was going to try to get a ride out there, but they wouldn't let me. They sent a coach to come pick me up! It was a nice one, too. I'll never forget coming up the path to their house. I was in shock. Well, I guess shock isn't exactly the right word. It was more like some sort of hallucination.

"The house, the farm, the barn. It was ridiculous. And, I've always loved dogs. Ever since I was a kitten, I've ridden every chance I had. It wasn't long before I was going off riding with the girls almost every weekend. And with Eddie. Eddie Arcato was in charge of their barn and all of their dogs. EDDIE ARCATO. He's a god! The best jockey in the history of ever, and here I am riding with him almost every weekend." Elvis just looked and kept nodding. She said, "Of course you know him. I mean, you must know I followed him out here."

If I could, I'd give you a short break from all of this. I know Elvis wouldn't have minded a brief respite himself. But, Calli was on a roll and you do need to know this stuff. She continued, "The girls actually wanted to fix me up with Clevin back then. I'm probably an idiot for not taking them up on that one. I mean, I know he isn't as bright as they are. Not even close, really. He's plenty cute, though. Adorable is more like it. And he's such a sweetheart! I certainly wouldn't have to worry about money ever again. But, he already was dating Melba then, and his mother was all about her for some reason. I don't know what happened. It was just bad timing.

"I was there in the kitchen and I couldn't believe what I was hearing. Melba told Hardcrass that she would pay him a hundred thousand dollars if he would kill Clevin!" Elvis' eyes stretched open to what appeared to be their limit, and he was shaking his head back and forth in disbelief. Calli continued, "She was sitting right there with a big wad of cash stuffed in her purse, talking about how they were going off to the lake house for a few days and she was going to send all of the help away. She said that Hardcrass and his bunch should beat her up, too. You know, to make it look good. He said that they'd have to rough her up really bad if it was going to look legit, and she was perfectly fine with it. That BITCH!

"I had no idea what to do. I wanted to run out and shoot them both right then and there. We always keep a rifle behind the bar in case trouble breaks out, but then I thought better of it. There was nobody else around to hear what they had said, and who was going to believe me? They all would have said that I was just some crazy jealous girl trying to get Clevin for myself, and then sent me off to the nut house. If somebody had just been there with me!

"They were really going to do it. She gave him every bit of that cash. It had to be fifteen, maybe twenty thousand dollars. Then she just got up and walked out. It sounded like a done deal. She was going to bring the rest of the cash to the lake house and he was going to take it after he did the job." Elvis said, "You're right, I wouldn't believe it either. I'd send you off to the nut house, too. Some little hoodlum and maybe another thug or two sneak into that place up at Claw, and the guards and all of the rest of the help just happen to be gone somehow? Then, he – or they – beat the hell out of the only son of Morris Pusserschmott IV, and his wife, and leave the boy there for dead? All for a hundred grand?"

Calli said, "Exactly! Who would believe it? And from a girl who Clevin's sisters wanted to fix him up with a couple of years ago? They'd send me up the creek. The only thing I could think of was to tell the girls, Jeanine and Sarena. I mean, I know it would sound far-fetched, but they both know that Melba is a good-for-nothing schemer. They might think that this is a little over the top even for her, but they know I wouldn't make up anything like this. And, it would be easy enough to smoke out. All we'd have to do is bide our time and wait to see if she and Clevin were going to go out to the lake and stay there all alone. No guards, no help. That never happens. It would have been a dead-on telltale. Just my luck, the girls were out of the country until three days ago."

Then she said, "Oh, wait, it gets better. Maybe not better, but there's more." Elvis just looked at her with his chin propped up on his forepaw, not really knowing what to think. All he could do was watch and listen as Calli kept on, "Two nights later, Hardcrass is back there again all by himself at the end of the night. I remember it was a Monday, because it wasn't that late. I had the place cleaned up and I was ready to go.

"I figured maybe Melba was coming to meet him again, so I hung out in the back going through some recipes for a while. I was just about to give up and go kick him out, and then I heard the door. It wasn't her, though. Some guy comes in, smoking a cigar, and he's missing an ear and one of his forelegs. He's got some big guy with a rifle following behind him. His lackey goes over and stands at the door, and he limps over to the bar and sits down next to Hardcrass.

"Hardcrass tells this guy the whole story and says he needs help, because he doesn't have the right guys that far away to pull it off. They were talking for a little bit and I heard Hardcrass call him 'Fatscat.' It was! It was him. The mob guy. Well, Fatscat tells Hardcrass that he's a complete idiot. Tells him that it's crazy to kill a Pusserschmott, even for a hundred thousand dollars. He said that the local cops would be everywhere and the feds would be all over it. He told Hardcrass no way would he help with something that stupid, not even for half. I remember Fatscat saying, 'A lousy fifty grand. You've got to be out of your mind.'"

Calli continued, "I couldn't believe it was Fatscat. If that guard of his hadn't been standing watch, I would have gone out there and blown both of their heads off. I swear I would have, Elvis. That bastard! He had my father killed last year, I know he did. My daddy had a little importing business. He worked so hard at it all of his life. Fatscat had been wanting to get his paws on that business for a while. I don't know why. He kept making offers, but my father always politely refused. Dad had been saying for some time that he would love to sell the business and retire, but he always said that he'd never sell out to someone like Fatscat.

"About four months ago, a group from Leashing met with my dad to talk about buying his business. They were for real, a big operation. He was going to stay on and help them run it for a few months and then he'd be done. It was his dream come true. I was so happy for him. Just a few days before everything was going to be finalized, Daddy was working late one night. I woke up early the next morning for school and he wasn't home, so I went to the shop to check on him. He was lying on the floor in his office. He'd been shot three times. The register was open and it was empty, so the police said it must have been a robbery.

"The police kept saying that they were looking into it, but nothing ever came of it. I know it was Fatscat. Maybe not him, but definitely his gang. They had to be behind it. The cops over there, they're all in Fatscat's pocket anyway. It was like they didn't even care. Ever since that morning I found Daddy lying there, I swore to myself that I would get that SOB. Somehow, someway, I was going to do it."

Elvis got up and started walking away. Calli said, "Elvis, please. Please don't leave! I'm not making it up. I swear." Elvis said, "It's okay. I believe you. At least I think I do. I just have to pee."

CHAPTER TWENTY-SIX

SUCKERS, ALL OF THEM

The Erry Brothers, their slightly suspect partners and the essentially worthless safe had traveled very slowly, but unimpeded, along the northern foothills for the better part of six hours when it finally was time to make camp. As soon as they got a few minutes to themselves, Terry and Perry shared a laugh about how obvious Greysome and his surveillance crew had been. Trailing "secretly" from behind. Walker's troupe up ahead certainly were no better – they might have been even easier to spot. Hopefully, they wouldn't completely scare off the potential perpetrators of any ambush that might have been in the works. At least it was dark.

The transport team had brought dinner along for themselves and for their dogs, so not much time transpired between when they pulled off of the trail and when they all were ready to lie down for the night. Terry took the first shift on watch and it wasn't much past midnight before he was the only one left awake. Well, the only one awake in this particular group. Greysome, Walker and their respective contingents? Those were other matters entirely. They all were waiting with baited breath for the slightest hint of foul play, and sleep was the last thing on any of their minds. It would have been only fitting if they had been forced to wait a good, long while for anything to materialize, but the Barncat had picked an almost perfectly vulnerable spot for her team to sleep over.

And there they went. The Barncat Prophecy was on the verge of fulfilling itself. You couldn't tell for sure, because they were sneaking down from the higher elevations, but there didn't look to be too many of them. Unless there were more coming in a second wave, surely there were no more than ten. They were as sloppy "sneaking" down on the wagoneers as the cops had been during the trail ride, and it wasn't out of the question that the Erry Brothers alone might have been able to take out the crooks if they had been so inclined.

Terry had heard them coming for a few minutes now, but resisted the temptation to put himself at much risk for an empty receptacle. When things finally got a little too close for comfort, he fired a shot into the air. Perry had heard them approaching as well and he already was awake when the sound rang out. The other two flew into the air like they had been sent up with a slingshot.

It was pandemonium after that. Cops were coming in from both sides at every angle, zig-zagging across each other's paths. Guns were blazing for a moment there. Not hitting much of anything besides trees, but blazing nonetheless. The Erry brothers and their fellow agents were holed up safely under the wagon, firing a shot every now and then to make it look good. Kathy had told all of them that, if anything did happen, she'd want everyone that they could get their paws on brought back to HQ alive.

With their lopsided odds of roughly three good guys for every one bad, it should come as no surprise that the party was over almost before it had started. One or two may have escaped, but probably not. It was exceptionally steep there above the trail and running away back uphill was a slower and more tedious proposition than the downhill approach had been.

Between their bad aim and not wanting to hurt anyone in the wagon crew with a misfire, the cops had not inflicted a single serious injury. That wasn't all bad. It was somewhat unbelievable that no one was hurt by friendly fire. As for the would-be thieves, it certainly made harnessing them a lot less messy.

After all of the disarming and restraining was completed, Parker and his Collarsport squad turned and ventured back from whence they came. To say that Greysome and his crew were a little too excited to even consider sleep would fall well below what most of us would characterize as an understatement. A little snooze wasn't buried somewhere near the bottom of their list of things to do. It just simply wasn't on the list. They immediately commenced to escorting everyone back to South Sebastian, both the feds and the scumbags alike. Carrying a banner and randomly firing shots into the air as they rode, you'd think that they had just won a war.

For barely half of a moon, it shone very bright, and when they came to the first big clearing along the trail, Perry fell back to see if he recognized any of what had been rounded up. All of the captured had their forelegs tied behind their backs and most were riding double on some of the dogs that had been impounded after the melee. Perry was surprised to have made it almost to the end of them without encountering a single familiar face.

The last prisoner was riding single and looking down at the trail. You couldn't see his face for the brim of his hat, so Perry used the barrel of his rifle to push up his chin. Perry's eyes then stretched open about as far as they could go. He didn't say anything, but he was back at Terry's side about as fast as one could get there without appearing to be in a rush.

Perry didn't say a word when he got back to Terry. After a few patient moments, Terry finally gave in and said, "Well?" Perry smiled and whispered, "I'd give you three chances, but you probably wouldn't get it in ten. Wanna hazard a guess as to who's back there at the end of the prize line?" Terry started whispering back, throwing out various names, but Perry finally waved him off and said, "Why don't you just go back there and take a look for yourself?" Terry said, "I think I will," as he turned his dog and started toward the back. Terry wouldn't need a rifle barrel. As he neared the end of the line, the last prisoner fortuitously looked him square in the face.

Terry did a great job of not flinching. He didn't even change his facial expression for that matter. He just kept riding right on past the cops behind the prisoners, and then rode back up along the other side of the entire line. When he fell back in next to Perry, he said quietly, "Wait until mama sees what the kittens drug in." Perry said, "My thoughts exactly. Let's keep this to ourselves. I don't want to make a big deal out of it in front of big Will or his boys, or they'll be wanting to take him in for questioning or something. The boss lady probably will let them have all the rest, but she's going to want us to keep that one. Don't you think?" "Oh, yeah," Terry said, "oh, yeah!"

They didn't stop to stretch, they didn't stop to eat and they didn't stop for any other call of nature. Will Greysome absolutely could not wait to get back home and show off what they had, and his guys might have been even more fired up than him. You do have to feel at least a little bit sorry for the rookies, whose minds easily could have wandered into thinking that their careers were going to be chocked full of exciting nights like this. Who knows, maybe times would change. If only they had known what a great service that they had done for the community. Bravely about in the wee, dark hours, thwarting a major heist. Of a box full of worthless paper! Oh, and a few pieces of scrap metal.

The ride back to town was completely uneventful and it was almost sunrise when they were about to pass right by East Coast HQ. Only this time, they hadn't come in by way of some lightly-ridden back trail. Greysome had been marching the whole lot of them down South Street since they reached the eastern edge of downtown. It was like a parade.

Publicity, it wasn't exactly what the Barncat was after, but she did take solace in the fact that she was among the one percent of townsfolk, maybe fewer, who were up and about at this hour. Some farmers on the outskirts may have been at it for a while, but not those fancy downtowners. Kathy was in slight disbelief at how quickly the whole thing had come full circle, and she walked out into the middle of the street as big Will and his dog led the long line right up to her.

She said, "Now, that is some mighty fine work there, Chief. I can't tell you how much I appreciate you bailing out my men. And whoever was supposed to be getting that safe, I'm sure they're going to have some fine words for all of you, too. I sure do owe you one, Will." He responded with the standard, "It's no trouble, ma'am. It's our job." Kathy still made a point to raise up her voice like only she could and announce to the entire crew, "I MEAN IT, MEN. THANK YOU SO MUCH. WE REALLY, REALLY APPRECIATE THIS."

She walked back along the lineup to where the Erry Brothers had halted their mounts, and said, "Hmmm, where did you two get those dogs?" Perry said, "We borrowed them from some of those rats back there. They didn't need them anymore." She said, "Nice! So, is this just all about you two or did you bring back any souvenirs for me?" Terry leaned down and whispered in her ear. She looked back up with a smile and said, "Oh, really?"

Kathy Barncat then proceeded to waddle down along the line of the roped and tied, observing the catch one-by-one until stopping at the very end. Without much expression. Scratch that. With no expression whatsoever on her face, she stood up on her hind legs and used both forepaws to push Albert Hardcrass off of the dog that he sat upon. He landed with a dull thud, his left shoulder and the left side of his face taking the brunt of the impact.

She jerked Hardcrass up from behind by the rope that bound his forelegs, and she started shoving him in the back as he stumbled and moaned a few steps at a time. The Erry Brothers kept their heads down, trying not to laugh out loud. When she had gotten Hardcrass up to the front of the line, the Barncat said to Greysome, "If you don't mind, we need to keep this one here, and we'll get that safe back over to the bank, too. You and your team can take the rest and do what you want with them. Deal?" Big Will replied excitedly, "Deal!"

She resumed to shoving Hardcrass around, this time in the general direction of the HQ building. As she was about to "escort" him through the front door, she turned and yelled to Greysome and his crew, "AND NO PRESS ON THIS NOW. YOU HEAR ME?" They all nodded as she continued, "We've got some friends out there who might be in real danger. Now, don't you all get to worrying. We can tell the whole world all about it soon enough, okay? I promise. I'll let you know when." Greysome said, "You got it, Mrs. Barncat," and then he turned to his team and yelled, "YOU ALL HEAR THAT?" They all continued nodding.

It wasn't long before Oliver was in the bank pulling paper and metal out of the safe, and Hardcrass was locked up in a small room in HQ, sitting on a chair behind a table. If you can believe it, the

Barncat had taken a smidge of pity on him and allowed him to sit untied, so that he could tend to his new scrapes. After she and the Erry Brothers engaged in a quick debriefing session in her office, they all went down the hall to pay Hardcrass a visit. She sat down in a chair directly across the table from Hardcrass as the boys followed her in, shut the door and proceeded to stand by it.

"Albert," she said, "long time, no see, eh?" Hardcrass just shrugged and grunted. Kathy responded, "Articulate as ever, I see. Albert, my friend, I really don't have much time today for fun and games, so I'll get right to it and maybe we can do this the easy way. Who was that crowd you're with and what were you doing out there?" Hardcrass said, "I don't know what you're talkin' about. You ain't got nothin' on me." The Barncat was a master interrogator, one of the best there was, due primarily to her ability to remain patient. She knew that the real trick to getting all that you can get is making sure that your subject is relaxed and comfortable.

It was just Hardcrass' luck that this was one of those special days when the Barncat really wasn't in the mood to go through the usual motions. She didn't look to be furious when she stood up. You certainly wouldn't have gotten that impression from the Erry Brothers, who weren't acting funny or looking startled. She just walked around the table, grabbed Hardcrass by the throat with her right forepaw and slung him off the chair.

His back landed squarely against the wall behind him and the back of his head followed quickly. It was hard to tell which was louder, Hardcrass slamming into the wall or the two wall hangings that had been on either side of him simultaneously crashing to the floor. No one knows for sure how many of his original nine lives he had remaining when the day had started, but between the fall from the dog and the jolt he just took, he probably had exhausted at least one of them in the last thirty minutes.

She picked him up by his vest with both forepaws, threw him back into his chair, got right up into his face and yelled, "I GOT NOTHIN? YOU SON OF A BITCH!" Then she unleashed a right backpaw that landed on his jaw and nearly knocked him off the chair sideways. "You call trying to steal five million dollars from federal agents nothing? And that's just for starters."

Hardcrass still was dizzy from the wallop and had to gather his thoughts while the Barncat rubbed the back of her right forepaw with her left. She reached back again, ready to take another swing, as Hardcrass flinched and blurted out, "Five million? What are you talking about? I thought it was two million." He paused and said under his breath, "Fatscat, that bastard."

Kathy said, "I thought you might be in on it. Yeah, ol' Fatscat. I don't know what he told you, but that was five million in ransom money that you and the rest of those idiots just tried to pilfer, not two million. I'll give you two choices. You tell me right now what's going on way up there and maybe I'll see if we can't work something out for you. If not, we'll take you down to the federal pen in a few hours, and you can wait there for your trial. You *do* know that Fatscat's got a few crumbs on the inside over there, and I'll make damn sure he knows that the only reason he isn't getting that ransom today is because you bums tried to steal it from him. It'll be a miracle if you last a week in that place."

She spoke the truth and Hardcrass knew it. He grumbled for a moment and then, like any good coward, he began to sing. He was careful to leave out some important details, like the original plan with Melba paying him to kill Clevin, and the boat he had lined up for him and Fatscat to escape on. But, he laid the rest of it all on the table.

He fingered everyone involved in the catnapping – two of his own and Fatscat's top three lieutenants. He told how he and Fatscat planned to split the ransom, but that he didn't trust Fatscat, so that's why he tried to steal it all for himself. He described a litany of other jobs in the works that had absolutely nothing to do with any of this. It was a veritable rat fink information overflow that would keep her entire roster of agents occupied for possibly the rest of the calendar year.

It all was good stuff, except for the last part. That Hardcrass already had paid a first installment of five hundred dollars each to over fifty hardened thugs. Real fighters. They were on their way as he spoke, riding dogs to Fatscat's compound with as many pistols, rifles, catling guns and carts of ammunition as they could haul. It would be enough to take on a small army and they'd all be there before sundown to lie in wait for Elvis and anyone else who might come up there after Fatscat and the ransom. Fatscat would pay them each another five hundred after all of the shouting was over.

The Barncat, she was right. There was a backstabbing. She had just assumed that it would be one of Fatscat's own and never expected an outlier. The decoy, it worked out pretty much just like she had hoped. It distracted everyone from the real money and she had tons of fresh dirt to work with. A lot of good that would do Elvis and Frank, though, and she felt sick about it. As badly as she wanted to, there wasn't a thing that she could do. She had her orders and there was no way she could send help until she had it on good authority that the Pusserschmott boy and his wife (speaking of backstabbers) were completely out of danger.

If Frank and Elvis really were going to take a run at Fatscat after the actual exchange, and she knew that they would, no one would be able to warn them in time. Unless there was something going on that she didn't know about, they were heading straight into a trap and it was a big one. Had it been anyone else, she would have gone back to her office and started choking up hairballs. For the Gunslinger, she at least held out a bit of hope. Even if only a little bit.

CHAPTER TWENTY-SEVEN

EVERYBODY'S GOT A PLAN

Just about the time when Greysome, Walker and their "troops" were descending on Hardcrass and his little posse, Elvis returned from relieving himself. He sat down beside Calli and she recounted, as best she could, the rest of the conversation between Hardcrass and Fatscat. She couldn't remember it verbatim, so I'll step in here and cover for her. It went something like this:

Fatscat: The whole thing is stupid. She's really going to send all of the help away?

Hardcrass: That's what she said. If she doesn't, then to hell with her. If the coast ain't clear, I'll just scram and keep her twenty grand. That's her problem. What's she going to do, tell the cops?

Fatscat: Yeah, maybe you should just keep it and forget about the whole thing.

Hardcrass: I thought about that, but another eighty grand, that's not chump change. I could really use that. It's certainly worth going up there and taking a look.

Fatscat: No, it's not chump change, but like I said, you can count me out. No way am I getting involved in killing a Pusserschmott for anything like that. You know, though, we could make something really big out this.

Hardcrass: Big like what?

Fatscat: The way I see it, to hell with Marva.

Hardcrass: Melba?

Fatscat: Melba, Marva. Who cares what her name is? All you've got is another eighty grand coming. And that's if she brings it. It's not a bad payday, but why don't we snatch both of them and tell the family that they're goners unless they pay up? Now you'd be talking about real money. A million at least, maybe two.

Hardcrass: Are you serious?

Fatscat: Hell yeah, I'm serious. If there's nobody else there, then why can't we? Instead of getting stuck with whatever cash that wife of his secretly is scraping up, we can tap into the old man. He's as loaded as they come.

Hardcrass: You're right about that.

Fatscat: Of course, I'm right. If we're going to take this kind of a chance, it better be worth it. Really worth it. We've got a few problems, though.

Hardcrass: Like what?

Fatscat: Like first of all, I can't trust one of my crews on something like this. I can't keep 'em all herded in anymore. Somebody will slip and say something. It would have to be just my top few guys on something like this. You got a couple that could help them out? A couple you can really trust?

Hardcrass: Yep.

Fatscat: If we can get as much as I think we can, I might get out of here and never come back. I mean it. I'm getting too old to keep up this pace much longer. The whole thing is getting ridiculous. I never thought I'd say this, but it's almost not worth the money anymore. This is your territory. Can you line us up a boat out of here? A fast one? And a crew that will go anywhere and stay shut up about it? I'm not talking about just down the coast a few miles. I mean Catagonia or something like that.

Hardcrass: As long as we pay them good, I can do it. They'll go anywhere.

Fatscat: Good. There is one more thing, and I don't know if we can cover it. You know if we do this, they're going to send the Gunslinger out here.

Hardcrass: Who, Elvis? Isn't he all the way over on the West Coast? What would they do that for?

Fatscat: You know, you really are a dumbass. What would they do that for? We're going to catnap a freaking Pusserschmott and his wife, and ask for two million bucks. Just taking the kids is bad enough. And, you know they're going to think that we're up to something big if we're asking for that kind of money.

Hardcrass: So what if they do. He's just one guy.

Fatscat: Asshole! Do you have any idea why I don't have this leg anymore? What happened to this ear that used to be here? There's way bigger fish out there than us that he's had locked up for good. We're gonna need to be ready for him, just in case. If he doesn't come, then great, but if he does. Boy, would I love to take out that SOB on my way out of here. Now, that would be something. I've been owin' him for a long, long time.

Hardcrass: Harold, enough already!

Fatscat: What do you mean enough already? You want my help or not? What if they do send him out here, then what?

Hardcrass: Aren't you way up there in those peaks? Hell, I don't even know how to get in there. Nobody does. And, don't you have a crew up there already? Get more. Load the place up with everything you've got and let him have it. I don't care who he is. And you'll be long gone if you play your cards right.

Fatscat: I like that, but I can't use my guys. I can't let anyone know about this until it's over. If they even start to think I'm running out on them, the whole operation will fall apart in two days. It's got to look like business as usual, up there and down here. How many guys can you round up? Not just anybody, I mean tough. Guys who can battle and won't run scared if a bunch of feds come riding in.

Hardcrass: That depends. I can get five, maybe ten good ones easy. They're tough and they're pretty cheap. But, if you really want to plunk down some cash, I know exactly what to do. I'm talking about real pros. These is some ex-catvalry riders who got tired of getting bossed around. They love shit like this. It's all they do. And, they'll keep their mouths shut about it, too. Problem is, they ain't cheap.

Fatscat: That's exactly what I'm talking about. Can we get fifty, sixty?

Hardcrass: Probably fifty, but I think that's about all there is. Those guys are almost a grand apiece, though. Half up front and half when the job's done. I know, it's ridiculous, but they bring all of the weapons and ammo, too. You don't pay the cash, they don't do it. You pay the first half and stiff them after the job, they hunt you down and kill you. I don't care who you are. Even you. Either way, I ain't got that kind of money.

Fatscat: Damn, that ain't cheap. But, if they're worth it. Boy, would I love to see that little rat get thrown into the ground for good while I go sailing and fishing.

Hardcrass: There's no guarantees on something like that, Harold. If he comes, they'll fight him off, and all the rest of them. But, we can't do anything if the feds just turn and run. He could get away if he's as slippery as you say he is.

Fatscat: That's okay. As long as they can stop him, that's the important thing. If they can take him out, then all the better. I can't make him walk into it. Okay, Hardcrass, here's the deal. You don't talk to anyone about this but my three boys, Bruno, Carlo and Hiram. I MEAN NOBODY. I'll let those three know what's up. Word gets out on this, then I pull the plug right away and you're a dead man. I'll overrun everything you've got. I swear I will.

Hardcrass: I get it. I get it.

Fatscat: You put up at least two of your best to go with my three and they go get those kids. So long as the coast is clear, that is. If not, the deal is off. I'll take it from there. We can keep them way up in the hills. I'm saying two million bucks or they're goners. If the family refuses, then we go from there. I don't think they will, though. I bet the old man will pay as long as he believes he'll get the kids back.

Hardcrass: You're going to give them back?

Fatscat: What are you, Hardcrass, some kind of nut job? We don't give those kids back, then I don't care what sort of militia, or whatever this group is, that you've got. They'll send a damn army up there. Not part of an army. The whole army. Nobody will be able to stop them. The whole place will blow sky high. Hell yeah, we're going to give them back. We just need to run as soon as we do.

Hardcrass: Whatever you say.

Fatscat: I can hold the kids and deal with the ransom demand. We just have to be ready. Sunrise after the payoff, we meet here, jump on a boat and we're gone. We split the money. You want to stick around, get dropped off somewhere else, that's your call, but I'm gone. Way gone. I'll decide where once I get out there.

Hardcrass: That all sounds good, but this twenty grand I got ain't enough to take care of all of this. Getting that group up there to fight, lining up the boat. Making sure we've got the right guys who stay shut up about it.

Fatscat: (He grumbled.) Yeah, I know. It's always the money. Well, we just pulled off a big job up North. I've got the cash. I'll have somebody contact you tomorrow and let you know a spot. He'll have a map. I'll be there Wednesday at high noon with fifty grand. That makes seventy with what you got from what's her face. That's way more than you'll need. I don't want to hear any bitching and I don't want anything getting fouled up. When we meet at the boat, I'll take the seventy out of your share. I'll make sure that this fighting squad gets the rest of their money after it's over. You screw me on this, Hardcrass, and you're finished. If it's the last thing I do, I'll hunt you down like a rat.

Calli said, "And then Fatscat got up and limped over to the door, and he and his guard walked out. I never saw him or Hardcrass again." Elvis said, "That's it? They didn't talk about anything else? No big job they're going to pull off, nothing like that? All they're going to do is take the money and run?" Calli said, "As far as I know. I mean, I don't know what they might have discussed after that, but that's all I know. Like I said, I never saw either of them again."

She continued, "I didn't know what to do, Elvis. All I could think of was how bad I wanted to kill that SOB. First, Daddy. Now he's going after Clevin. I didn't know where to turn. I remembered how Jeanine and Sarena used to talk sometimes about this guy, Elvis. Like he's some sort of a legend. How he can take on anyone, how he's the best shot anyone's ever seen. And so good looking. I figured it had to be you that Fatscat was all worried about.

"So, I started asking around. I found out that you live in Woodville, that your uncle owns the grocery store. I figured why not? The rail line was looking for another cook anyway, so I went over there and started right away. When I met you in your uncle's store, I had just come in that day on the train. I didn't even have a place to stay. I was hanging around hoping that I might bump into you, and there you were. I was so nervous I could barely speak. And then you came up and started talking to me, and you asked me over.

"I wanted to say something so many times, Elvis, but I just couldn't get up the nerve. I was afraid that you'd think I was some sort of lunatic, or that maybe I was in on it. You know, working with Fatscat or Hardcrass. I had no idea what you'd think. That morning after the fire, I was just about to say something at the table, and then there's Frankie knocking at the door. You said you were leaving. I figured it must have something to do with Clevin. I didn't know what to do, so I just went back to the station and picked up the run back to Littermark. The other chef wanted the weekend off anyway.

"I figured maybe I could at least follow along and stay close, even if I couldn't risk saying something to you. All I care about is seeing that scumbag Fatscat get what's coming to him. I knew there was no way you'd ever let me tag along. I couldn't even bring myself to ask. You'd think I was some kind of nut case. Even if you would have been okay with it, what about Frankie? No way would he go for that. I wouldn't blame you guys. I wouldn't let me come if I were you.

"Anyway, I sneaked over to Jeanine and Sarena's early this morning. After you all left, I was going to ask to borrow one of the dogs for the weekend and then try to follow along. When I got there, everyone was long gone. The girls still were in bed, and Barry told me that all of you left at sun-up. I was afraid I'd never catch up. So, I asked if I could take Catfleet for a few days to practice for a race, and he said it was okay. They like having someone help keep the dogs in shape." She pointed at her dog and said, "That's who this is. He's the fastest dog in the barn, except for maybe Catation."

Elvis sat there wondering if he'd ever sleep. At least the search had taken him only ten minutes, so he did have that going for him, but he was starting to worry that his absence could become a concern back at camp if it were to extend too much longer. Calli continued, "I rode into town, but I didn't see anyone. I looked all over. Finally, I went over to that headquarters building where I figured you guys might be. All I could find was Catation in a stall in the barn out back. I was so worried, I thought maybe I missed everyone. I waited and waited and waited. I must have been there for five or six hours. It was going to be dark in a few hours and I had just about decided to give up. It was making me sick.

"Then, probably around five, maybe five-thirty, Eddie came running out of the building and went into that barn. Then he went back into the building again. A couple minutes later, he goes back into the barn and he comes flying out on Catation. They just took off, and they weren't on their way back home. I figured he had to be chasing after all of you. I mean, where else could he be going like that? I came after him as fast as I could. If I hadn't been on Catfleet, or if it hadn't been me riding, we never would have been able to keep up. He's so fast, and I'm lighter than even Eddie. I tried to stay back far enough to stay out of sight, but I was afraid that Eddie might have seen us a couple of times.

"I saw him catch up to all of you and I could hear everyone talking. Catfleet and I just stayed back here and plopped down to get some rest. We were completely worn out. Eddie had Catty running wide open almost the whole way. That pork, we could smell it all the way over here. I was dying to have some and I know Catfleet was, too. We both were starving, but I couldn't chance showing us.

"Like I said, even if you believed me and even if Eddie did, too, Frank probably would freak out. I don't think Warren would be too happy about any of this either. Especially once he found out that I'd heard all of this stuff between Fatscat and Hardcrass, and never came to tell him about it. Anyway, Catfleet and I just fell asleep, and the next thing I know, there you are holding that gun in my face."

Elvis said, "Please tell me that's everything." Calli replied, "That's it, Elvis. I swear that's everything. I just want to see him die if it's the last thing I do. Please, can I ride with you? I can help, Elvis. I really can. I'm quiet. I'm a good shot. I won't hold anyone up. I won't give anyone away." Elvis sat silently for a moment, turned to her and said, "I can't promise anything, but maybe we can work something out. You're all the way out here now, and I don't like the idea of leaving anyone alone out here anymore than I like having to bring someone else along. I'll tell you what. Can we take a break for a little bit? I can't talk or listen anymore right now."

Elvis put his forelegs around her and pulled her down to the blanket. She started to kiss him and all (well, almost all) that Elvis could think about was how Frank likely would say that her trailing Eddie all the way out there must have been Elvis' idea.

CHAPTER TWENTY-EIGHT

THE START OF A BIG DAY

After their interlude, Elvis told Calli that he thought it would be best if she didn't return to camp with him. He didn't have the energy or the inclination, even with her help, to try to lead everyone through that saga, and he had no idea how Warren or the guys from HQ might react to her being there. Frank? Oh, he'd definitely be ticked off. Way ticked off. But, he likely would get over it sooner or later. Unless Calli was lying, and Elvis didn't think she was, then at least she wasn't on the wrong side of the affair.

Still, even if she meant well, an inconvenience of this sort certainly wasn't paradigm and no one would want to deal with a surprise like this at the eleventh hour. Frank almost certainly would be spouting myriad valid reasons for sending her back summarily, or for just leaving her out there alone if she refused to return. Assuming what she said was true, though, Elvis knew that they would be able to put an extra body and another capable dog to good use out there, so long as Calli didn't screw up somewhere along the way.

When Elvis and Daisy returned to camp, Eddie's shift on watch nearly was over. Eddie started to ask Elvis what had happened, but Elvis responded by cutting Eddie off and asking him to stay on lookout for a few more minutes. Then Elvis put Daisy back into the paddock, ran over to the spit, pulled off a huge pile of pork and stuck it in a sack. Eddie just sat there staring with a perplexed look on his face. Elvis looked over at Eddie, put his free forepaw up to his mouth and made the "shhh" sign. Eddie shrugged and silently mouthed, "Okay," and Elvis took off back into the woods.

Eddie was dying to know what was going on and Elvis knew it. As soon as Elvis re-returned, he went straight to Eddie's side and began to whisper, "Sorry about that, partner. Everything's okay. It'll take way too long now, but I'll explain in the morning. Remember, don't mention this to anyone. Oh, and remember when I said it's okay to tell Frankie if you need to?" Eddie looked and nodded, and Elvis said, "Well, forget I said that. No telling Frankie either, okay? Not for now at least." With yet another surprised look on his face, Eddie just nodded and whispered, "Okay, Boss." Eddie went over to lie down in his spot and Elvis woke Frank for his turn on watch.

Frank's and the four shifts thereafter were not nearly as eventful as Eddie's had been, and sunrise quickly was upon them. It was cool on the western side of the peaks, and Elvis uncharacteristically was up first, rekindling the fire to get some heat cranking. Frank wasn't far behind and his first order of business was tending to the spit, where he began rotating in anticipation of morning fare. Benji got up and began making coffee, and the others started milling around and getting their gear together.

After everyone was seated around the fire, Elvis began to show off the map that he and Frank had pilfered on the train with all of the trails in the upper Longtails. Eddie was next on the podium and he revealed to everyone the exchange location that Fatscat had specified. Elvis then described the events that recently had unfolded at his house and on the train, and he said that he thought it might be best for the group to split up. He was concerned (not so much, but his plan needed him to act the part) that him being involved in the exchange might be problematic, and he didn't want to chance scaring off anyone or causing something that might endanger the kids.

Elvis suggested that it might be best for Warren, Benji, Burt and Timmy to take Amos with them to the exchange location. Amos could carry the cash that Elvis and Frank had been carrying, and he would be needed for the return trip anyway. Unless, that is, the plan was for Clevin and Melba to walk all the way back to town after they were freed. Somehow, no one had bothered to give any thought to that, which was convenient for Elvis as he proposed his plan. Frank, Elvis and Eddie would take Amos' load and split it up amongst themselves, and then follow one of the northern trails around to the other side of the peaks. They would need Eddie not only to help shoulder Amos' cargo, but also in case something went wrong and they needed to send him back to deliver a message or to get help.

The timing did seem a little curious, certainly to Frank and Warren, but neither they nor anyone else objected. Everyone was in agreement that Fatscat was too much of a paranoid control freak to chance missing the exchange ceremony. With Fatscat already having engineered a couple of attempts to interdict Elvis, there was a strong possibility that Elvis being in attendance for the exchange might create a bit of a stir. Fatscat would be nervous at a minimum, if not downright alarmed, and everyone did share the same goal – for the exchange to go off smoothly, with little or no ado.

Warren, Benji, Burt and Timmy were fully capable of handling themselves, and it definitely would look more innocuous with only them there. Plus, everyone knew that, after the kids were returned safely, Elvis' next order of business was to get up into those hills to find out exactly what was going on with Fatscat and whoever else might be there with him. If Elvis thought that this was the best way to approach it, then everyone else seemed willing to go along with him.

As they were swapping the cash from Daisy's and Stella's saddlebags for some of the cargo that Amos had been toting, Frank couldn't help but think that something else must be at work. Elvis surely was capable of hatching a plan on his own, but on a matter of this importance, he almost invariably would have discussed something this drastic with Frank before proposing it to the others. Eddie, of course, knew that something else was up, but he didn't want to raise any suspicion by initiating a whispering exchange right there in front of everyone.

Camp was completely cleared out by eight-thirty. Warren, Benji, Burt and Timmy (who had Amos in tow) were off on their way to the exchange site, carrying a cool five million in cash. Elvis, Eddie and Frank had just started down the trail in the other direction when Elvis abruptly turned back and chased down the other four. He rode up to Warren and said, "My man, I hate to ask this, but I'm going to need to take one stack of those bills. Fifty grand." Warren took one from his saddlebags, handed it to Elvis and asked, "Whaddya need that for?"

Elvis said, "Where we're going, we might need some bribe money and I didn't bring that kind of cash with me. Sorry, but it might be the only way. You can tell Fatscat. He won't like it, but I guarantee he'll take forty-nine-fifty. Just tell him that's all the cash that the bank could release. I'm sure he'll cry about it a little, but he'll understand. If you see the old man before I do, tell him that I'll get it back for him somehow if he really needs it. Good luck, guys. As soon as you get those kids, you get the hell out of there and get back home as fast as you can."

Elvis quickly caught back up to Frank and Eddie, told them where he'd been, and then took an unexpected turn off the trail and started straight uphill. Frank and Eddie followed, but they really were wondering whether the man was starting to lose it. Breaking up the group, taking fifty grand for bribes, now riding right off the trail. All before nine a.m.! Who knew what the rest of the day might bring?

They rode behind Elvis for a few seconds more, turned a corner past a thicket and, just as Frank finally was about to break down and ask where they were headed, there was Calli straight ahead, sitting on Catfleet. Eddie's jaw might have hit the ground had his saddle horn not intervened and Frank's eyes bulged out about as far as Elvis ever remembered seeing. After Frank leaked out a string of choice expletives under his breath, he finally was able to assemble a clean phrase and blurted, "You *cannot* be serious!"

Elvis promptly jumped off of Daisy and began shifting into Calli's saddlebags some of the load that Daisy, Stella and Catation had just begun lugging. Neither Frank nor Eddie could take issue with that. Calli said hi to them, as nicely as anyone could, but the vibrations appeared to travel undetected through their apparently preoccupied auditory canals, as they both sat there staring, still and speechless. Elvis knew that it would be best to not give them the chance to start firing off questions or comments, but instead to quickly take to the offensive while they still were dumbfounded.

He jumped back onto Daisy, started downhill toward the trail and turned back in his saddle to look at the others. Calli was last in line and Elvis quickly hollered back to her before anyone else could get a word in. "Young lady," he said, "I'll jump in if you need me to, but my advice is that, if you're going to have any chance at riding with us today, you'd better tell these gentlemen everything that you told me last night. And, yes, I mean EVERYTHING." Elvis quickly turned back around, hoping to hear her voice before the others started chiming in with who knows what.

It would be folly to think that Frank and Eddie could withstand, without at least a few of their own interjections, the onslaught of recounting that Elvis had endured the night before. To be sure, they did interrupt from time to time, but those occasions were surprisingly rare. Believe it or not, they pretty much sat idly in their saddles as Calli essentially repeated for them the entire rendition. It was a lot to digest, and Eddie and Frank had widely differing viewpoints. Not necessarily opposing, but different nonetheless.

Eddie was somewhat in shock. Quasi-shock might be a better way to put it. He knew Calli quite well, but only as a friend of the family, albeit an extremely attractive one. He had no idea that she could have gotten intertwined in anything of this nature. Frank, on the other hand, had been skeptical about Calli's motives since nearly the moment they met, and he almost had been expecting something. Even he, however, couldn't have anticipated anything rising to this level. In her defense, it wasn't that she was involved in anything untoward, but what she knew definitely was startling.

In a perverse way, the outrageousness of it all served to bolster her credibility. Even a full-on psychopath would have been incapable of scheming up something of this magnitude or with this level of detail. Yes, it had to be true, because you just couldn't make up something like this. Layer upon that the various bits and pieces that obviously were true. She clearly knew Eddie well, she hadn't stolen the dog, and all sorts of other things that they could verify were, in fact, consistent with what they knew to be the case.

As much as Frank might have wanted to when he first saw Calli sitting on Catfleet, there really was no casting her off at this point. No, she shouldn't have followed along. One even could claim that her doing so could have put the entire operation in danger. As a practical matter, though, that was a stretch and no real harm had been done. Under the circumstances, Calli really hadn't done anything that justified a punishment as drastic as excommunication.

Plus, leaving her behind now didn't make sense for other very good reasons. For starters, whatever it was that Amos had been carrying in those bags was really, really heavy, and it was a big help having another dog along to assist in shouldering the load, especially clambering about in those hills. And, if they did send her off, what if she were to get caught? If she fell into the wrong paws, who knows what they might be able to find out?

After all was said and done, she was in. Even if for no other reason than by default. No one even bothered to declare it. It was one of those things that just sort of happened on its own. They would, in fact, be better off with her than without her. As a practical matter, Calli didn't much care how or why she survived the cut. She was just happy to be able to stay, and what she hoped for most was to get an opportunity to prove her worth and not be thought of as nothing more than surplus baggage. She would have her chance soon enough.

CHAPTER TWENTY-NINE

A COLORFUL EXCHANGE

The ride to the exchange location was a quiet one, almost silent, for those porting the cash. It was an easy ride, there was only so much to discuss and, truth be told, they all were a little bit nervous. You would be, too. Unless they stopped for a lengthy spell, they'd easily arrive before three o'clock, which was the original exchange deadline, at least implicitly. Of course, Fatscat was over two hours late with his wire specifying the drop-off location. Did that mean that the new deadline was five o'clock or shortly after?

If I ever find out the answer to that, you'll be the first to know. The fact of the matter is that there are times in life when you can't get a good answer, and you have to suffer your way through as best you can with a little bit of uncertainty hanging over your head. Well, this is going to be one of those times. If you're having a hard time dealing with that, I'll let you in on a little secret – it won't really matter.

There was a little more excitement for those coming down from the top, at least at the beginning of their ride. Fatscat had summoned Bruno, Carlo and Hiram to the compound the night before. They deservedly were his top three lieutenants, for lack of a better term – veteran, seasoned, extremely competent thugs. They were the real deal and each of them had his paws completely full managing a substantial territory. Their slimy cups, they did runneth over.

Fatscat's job of keeping everything in check for the entire organization surely was not an easy one. However, having to direct and keep tabs on the oft-transient Tin Roof front linesmen in any particular territory probably was even more challenging. Good help, it was hard to find. Bruno, Carlo and Hiram each had his work cut out for him on a daily basis and, to a man, they considered themselves way overworked and far underpaid. Predictably, Fatscat had an entirely different opinion on the matter, being of the mind that they were lucky to have the positions that they held. The truth, as always, lied somewhere in between.

Each of the three was more than perturbed about having to shove aside everything that he was in the middle of, in order to make another "secret" run to the compound with virtually no notice. Fatscat had demanded that they do the same less than two weeks ago, when they had to drop everything to help Hardcrass' boys execute the Pusserschmott catnapping. They originally had considered that to be some sort of disguised suicide mission. To their credit, they had since kept that entire job a complete secret. Not that they had any choice, having been told by Fatscat that any leak, anywhere, would result in certain death to them all.

Here they were again. Not having received their orders until late the night before, it was almost sunrise by the time they all had made it to the compound. With barely a couple of hours of sleep under their gun belts, Fatscat roused them just after eight a.m. If they had to guess, they probably would have surmised that it must have something to do with that Pusserschmott couple again. What else could it possibly be? Still, they didn't have the slightest clue about where they might be going or what they'd be doing.

With their whiny attitudes and pouty faces, Fatscat thought briefly about sending them home right then and there, and cutting them out of the whole thing. "Ungrateful bastards," he said to himself. At the moment, though, they didn't even know that they were in on something to be cut out of. Don't get the wrong impression, what Fatscat was about to do for them wasn't a gesture of kindness, but something wrought mostly by necessity.

Fatscat knew that he would need help with logistics alone, even if nothing else. Carrying that much cash back up into the hills at anything resembling a decent pace, managing the prisoners on the way down, not giving the appearance of being (much less actually being) alone, and therefore completely vulnerable, when the exchange did go down. No way could he possibly do it alone and even he wasn't greedy enough to risk trying it.

True, he could have chosen others to help, but he had been around long enough to know that this was too important to take any chances on. He needed to have with him the toughest, most grizzled crew that he could assemble and he was willing to pay for it, even if it was someone else's money as a technical matter. It was *the* once-in-a-lifetime shot and, to his credit, he made sure that there was a big incentive for everyone to get it done right.

While most everyone in the compound was occupied with breakfast, the four of them sneaked over to the barn and saddled up their dogs. They extracted Clevin and Melba from their little room, bound them together and tied them onto a saddle atop a big Doberman Pinscher. The Dobie was on a long lead line, so that Fatscat and his cohorts could ride ahead and speak privately, and it had strict orders to kill the hostages if they tried to make a run for it. Bruno, Carlo and Hiram sat in utter disbelief, flabbergasted, when they started descending the western side of the peaks and Fatscat told them what was on tap for the ensuing twenty-four hours.

He said, "If everything goes to plan today, and you better be damn sure it does, us four leave late tonight and ride to Catina Town. Don't blow it and each of you walks with half a million bucks. We meet Hardcrass at the marina at sun-up to take off on a boat, and I'm going as far as they can take me. Come with me if you want or get dropped off somewhere else along the way. Either way, it's going to be all over after tonight. Now, get back there and make sure you keep an eye on those kids. Keep an eye out for anything else, too. We have a pretty good ride ahead of us. And like I said, don't blow it."

The trio suddenly sloughed off their angst like a worn overcoat and they immediately fell back, newly bright-eyed and bushy-tailed, to surround the Doberman. It smelled a good bit better back there anyway, although they were victimized by the breeze, which intermittently rolled uphill nearly the entire morning, carrying fresh batches of odeur du Harold.

Fatscat was dead set on getting to the exchange location hours ahead of the appointed time, so that a full-on scan of the surrounding area could be conducted to make sure that no advance team had been sent to try and ruin his payday. That was the real reason he had delayed in sending the exchange location instructions to begin with. So that he could be sure to beat out the cash arrival by a wide margin. Of course, Fatscat had no idea that those on the money train already had put fourteen miles behind themselves before the day even began.

The sky was clear, the trail was dry, the help had major newfound motivation and they stopped literally for nothing. Had it been a family road trip to a frequented vacation destination, Dad would have bragged for days about how he had obliterated the all-time speed record. It was barely after twelve when they arrived, and they went straight to riding in concentric circles three at a time, with one always staying back to stand guard on the hostages. Fatscat was as satisfied as he would let himself be that no one appeared to be lying in wait for them, but he clearly was taken aback when Warren and his convoy came riding in at two o'clock on the dot. If he wasn't, he did a bang-up job acting the part.

The scumbags took their positions. The Doberman was stationed uphill, about twenty yards above a small clearing. Bruno was next to it on his dog, holding a pistol to Clevin's head. Fatscat sat on Louie in the middle of said small clearing. Carlo and Hiram sat upon their mounts on either side of Fatscat, about five yards back, each with a rifle trained on one of the good guys riding toward them. Fatscat threw down his sloppy cigar to free up his forepaw for his pistol and yelled, "WHAT THE HELL ARE YOU DOING HERE ALREADY?"

Warren was as cool as a cucumber and replied without hesitation, "Never mind that, asshole. And before we do this, let's get one thing straight. I can't tell you how lucky you are that I'm under orders that I am not at liberty to ignore. Not unless you try something really, and I mean really, stupid. If it weren't for those two kids sitting up there, I would take your fat ass out of here so fast, it would make your one-eared head swim."

Warren nodded toward Fatscat's crew and said, "I don't care who these chumps are or anyone else you've got hiding out up here in these hills with you. You think y'all are bad, huh? Yeah, you're real tough. Sitting there with a pistol to the head of a tied up kid. I shudder in your midst. Ooohhh! Look, if I ever get the chance, EVER, I'm gonna light you up like there's no tomorrow. You better run and hide for a long time, you bastard. You make one mistake, just one little slip up, and you're mine. You'll wish it was the feds or some cops if I ever get a hold of you."

Fatscat commenced to talking big, but he knew deep down inside that Warren was right. Warren was a certified bad ass and pretty much everyone on the entire East Coast knew it. Fatscat said, "Blah, blah, blah. Just gimme the cash and you can take these little rich kids back to Daddy. It all better be there, too, you hear? And hey, where's the Gunslinger? I know he's coming."

Warren replied, "Sorry to disappoint you, lard ass, but he wasn't allowed to ride here with us. And believe you me, he was dying to come. Everyone else was afraid that it would give you flashbacks about the last time you two met up, and nobody wanted to take the chance that you might roll around and start crying, or snap and hurt those kids. Don't worry, he's no different than me. If they ever cut him loose to come after you, he'll hunt you down and kick your fat ass as bad as I would. Probably worse. I'd just blow what's left of your ugly head off, or maybe knock it off. He and his buddy are way more creative than I am. Who knows what they'd do?"

Warren said, "Oh, there is one other thing. Actually, it's not all here." "WHAT DO YOU MEAN IT'S NOT ALL HERE?" screamed Fatscat. Warren said, "Just shut your trap and quit griping. It's fifty thousand short and there wasn't anything that any of us could do about it. It's all the cash that the bank could release without having to call in its loans to other banks. We didn't want anyone to start asking questions and chance having the press find out about all of this. Then it's the cops, then maybe even the army. It's your call, fat boy. You want it or not? If not, we can take it back and try to do this again later, but seeing that it ain't your money to begin with, you might want to take it and run before I change my own mind and blow you away right now."

Warren nodded toward Burt and Timmy and said, "Men, if you don't mind, pull those sacks off of Amos there and finish loading 'em up with the cash from our saddlebags." They instantly jumped into action, as Warren turned to Benji and said, "Brother, could you please do us all a favor? See that little cone up in that tree over there?" Warren pointed up into a pine tree about forty yards away, and Benji looked up in that direction and then nodded. Warren said, "Take your rifle and shoot that thing down for all of us, please." Benji pulled his rifle out of the holster, raised it up, closed his left eye and squeezed the trigger. The pine cone shattered into a few chunks and a small cloud of dust, and Warren said, "Not bad, dead-eye."

Warren raised his voice out toward Fatscat and his bums, "I trust that all of you dirtbags saw that. Now, don't anyone get alarmed. No false moves and nobody will get hurt." Still facing in the scumward direction, he said loudly, "Benji, now take your rifle and point it at his head, right between the eyes." Warren pointed at Bruno, who still had his pistol trained on Clevin's head, and then continued, "If I say the word, you blow his brains out. Okay?" Benji said, "Got it, Boss." Warren pulled his pistol from his holster and said to Fatscat, "And if you don't mind, I'm gonna keep this pointed at your ugly face. And I mean ugly, Fatscat. Damn, if that's not one of the ugliest faces I've ever laid eyes on!"

By now, Burt and Timmy had emptied all of the saddlebag cash into the two bags that Amos once carried, and each of them was standing there holding one. They still were nervous as ever about the whole situation, but they clearly were enjoying the unexpected entertainment that Warren was dishing out. They already couldn't wait, assuming that they would make it home alive, to recount for the boss lady the unadulterated verbal lashing that Warren was laying on ol' Harold. It was right up her alley. True Barncat-style insultory bludgeoning for someone who completely and unequivocally deserved every word of it.

Warren said to them, "Now, please take those bags and set them down over there next to Harold's dog." Burt and Timmy started for Fatscat, but halted quickly when Warren yelled, "WAIT! Before you go over there, you might want to take a deep, deep breath and then try to hold it until you get back. If I can smell him from all the way over here, you know it's gotta be bad where you're going." Even Carlo and Hiram had to suppress giggling after that comment. Fortunately for them, Fatscat was facing away and didn't see their smirks.

Warren said to Fatscat, "Count it up if you want. You, your boys, whoever. Like I said, it's fifty grand short. Fatscat jumped off of Louie and began pulling stacks from one of the bags. He fanned through a few of them, took a couple of whiffs, dug back through the bag a little more and then looked skyward as he struggled to do some quick math in his head. Warren yelled, "Sorry, dumbass, I didn't bring anything to write with. You can write, can't you? Maybe you can just scratch some numbers in the dirt if counting by fifties is a little too much for you. You know, they say that arithmetic is a lot harder if you're missing an ear, especially the right one."

As much as they hated each other, there was some sort of implicit trust at work. Fatscat knew that if they had come all that way, and then made a point to acknowledge a one percent shortfall, the rest of it probably was there. And, with all of the plans he had made, what could he do if it was short, or even counterfeit for that matter? It wasn't like he carried some sort of portable currency analytics device for testing. He knew that there was only so much that he could do at this point. So, he rummaged through the other bag to make sure it looked about the same. When he appeared to be through, he waved Carlo and Hiram over toward himself.

Warren was quick to resume his monologue. "Not just yet," he said. "You've got your money, crudball. Before any of you takes one step with it, you cut those kids loose and you do it right now." Fatscat started to grumble. Warren responded by cocking his pistol and Benji did likewise with the hammer on his rifle. Warren said loudly, "Ten seconds, Fatscat, or your face goes up in smoke and your boy's head goes with it. I don't care who else you might have up here with you. Maybe I die. Maybe those kids die. Maybe we all die. One thing I can guarantee you, though. You and your boy up there next to those kids, you're goners no matter what."

Fatscat yelled over to Bruno, "Untie the little runts and let 'em go." Bruno hit the ground before Fatscat had finished his sentence, delighted to be anywhere other than wedged in the cross hairs of the sniper kid's rifle. He quickly untied Clevin and Melba, and Warren told them to come down the hill. Both of them were shaking, and they knew that it probably wouldn't get much better for them anytime soon.

Don't get me wrong. Being upgraded from hostage status certainly was their paramount wish. Still, freedom would not come without cost. Warren may not have posed the same type of threat as did Fatscat and his gang, but Clevin and Melba knew that it was only a matter of time before Warren turned his attention to them. The ride home would start with a brief celebratory period, followed by the obligatory honeymoon stage, but the gloves would come off sooner or later. With hours of trail to kill, no one could predict how long Warren would spend laying into them with a vengeance for sending his security team and the rest of the help away from the lake house that fateful night.

Warren asked Burt and Timmy to help Melba and Clevin up onto Amos, and they complied quickly. It had been several minutes now since Warren did not have his pistol aimed at Fatscat's head. He even had to switch paws a couple of times for fatigue. Bruno was back on his dog, riding toward the others, Benji's rifle was back pointed at Bruno's head, and Burt and Timmy were back on the trail, going the other way with Amos and the kids. Warren yelled to Fatscat, "As much as we'd like to use your heads for a little target practice, we can't. I mean, unless you want to try something fancy here at the last minute. Go ahead, tough guy. Make a move." Fatscat just shook his head and spat.

Warren suddenly jerked his pistol and Fatscat jumped about as high as he could go on a three-legged launch. Warren started laughing and Benji quickly joined in. "Now, get out of here," Warren said. Warren and Benji watched intently, guns still pointed, as Fatscat, Bruno, Carlo and Hiram divided up the money stacks, loaded them into their saddlebags and remounted their dogs.

Fatscat and his crew ordinarily would have waited for Warren and Benji to ride well out of sight before moving on in the direction of the compound. For some reason, they just seemed to want to get out of there as fast as they could, and they barely bothered to look back. Warren yelled, "DON'T WORRY, PUNKS. WE'RE NOT COMING AFTER YOU. MAYBE SOME OTHER TIME, BUT WE'VE GOT TO RUN OURSELVES." He started riding down the trail, and then he turned back and yelled, "OH, HAROLD." Fatscat turned back with a grimace and Warren shouted, "DON'T SPEND IT ALL IN ONE PLACE."

CHAPTER THIRTY

DOWN AND DIRTY

For most, the early rides were a breeze. Fatscat and his scumbuddies, they were going to pick up (almost) five million dollars and it was all downhill, literally. If that wasn't enough to get them fired up and keep them on or ahead of pace, what would be? Not only did Warren and his squad have a big head start and an open trail, but they were anxious to get there as soon as they could to get those kids out of hock. And as it turns out, no one was in more of a hurry than Warren, who couldn't wait to give Fatscat a piece of his mind. For Elvis, Frank, Eddie and Calli, however, morning travel was more in the nature of a slog than a breezy jaunt.

It wasn't that the company was bad, even if Frank initially was less than thrilled about Calli tagging along. They also had the benefit, or at least the distraction, of listening to her story for the first ninety minutes of the ride, which helped keep their minds off of most everything else. It being the first time through for Eddie and Frank, they had no trouble staying engaged with that sort of material. And though it no longer was fresh news to Elvis, he still paid close attention, on the lookout for any inconsistencies between the story she had told the night before and what she now was saying. He was relatively certain that Calli was completely on the up and up, but this was no time for getting sloppy, and he wanted to be as sure as he possibly could.

Not the company, and not the weather either. It was another gorgeous summer day in the Longtails. The terrain, though, it was tough. After Calli finished divulging, and after Eddie and Frank were satisfied with her answers to the few questions that they did have, the trail was all that remained for anyone to focus on. You could sort of call it a trail. It was depicted as such on Tony's map at least, but it was a trail pretty much in name only. Tough as it was, they still felt lucky to be on it. They were meandering easterly, trying to traverse the northern edge of the lower peaks and get themselves around to the eastern side by mid-day.

Although the undulations weren't overly severe, they were frequent. Almost constant. And, it was rocky in lots of places. Most stretches were too overgrown to have been traveled with any frequency. What they were riding probably was more of a getaway route than anything else. It was pretty heavy work for the dogs, with the only bright spot being that this route did shorten the distance that they'd have to cover by more than half. Traveling the conventional way to get where they were going would have been more than a full day's ride, even for these dogs. They couldn't spare that kind of time.

They broke for lunch, mostly as an accommodation to the canines, each of which was carrying a heavy load in addition to its rider. Frank had brought along enough food to get both canines and felines alike through at least a couple of meals. It was not anyone's preference, but there was little choice today. There wasn't time for the luxury of a hunting expedition, and even if there had been, they were approaching the point where they didn't want to spoil the quiet mountain air with gunshots. They may have had a little bit of cushion to work with, but there was no way to tell for sure with the way the map had been drawn. Stealth soon would be a high priority and they couldn't take any chances on giving themselves away.

Not long after lunch, the "trail" did begin to open up a little. It was nothing to write home about, but still a definite improvement. By the time Elvis' watch struck two, they had fully made it around the top end and were moving south along the eastern edge of the range, just below the upper peaks. Assuming that Fatscat and Hardcrass hadn't since changed the plan that Calli had heard them hatch, there should have been some mercenary types ascending the hills sooner or later. The trick would be to find a group that was small enough to take without having to resort to gunfire.

Unless Tony's map was sorely out of scale or kilter, or both, they should have been coming up on a trail that appeared to be almost due east of Leashing. They kept their claws crossed, hoping that it would turn out to be something more substantial than the broken way they had been relegated to for most of the day. They needed it to be the kind of path where they might expect to see some activity and it turned out to be just that. Everything below it for at least a hundred yards was thickly forested, which they expected. Up above, though, the road was clear, even if steep, and it looked to be pointing straight to the top of the high peaks.

With Fatscat carrying a pile of ill-gotten gain back up the other side of the range, and Warren leading the way home with two uninjured former hostages, it would be only fitting for the remaining travelers to get a little break of their own. Voila! It was just what the doctor ordered. No one could see anything yet, but sounds definitely were creeping their way uphill, and the volume was progressively climbing. It was hard to tell exactly what was being said, with voices being muffled by the steady sounds of canines pushing through brush. Cussing, it sounded like mostly, which would have been entirely understandable. Where those noises were coming from, it was very steep and the brush was just as thick. A perfect combination for enhancing rider consternation.

Everyone that we know huddled up, took cover and started whispering amongst themselves, as they watched downhill until the images began to come into focus. There were three riders, trailed closely by a fourth dog that was loaded up with what looked to be bags. Almost instantly, Elvis, Eddie and Frank had disappeared, and their dogs were lying down in complete silence on the other side of a thicket. Just as the riders finally made it out of the rough, they got their own reward, or so they thought. There was Calli sitting on Catfleet under a huge oak tree, not twenty yards away. She had her face in her paws and was sobbing away as if she had gotten lost. As soon as their dogs caught their breath, they started riding toward her.

Although having a pack dog that carried a full complement of nothing but pistols, rifles and ammunition sort of gave them away, they otherwise looked to be ordinary, average guys. One of them politely asked Calli if she was okay and whether there was anything that they could do to help. She almost felt bad when Elvis, Frank and Eddie dropped about fifteen feet from a huge limb, each of them landing squarely upon the back of one of her valiant would-be rescuers. They all were driven straight, and hard, to the ground and each of them now was enjoying a pistol to the side of the head.

Elvis and Frank both winked at Eddie and commented on his nice work. They knew that this wasn't his usual cup of milk and he had performed flawlessly. Frank quickly looked over at Calli and said in an angry tone, "I've got two things to say to you, girl." A disappointed expression came over her face and it looked like she might even cry for real.

Frank broke into a smile as he continued, "First, despite what you might think, I'm very glad we have you in our group. No way could we have pulled off something this smooth without you." She felt relieved and countered with a smile of her own. Then he said, "Second, I need you to go to my saddlebag on this side of Stella. Inside, there's a small leather case and I would really appreciate it if you could bring it over here to me, along with one of the canteens. Any of them will do."

As Calli happily started toward Stella, Elvis took the opportunity to lecture the captured. He said, "Gentlemen, we are so sorry to have to do this to you, especially after you were so nice to try to help out our very cute friend here, but, we don't have much choice. As much as we'd like for you to go to that party tonight, we're going to have to sub for you and I'm afraid there's no way around it. We go, you don't. That's just the way it has to be. Now before you all get your butt hairs in a big wad about it, I do have some good news. When you wake up, and I'm not exactly sure when that's going to be, each of you will have one thousand dollars in your holster, right where your pistol used to be. Yes, boys, I did say one thousand."

Calli was back right away, standing in front of Frank with the case and a canteen. As she awaited her next orders, Elvis continued, "Don't any of you try coming up this hill, and none of you says a word to anyone. NOTHING. You hear me? Just go back to where you came from and all of this will be our little secret. If we see you again, ever, you die. That ought to be more than enough cash for each of you to get a good new dog and a new pistol. As long as you don't go too far overboard, each of you should have way more leftover than the five hundred you were slated to get for finishing this job. Catpeesh?"

All of the fallen nodded their heads as best they could, while the down sides of their faces ground back and forth into the forest floor. Elvis said, "And don't worry. I promise you're not going to miss out on anything good. Actually, there's a damn good chance we're saving your lives now that I think about it. Please accept our apologies in advance for whatever might happen to any of your friends up there. Like I said, we don't have any choice, so just consider yourselves the lucky ones."

Frank looked up at Calli and said, "Excellent. Those are exactly what I'm looking for. If you unzip that pouch, you'll see some small vials of powder. Near the top, there's one with a little bit missing." She held one up and Frank said, "Correct. If you don't mind, kneel down next to me and pour a little bit of that into this fine young man's mouth. Maybe about a third of what's left in there. He's going to swallow it like a good boy and then we'll let him chase it down with a teeny swig of agua." With his free forepaw, Frank pulled a knife from a sheath on his hip, pushed the blade up against his counterpart's neck and said, "Or maybe he won't cooperate and I can just cut his throat instead."

Frank's captive kitty was quick to interrupt, as out from his contorted mouth came some noises that resembled the words, "You don't have to do that." He opened wide as Calli sprinkled in some dust. Then she opened the canteen and poured in a few drops to help wash down the chalky stuff. Frank looked back up at Calli and said, "Perfecto."

She stood there smiling and Frank said, "Well, don't stand there looking at me. You know what to do." Calli stepped over to the cat that Eddie had pinned and repeated the procedure, and then moved over next to Elvis to finish off number three. Each of them was out cold inside of a minute and all of the waking felines promptly whipped into action.

The recently vacated dogs truly were a godsend. In just a few minutes, everything that at one time occupied Amos' back had been neatly transferred over to the new team members. Despite their athletic prowess, Daisy, Stella, Catation and Catfleet already had worked what would be more than a full day for most dogs, and substantial climbing still lie ahead of them. They would have suffered through it like the troopers they were, but the new hires definitely were going to be a major boon to the pace.

Next, Frank had his way with the dozers. Maybe not in the traditional sense, but he did strip from them everything that they had, leaving each of them with only an empty gun belt. After the loot had been safely stowed, Elvis and Eddie helped Frank drag the trio over to an out-of-the-way indentation in the ground. True to his word, Elvis made the first deployment of his bribe stash, stuffing ten hundreds into each of their holsters. Everyone not asleep then pitched in to help tuck in the slumber party attendees by piling on a bunch of sticks and leaves until they were good and covered.

Elvis, Frank, Calli and Eddie quickly were back on their mounts. While each of them was very excited to have a private pack dog, their joy paled in comparison to that of their dogs. None of them ever had a Sherpa to assist with a hike, and there would have been no better day for it than today. The trails ahead were some of the steepest they'd ever been asked to navigate. Eddie was the first to make mention of it, saying, "No wonder no one ever rides up here!" All of the others were quick to nod in agreement.

After about an hour of heavy climbing, they came across a narrow stream. It was a perfect time for a break and from the way things looked up above, they might have less than an hour to go before they'd be riding up on Fatscat's compound. It was hard to believe that they hadn't yet encountered anyone else on the trail.

With their luxurious ratio of two dogs per rider, they were keeping a rapid pace, and it wasn't likely that anyone would creep up on them from behind. But, they were bound to cross paths with one or more groups up ahead before long. Especially once they passed the area where several of the trails converged near the top. From the looks of Tony's map, that location wasn't too far off, and they needed to start giving some consideration to disguising themselves and maintaining a low profile.

Though several hours of daylight remained, the sun by now had crept over the top of the peaks. Not a big deal for most purposes, but it soon would take on greater importance. Frank had just announced that everyone was going to need to get into the bed of the stream to do some good old-fashioned mucking up. He was right. Maybe they weren't dressed for church or court, but everyone was clean and reasonably well-appointed. It certainly wasn't the thug-for-hire look that they would need for a proper blending in.

They wouldn't be able to formulate a complete plan until they got on-site and had a good look around. Whatever it was that they might devise, heavy mingling with the mercenary crowd likely would not be part of the itinerary. Still, they had to assume that it would be difficult to keep entirely to themselves throughout the afternoon and evening. There was going to be at least some interaction and they would need to look the part. Or, at least look it a little better than they did at the moment. It was now that the direct sunlight would have been a positive force. Streams at these elevations run cold, even in the summer months, and dogs and cats alike all shivered as they haphazardly smeared mud and gunk all over themselves.

After they had gotten their bodies, their hats and their garments good and yucky, they covered their faces with bandanas and got back on the trail. While they would make every effort to avoid being recognized, they had to at least be prepared for the possibility. Elvis was not an unknown in these parts, and in a crowd likely to include a substantial number of criminals, there might well be a handful who had seen a photo, if not actually made his acquaintance.

Calli also was a prospect for recognition. First of all, any male who frequented that bar in Catina Town couldn't help but remember *her*. And even if she did go unrecognized, she still was conspicuous for no reason other than gender. It wasn't unheard of for a woman to enter this line of work, but it surely wasn't the norm, especially a woman who looked like she did.

Eddie may have posed the greatest risk of all, certainly so here on the East Coast. He possibly was the most famous jockey who ever lived. Though his career had been over for a couple of years, hundreds of thousands had seen him race and he was highly decorated at some of the eastern tracks, where he had done almost all of his riding.

It was nearly six o'clock when they finally hit paydirt. They did encounter a couple of small groups during the last mile of their ride, but they enjoyed great success keeping to themselves and avoiding getting dragged into any lengthy conversations. They stayed below the compound when they arrived, and were able to work their way over to an out-of-sight area just thirty yards below the northwest corner of the paddock. Though it was a spot that the guards would have checked once or twice during a routine day, today was anything but routine. With all of the arrivals coming in and Fatscat nowhere to be found, no one had bothered to make the usual rounds. Did I mention that good help was hard to find in these circles?

After the gear had been offloaded, they put all of the dogs in a secure place and climbed up to just below the paddock. They lied down on their bellies in the warmth of the waning sun, a few yards below the line of sight from the compound, and they proceeded to look around and start scheming.

CHAPTER THIRTY-ONE

ALL PAWS ON DECK

If ever there was a day for the uninvited, much less the unwelcome, to drop by Fatscat's compound and say hello, today was the day. The entire joint was overrun with strangers, and virtually none of the usual or semi-usual occupants ever had crossed paths with the vast majority of the visitors. Everyone got the benefit of the doubt, and the only sure way to raise an eyebrow probably would have been to show up in uniform.

From a low vantage point on the immediate outskirts, Calli, Frank, Elvis and Eddie had no trouble circumnavigating the entire compound in just over an hour, and they had a solid grasp on where everything and everyone was. It wasn't a huge place, mind you, but they still thought it appropriate to pat themselves on the back for making such efficient progress.

Being the least likely to be recognized, Frank had gotten the nod to serve as emissary from time to time, and he had been busy during the entire excursion making his case for MVP. While the others circled the perimeter step-by-step, Frank darted almost at will into and out of myriad buildings and impromptu conversations. He gathered all sorts of useful information, not the least of which was that an all paws meeting was set for nine o'clock in the mess hall. Attendance was mandatory for everyone who wasn't either working in the barn or manning the telegraph.

They barely had arrived back at their little hideout when Frank ran off again. He ducked into the barn completely unnoticed and essentially waltzed right out with a huge bag full of food that he had pilfered for the canines. So easily and breezily that he decided to go back and do it again for good measure. Well, not *just* for good measure; actually, he had to. Frank could carry only enough food at one time to give half of the dogs their fill.

With almost sixty more dogs on the grounds than usual, Felaine was absolutely overwhelmed, and it was all that she could do just to get them fed and watered. The barn was bursting at the seams with dog and the paddock was in full overflow mode. No wonder she had been exempted from the assembly! The guards (who had been doing anything but guarding) had been kind enough to pitch in and help her with various tasks throughout the day, but their surveillance skills were no match for a master thief like Frank.

Despite getting off to a much earlier start than they had expected, it still was a long ride back lugging all of that cash uphill, and Fatscat and his trio didn't return to the compound until nearly eight o'clock. They went straight to Fatscat's office, into which they dragged their saddlebags and shoved them all under his desk. Fatscat ordinarily would have been livid to find no one at the hilltop keeping watch over his office, the telegraph room or his quarters, but he was happy to have the privacy at the moment. They all could hear the noise bellowing out of the barracks and the mess hall down below, as they started for the barn to drop off their dogs.

It was Eddie's turn on watch and he came dashing over from his lookout post to report that a cat on three legs had just left the barn and was going toward the mess hall with a few others. It seemed that virtually everyone else in the compound was in the mess hall by now as well. There had been some half-hearted discussions about Frank possibly taking a run at the mess hall and trying to sneak out some food, but they all knew that it was more fantasy than anything else.

With all of the good fortune they'd had during the past few hours, they weren't about to get greedy and chance making a mistake that they would regret. They finally faced up to reality and resorted to more of the canned stuff that Frank had gotten from Uncle Sam. It wasn't fresh roasted boar, but it wasn't bad, and a bit more of the old man's bourbon was just the thing to make it all the more palatable.

They all lied around digesting their meals while they waited for darkness to set in fully. Except for Frank. He had been fooling around with his gear for over half an hour now and no one knew exactly what it was that he was doing. When it finally had gotten dark enough to strike out, Frank and Eddie were the first ones to go. They took a couple of the "borrowed" dogs and led them away toward the upper reaches of the compound. Elvis said to Calli, "It's time that you and I paid a visit to the barnmaster." Calli just nodded as she got up and took off after Elvis, who was sprinting through the dogs in the paddock. He stopped just short of the barn and waited for Calli to catch up.

They looked through a window on the side of the barn and could see Felaine walking quickly down the aisle, leading a saddled dog into a stall at the front of the barn. They sneaked around to the back doors of the barn and peeked in. There she was again, hitching another dog to a cross-tie in the center of the barn. She stepped into a nearby room and Elvis dashed down the aisle.

Felaine came back out of the room with a saddle in her forelegs, and Elvis grabbed her from behind, put his left forepaw over her mouth and held a pistol to her head with his right. Calli stood there in the aisle, frozen in her tracks with her mouth wide open and obviously worried about what might happen next. Not as worried as Felaine, mind you, but still quite worried nonetheless.

Felaine was shaking almost uncontrollably, and though the sound was a bit muffled by Elvis' paw, you easily could make out the words, "Please, please don't hurt me. I'll do anything, just don't hurt me. I have six little kittens and they can't survive without me." Calli was almost in tears herself when Elvis said to Felaine, "Don't worry, dear. Unless you're dead set on helping all of these scumbags, everything is going to be all right."

Elvis loosened his grip on her mouth and let her slump down onto the barn floor. He sat down next to her and said, "First, I need some answers, and then we're going to need your help." Tears began streaming down her face as she tried to regain her composure. Elvis leaned over, pulled off his bandana and dried her eyes, and the following conversation ensued:

Elvis: Why are you saddling dogs at this hour?

Felaine: If I tell you, he'll kill me.

Elvis: Who, Fatscat?

Felaine: (She nodded her head rapidly.) He will. I know he will.

Elvis: Don't worry about Fatscat for now. Are these dogs for him?

Felaine: Yes, him and his buddies.

Elvis: What buddies? Do you know who they are?

Felaine: Some big shots from down on the Coast. They don't usually come up here. They were out together all day and they just got back. He told me to saddle up four fresh dogs, and take them to the top during the meeting and tie them up behind his office. He said that if I tell anyone, anyone, he'll kill me. And my kittens, too. (She started crying again.)

Elvis: Who else is up there now?

Felaine: If they started the meeting, then I guess just Tomboy.

Elvis: Who's Tomboy?

Felaine: She runs the telegraph. Fatscat told me to bring her back down here with me after I drop off the dogs. She usually sleeps up there, but she has to stay in the barn with me tonight to make room for Fatscat's buddies.

Elvis: What's the deal with her and Fatscat? Is she loyal to him?

Felaine: No, she hates him. We all do. She just needs the work. Her parents are really old and they can't take care of themselves anymore. She's all they have.

Elvis: Okay, let's finish saddling these dogs and get them up there like Fatscat said. (He pointed to Calli.) This is Calli. She's a very good friend of mine and she can help, too.

Felaine: (Still sniffling.) Okay. This is the last one. The other three are saddled up in that front stall.

Elvis: What about the Pusserschmott kids? The ones that were catnapped. Are they here?

Felaine: No, not anymore. Fatscat and his buddies rode away with them early this morning. I was up in the loft. They didn't know I was watching.

Elvis: Okay, good.

Elvis picked the saddle up from the ground, threw it onto the dog and began to tie his bandana back on. Felaine started to cinch up the saddle and Calli already was leading the other three dogs out of the stall and into the aisle. They made their way out of the barn, got as far away as possible from the mess hall and marched as fast as they could toward the hilltop. As they strode up the hill, Calli whispered to Elvis, "What are Frankie and Eddie doing over there by that building with a shovel?" Elvis whispered back, "Don't ask me. I'm just here to make love, pass out cash and shoot somebody every once in a while. They don't tell me about any of that other stuff." He looked at her and winked, and Calli smiled back and shook her head.

The telegraph room was the uppermost structure in the compound, on the back side of Fatscat's office. There was a hitching post directly behind it, where they tied up the dogs. They walked back around to the front of the telegraph room and Elvis insisted on being the first to enter. He walked up the three steps leading to the door, kicked it open and stood there, not five feet from Tomboy, holding a pistol in each forepaw. One was pointed at Tomboy's head and the other was pointed at the telegraph machine. Tomboy started to scream, but quickly covered her mouth with her forepaws.

She sat there silent, staring, with her paws still over her mouth. Even Elvis was at a bit of a loss for words. She started to pull her paws away from her face and Elvis was about to make some sort of authoritative declaration. Before he could get the first word out, Tomboy said, "Elvis, is that you?" He was at a complete loss for words now, so Calli took the opportunity to say, "No way! You're not doing her, too. Are you?" Elvis knew that he wasn't guilty as charged, but he still didn't really know what to say.

Whether or not he needed it, Tomboy bailed him out. She said, "There's a picture of you at my parents' house. You and my father. You're wearing that same vest. Carrying those same guns. My daddy worked for the railroad. You saved his life when Screech Tabby tried to hijack that big gold shipment last year. You're his hero. I mean, not just his. Mine, too." Elvis looked back at Calli and Felaine, and they looked back at him with blank stares. All Elvis could think to say was, "We need to get back down to the barn. We don't have much time."

He started to turn, but then stopped himself and asked, "What sort of messages have you gotten in the last couple of days? Anything weird? Anything unusual?" Tomboy said, "No, just the regular stuff." "Are you sure?" Elvis said. Tomboy looked around her desk and said, "Wait a minute. I did get one this afternoon. I just thought it was a mistake or something, or maybe it was in the wrong code. It said 'Dock 23.' That's all, just 'Dock 23.' Fatscat was looking for it a few minutes ago. It seemed like he understood it. I just went back to my work and forgot all about it." Elvis said, "Okay. We've gotta go now." With that, Elvis the Gunslinger took off down the hill, with three young ladies rapidly chasing behind.

- - -

Hey, if Elvis only had known that, as he stood there at the telegraph room door, all that separated him from the ransom were the back wall of Fatscat's office and approximately fifteen feet. Now, that would put a twist in our story. For better or worse, neither he nor Frank ever considered that sort of possibility. Imagine the look you would have gotten from someone, say Kathy Barncat for instance, if you said something like this. Oh, and you really meant it.

> *"Okay, this is what we'll do. First, we'll sneak all the way up there completely undetected. We'll make camp right outside of the place and no one will see us, because all of the guards are going to be goofing off that day. Later on, Fatscat will show up with the money, but he'll put it in some completely obvious place, and leave it unlocked and unguarded. Then, everyone in the entire camp – guards, visiting henchmen, everybody – will go lock themselves in a big room and we'll have the run of the place for about an hour. Completely unsupervised. We'll even get a couple of staff members to help us out. You know, show us around a little. They'll probably be cute girls. We'll find the money, load up the dogs and take back off for South Sebastian. No one will notice until it's way too late. Fatscat will lose his mind. Then, we'll all have a big party."*

Yeah, good one! They'd lock you up and throw away the key, my friend. At a minimum, you wouldn't be going off on any mission, much less be in charge of it. No, you can't make a plan like that. You might be able to talk someday about how you could have. One of those after-the-fact, "if only we had known," conversations that you have in the aftermath over a few beers or glasses of wine. You can even do that more than once. As many times as you want to until everyone gets sick of hearing the same story over and over again. Yeah, it would have been nice, but it doesn't work that way.

As a practical matter, even if Elvis had stumbled across the money up there, at least fifty seasoned individuals who were armed to the teeth might walk out of that big room down below at any moment. With another ten or fifteen who frequented the compound and were very familiar with the surrounding territory. Getting caught in the act or being chased down thereafter would have been a distinct possibility, even for Elvis and Frank. More likely than not would be my guess. And, at the end of the day, they did have a job to do.

Escaping with that cash and bringing it home? Now, that would have been a neat trick. Assuming that the Pusserschmott couple were safe, though, and it appeared that they would be, it was expected that our boys would accomplish something more. Putting a major dent in the Tin Roof operation was their implicit assignment, if not blowing the whole thing wide open.

CHAPTER THIRTY-TWO

THE FINAL COUNTDOWN

When he got inside the barn, Elvis ran straight to the back and ducked into the last stall on the right. The ladies were close behind him and everyone just sat for a few moments to catch their breath. Elvis peeked out to make sure that no one had followed them, slid the door shut and fell back against it. He looked up at the stall ceiling, looked around at the others and began speaking very softly, "I'm sorry I can't explain everything right now. If I know my partner, he's probably looking for me already, wondering where the hell I am."

He continued, "You can listen to me and do what I say, or you can stay up here and die. It's completely your decision." Elvis pointed at Calli and said, "This is Calli and she's in charge." Elvis looked at Tomboy and Felaine, and said, "You two need to act like nothing unusual is going on. Finish up whatever it is that you have to do, close up the barn, make sure that all of the dogs are taken care of for the night and get to sleep as quickly as you can."

Elvis looked at Calli and said, "You and Eddie are going to sneak in here at about three o'clock." He pulled out his pocket watch, glanced down and said, "That's almost six hours from now." He looked back at Felaine and Tomboy and said, "My friend, Eddie, and Calli here are very good with dogs. All four of you should take every dog that you can out of this barn and out of that paddock. All at once, in groups, I don't care how. You figure it out. Just be quiet and don't get caught. If you do, you're probably goners. Start heading down the northern slope and get as far away as you can. Any questions?"

Tomboy asked, "Are we ever coming back?" Elvis said, "Not if you know what's good for you." Felaine said, "My kittens, can they come with us? I can pick them up on the way if we go down the north side. I can't just leave them." Elvis said, "Of course, but make it quick. In and out. And, they need to listen.

"I don't know exactly what's going to happen up here tomorrow, but it's going to be dangerous and you need to be as far away as possible by sun-up. By the way, you don't have to take the dogs if you don't want to. It will be a lot riskier trying to take them than just leaving them behind, but there's a good chance that any dog stuck here is going to die. It's going to be entirely up to you four."

Elvis asked, "How much does Fatscat pay you?" Tomboy said, "Ten dollars a week." Felaine nodded her head in agreement. Elvis scrunched up his face and said, "Can you live on that?" Tomboy replied, "Up here in the hills you can. It's cheap to live and there's not much to do." Elvis said, "Okay, nobody move. I'll be right back."

He slid the door open a few inches, peeked his head out, slipped into the aisle and took off. He was back in virtually no time at all. He stepped back into the stall, closed the door behind him and said, "Take this." He went over to Tomboy and Felaine, and dropped a pile of cash on the floor between them. They stared down dumbfounded as Calli looked on, appearing to be somewhat in shock as well.

Felaine exclaimed, "How much money is that?" Elvis held his forepaw up to his mouth and replied quietly, "Shhh! It's ten thousand dollars. You two split that up, five apiece. I don't ever want you to work for someone like this again. Never! You got that? This should be more than plenty to take care of yourselves." He looked at Felaine and said, "And your kitties." Then he looked at Tomboy and said, "And your parents."

Tomboy and Felaine sat motionless, looking up at Elvis with their eyes glazed over. He said sternly, "I'm serious. Now, split that up and put it away. Just remember, if you don't cooperate with Calli and Eddie tonight, you're dead." They continued staring up at him and began to nod slowly, and then they started picking hundred dollar bills up off of the stall floor.

He looked over at Calli and said, "Let's go," and they quietly slipped out of the stall. Then, they took off out of the barn, across the paddock and down to the makeshift hideout. They could see Frank and Eddie coming toward them along the outside of the paddock, trailed by the same two dogs that they had left with. When they arrived, Frank asked Eddie and Calli to take the four dogs that they had hijacked earlier in the day and turn them loose into the paddock. While they were tending to that, Elvis and Frank saddled up Daisy and Stella, loaded up their saddlebags and made sure that everything was ready to go.

When Calli and Eddie returned, Frank and Elvis were sitting with their heads down, engulfed in weaponry maintenance. They didn't say a word or even bother to look up until every firearm was fully loaded and their belts were filled with excess ammunition. Elvis still sported the original hardware that he had taken from his closet four days ago – his two pistols and his rifle. I know, can you believe that was only four days ago? Well, four and change. Frank had supplemented his lone pistol with an awesome eight-shot revolver that resembled a small cannon, and a shiny, new Catmington rifle, all courtesy of the gentlemen they had jumped earlier in the day.

Eddie and Calli might have been anticipating that the next event of the evening would be Elvis and Frank imparting a detailed list of step-by-step instructions, but it was not to be. Elvis looked up and said, "Eddie, Calli knows exactly what to do. Frankie, do you have any of those little timers left?" Frank nodded, reached into his vest pocket, threw a little metal contraption over to Eddie and said, "It's set for five-thirty. Make sure you change it to three before you lie down."

Elvis said, "Remember, three o'clock. Get those girls, get those dogs unless you really don't want to, and get out of here. And make sure you're quiet about it. There's a big pile of rifles, pistols and ammo leftover here from those nice boys we met today. You and those girls take what you can carry and cover up the rest. You never know what might happen out there."

Elvis walked over to Calli, gave her a hug and a big kiss, and rubbed Eddie's paw. Frank did likewise, except that he had to settle for a peck on the cheek in lieu of the wet one that Elvis had applied. Elvis said, "Frankie and I have to go." They unceremoniously jumped onto their dogs and rode off, working their way along the outside of the paddock, toward the top of the hill. Their next stop would be tracing the wire out of the telegraph room, following it for a couple hundred yards and chopping it in multiple places to cut the compound off from the outside world. It would be a piece of cake.

- - -

Internal psychological struggles? That probably wouldn't top your list if I asked you to enumerate the maladies afflicting Fatscat this evening. Unlikely as it might seem, he had two of them front and center, and he had spent the entirety of the ride back to the compound mulling them over. The first was merely a garden variety case of stage fright.

Even though Fatscat technically was a CEO, albeit on the dark side, addressing large assemblages was not exactly his bag. He had a dearth of experience in the field, especially when it came to groups constituted primarily of total strangers. He didn't have anything complex to say and it didn't really matter whether the audience was impressed or not. But, he being the only speaker on the program made him the keynote by default, and he was more than just a little nervous about it.

It was as close to a party atmosphere as ever had been seen in the mess hall. Calvatore had done a bang-up job of churning out a veritable pile of food. Just as Fatscat had little experience in large group public speaking, there likewise was not often a particularly large group to serve in the mess hall. This was nearly thrice the size of the largest crowd that Calvatore had cooked for since the hall had been built.

Veal and lamb were the menu choices tonight and there was more than plenty of both to go around. It all was met with a very warm reception. As the last few were finishing their seconds or thirds, maybe even fourths, the putrid one finally summoned the courage to raise himself out of his chair and hop to the front of the room. His tablemates breathed, literally, a sigh of relief.

To take his mind off of things, he lit up a cigar and began slobbering and puffing on it. The murmur in the room had fallen nearly to a hush, and by now everyone was staring at him. He said loudly, "Gentlemen, thank you for coming. Not that you haven't been paid damn well for it, but thanks just the same. Last week, a few of my men kidnapped some rich folks. Today, I traded them back for a fat wad of cash, and we've got some really big plans for our future." Several in the audience stood to cheer and whistle. Fatscat, feeling a little better after the round of applause, continued, "But first, we need to be on our guard for a little while."

Everyone stared intently and that made Fatscat more nervous than ever. He said, "The feds probably will be up here soon. They'll be coming up to try to get that money or to try something else. I can almost guarantee you that the little bastard who shot my leg and ear off already is on his way, and I assume that he'll be bringing a lot of help along with him. All I can say is that they're going to be in for a little surprise once they finally make it up here!" Everyone in the room started screaming and whistling, and clapping their paws loudly.

Fatscat had time for several puffs on his cigar before the sound had quelled so much that he was forced to continue in order to forestall an awkward silence. He said, "You can do what you want tonight, but everyone needs to be ready first thing in the morning." Fatscat pointed to Treeclimb and said, "This is Treeclimb and he'll be sounding the alarm at seven. Get over here right away for breakfast and then we get this place set up for war."

He continued, "I don't know when they'll be here for sure. Maybe it won't be tomorrow. Maybe they won't come after all. Who knows? We'll give it a few days. If it turns out that they don't show up, then so be it. All of you still will get paid." Cheers again filled the room, even louder and longer than the last round.

Fatscat thought that he might have more important things to say, but he couldn't seem to come up with anything useful, so, he just took to some basic repetition. As the crowd quieted back down, all he could muster was, "Like I said, do what you want tonight, and Cal will have a big breakfast ready for all of you in the morning. After that, it's all business."

His nerves were about to get the best of him, so he turned and went straight for the door. Bruno, Carlo and Hiram followed after from an aromatically safe distance, and Treeclimb came trotting out of the hall to chase them down. When Treeclimb caught up, Fatscat said to him, "I'm going to let these three stay up top with me tonight. It'll be tight in there. I sent Tomboy down to the barn to stay with Felaine and you just hunker down somewhere around here, wherever you think is good. I want you to keep an eye on things."

Treeclimb nodded and said, "That will do just fine, Harold. I want to stay down here anyway and make sure that they all get to bed at some semblance of a reasonable hour. More importantly, though, are you certain that seven o'clock is sufficiently early for our purposes? Shouldn't we be initiating the festivities in the neighborhood of five or five-thirty, sun-up at the latest? I well understand that we have tremendous firepower, surely more than they'll ever expect us to have at this altitude. But, getting caught off guard? That could be devastating for us. There's nowhere to turn up here, and if we have to run, they'll be chasing us downhill."

Fatscat grumbled dismissively, "Nah, everyone up at seven. That's good enough. They ain't coming that early. They'll need daylight to see their way through the heavy stuff below the high trails. They don't know this place like we do." Treeclimb said, "Whatever you say, Harold. I just don't know that we ought to be taking any chances. We still haven't heard a word from the crew that we sent off on lookout the other day. If there really is a squad coming up here after us, they could be anywhere by now."

Fatscat said, "Don't worry about it. Oh, and if something happens to me in this fight, thirty grand will be in my desk drawer. Use it to pay all of the SOB's who live through this." Fatscat took off for his office, and as soon as he had bounced about fifteen yards uphill, Bruno, Carlo and Hiram started up themselves.

It was his other internal struggle du jour. Ostensibly preparing to lead the way in a noble battle. To destroy those who once nearly destroyed him, and to pummel countless other enemies who might dare to destroy all that he had built. All the while it was strictly façade, and his only real plan was to turn and run. Take a bunch of money and run as fast and as far as he could, before it all ever started, and leave the mess behind for others to clean up.

It wasn't that Fatscat was unexcited or unconcerned about the confrontation. He wouldn't have gone to all of the trouble or expense unless he was firmly convinced that a battle was about to ensue. And, he really did hope that Elvis the Gunslinger would meet his maker in the midst of it. Fatscat just wasn't willing to put his own life at risk and figured that he'd be better off leaving all of the dirty work to everyone else. Not only wouldn't he risk himself, but he also had resorted to forcing his own colleagues to take chances in order to improve his personal situation.

Treeclimb's point was an excellent one. The feds already had plenty of time to prepare if they were intent on making a move, and they easily could make the compound before sun-up (if they were coming, that is). Instead, top priority went to Fatscat's own cowardly plan. Even if it might well jeopardize his team's chances in battle, the last thing that Fatscat wanted was for someone in the compound to rise early and discover that he had abandoned ship in the middle of the night. He envisioned himself being well on his way out to sea before anyone had awakened.

Treeclimb just shook his head as he turned and started back for the mess hall. The crowd nearly was in a tizzy when he walked in. There was screaming, screeching, hissing, and lots of jumping up and down. Bottles were uncorked, cards were dealt and smoke began to fill the air. It was a genuinely raucous atmosphere. Treeclimb started thinking to himself that, with the way things were looking in the hall, seven o'clock probably was plenty ambitious for a start time. Not that getting an earlier jump wouldn't be a much safer bet, but given the crowd that he was dealing with, attempting to rouse anyone much before seven probably would be an exercise in futility.

When Fatscat, Bruno, Carlo and Hiram reached the top of the hill, they settled into Fatscat's quarters to have a drink and make sure that no one was going to come up behind them to bring news, ask questions or whatever. In about an hour, the time finally seemed right, and Fatscat told the others to go behind the telegraph room and make sure that fresh dogs had been delivered. Fatscat knew that they would be there; Felaine wouldn't have dropped a ball that big.

As soon as they left, Fatscat dashed into his office and shifted some money around. He loaded eight hundred and ten thousand dollars into each of three saddlebags. Just as he was finishing, the others came into his office. He said, "Here, each of you take one of these. There's a little over eight hundred grand in each bag. You each keep five hundred, like I said, and all the rest goes to Hardcrass.

"Maybe we'll kill Hardcrass when we get out on the water and then we can take his share, too. I haven't decided yet. I did promise it to him, though, and he's done everything that he said he would. So far anyway." Of course, Fatscat had no idea that, not twenty-four hours ago, Hardcrass tried to steal what he thought was the entire ransom. Fatscat likewise didn't know that, due to the failure of that attempt, he wouldn't end up having to split anything with Hardcrass. He waved the others out of his office and said, "Go put all of that on your dogs and make sure you tie those things down tight. I'll be right out."

As soon as they exited, Fatscat succumbed to his guilty feelings about running off like a coward and did what he could to compensate. He put five hundred grand in his desk drawer, covered it up with some papers and left the following note sitting on top:

Treeclime

Im reely sorry about running off.
It was sumthing I had to do. Thank
you for all yoor help. By the time
you reed this I'll be far away. Heer
is a lot of money. Do what you
want with it.

X

Fatscat quickly was out the door with just over two million dollars in his own saddlebags. He hopped around to the hitching post behind the telegraph room to meet his cohorts and the four of them began riding down into the darkness. The clock had just struck eleven.

CHAPTER THIRTY-THREE

A SLEEPLESS NIGHT

There was plenty of worrying going on tonight. A worrying epidemic, if you will, and one thing that almost no one was going to do was sleep. Kathy Barncat was tossing and turning, worried sick that Elvis, Frank and anyone else who they might have with them were on the verge of destruction at the paws of a small army of bad guys. Treeclimb lie awake himself, equally as worried that an army of good guys would ascend upon his army of bad guys before his bad guys would be ready to take on those good guys. In the end, their fears would turn out to be completely unfounded.

Eddie and Calli, what did they have to worry about? Oh, just a little matter of having to sneak out, steal about sixty dogs and lead them down into some steep, dark, unfamiliar hills in the wee hours of the morning. Right out from under the whiskers of their owners, who just happened to be a bunch of heavy-duty mobsters and mercenaries. Tomboy and Felaine, despite being more familiar with the territory, understandably were wide awake with the same sorts of concerns running through their own minds. Fortunately for all four of them, most of the crowd in the mess hall had been up pretty late hitting those whiskey bottles hard.

It wasn't the first time that Morris Pusserschmott IV had grown tired of hearing his wife snore. He went downstairs to spend the rest of the night on one of the couches, staring into the fire and wondering if he ever would see his boy again. His daughters were sitting up in their beds worrying just the same. Warren wasn't too worried himself, knowing that if they'd made it this far without a hitch, it probably would be smooth sailing the rest of the way. Still, he refused to let anyone sleep and he had no plans to stop until those kids were back at the homestead. Save for whatever rest might be necessary to keep the dogs from collapsing and possibly a quick stop by HQ to let them know that the youngsters were safe and sound.

Fatscat's innate paranoia was spun up way, way tight. It all was seeming just too easy and he worried on the entire ride down to Catina Town that someone must have been following them. It would have been difficult to do. It was dark in the woods and no one knew those trails like Fatscat. He had cut most of them himself back in the very early days, way before there was anything like a compound and there was only his little hideout up there.

He just had that eerie feeling that someone was sneaking through the woods behind them, and his head was on a swivel. He thought he heard noises. He thought he saw shadows. He didn't really know what to think and he was on perpetual high alert. Carlo, Hiram and Bruno? They were mostly worried that they would get lost on the trail, because Fatscat was moving so fast and not seeming to care whether they kept up or not.

For once, the only one who wasn't worrying was Frank. Not that he would have the luxury of sleeping tonight. No, they would be out and about alright. But, he pretty much had done all that he could do at this point, and the chips were going to fall where they may.

Elvis? Well, he wasn't much of a worrier himself, though he was wrestling with one significant concern. If Eddie and Calli did opt to rescue all of those dogs, the only logical place to put them until permanent homes could be found would be the Pusserschmott ranch. No, it wouldn't be a concern for the Pusserschmotts. They could well afford it and it would be just the kind of good deed that the family and their staff enjoyed doing, even if it entailed some work.

However, if Elvis and Frank did survive all of this, the Pusserschmotts almost certainly would insist on expressing their gratitude by having Frank and Elvis stay as their guests for at least a few days. Elvis wondered how he possibly could navigate if he were to end up with Calli and Jeanine in the same house at the same time.

Best of friends, no less! How, he asked himself, did he get into these situations?

- - -

It was almost four-forty when Fatscat and his crew broke through the edge of the forest and were gazing out into the harbor. The sun wouldn't rise for at least another hour, and there appeared to be no activity yet out on the docks. The appointed time to meet with Hardcrass was not until sun-up, but Fatscat had intended all along to get there early and check everything out. Check out the boat, the crew, even the tavern. It would open at five and Fatscat had every intention of being the very first customer, so that he and his pals could take a good look around and make sure that no one was hiding out. This was, in fact, part of Hardcrass' territory and Fatscat wanted to be certain that there wasn't going to be any funny business.

Bruno, Hiram, Carlo and Fatscat rode down to the water's edge, dismounted, pulled off their saddlebags and started walking out onto the pier, each with his pistol in paw. Except for the occasional board creaking under the weight of their paws, it was completely silent, and the water was still and dark. There was a nineteen-foot (average by cat standards) fishing boat moored at Dock 23, and when they arrived they could see what appeared to be two cats sleeping in chairs on the lower deck, each wearing a bandana.

In remarkably quiet fashion, Fatscat hopped aboard, bounced up to the cat sleeping by the steering wheel, pushed the barrel of his pistol up against his chin and said, "You boys know Hardcrass, do ya?" Both of them awoke and Bruno put his gun to the head of the other. The one that Fatscat had accosted quickly raised his paws into the air and said, "Yes, yes. Mr. Hardcrass hired us. Where is he?"

Fatscat said, "Don't worry about him for now. If I were you, I'd be a lot more worried about me. Now, how much did he pay you? You know, Hardcrass." The one that Bruno had at gunpoint quickly interjected, "Ten thousand. He gave us ten up front and said we'll get another ten when we drop everyone off. He wasn't sure where we'd be going exactly, but he said it might be a long trip." Fatscat looked over at him and said, "That all sounds right to me. Now where can we put these bags down? We've got a lot of very important papers in here and if anything happens to them, you can kiss this boat and your asses goodbye. You hear me?" Each of them nodded and said, "Yes, sir."

Carlo opened the galley door and stepped down, and Bruno, Fatscat and Hiram all followed him in. They made their way to the back of the galley, put down their bags, covered them up and came back out to the deck. Fatscat was the last one to emerge and he had some cash in his forepaw. He gave each of the boaters a few hundred dollars and said, "Here's a few bucks for now. Stay here and don't move until we get back. Make sure you get that engine started up soon and keep it running, just in case we have to go in a hurry. We'll be up there in the tavern looking out for Hardcrass."

Fatscat put his pistol up to the head of one of them and said, "Did you hear me?" Then he nodded toward the tavern and said, "We'll be right up there for a little while. You try anything. I mean ANYTHING. If something happens to those bags. If I see this boat so much as even peek its nose out of this slip before we get back. One false move and it'll be the worst mistake you'll ever make. I'll hunt you down for the rest of my life. I'll kill you, your family, and everyone that you ever cared about. You got me, boys?" In unison, they responded, "Yes, sir!" They even saluted, although Fatscat clearly was not military.

Fatscat started hopping back up the pier and the others came trailing behind as soon as it was safe. A light breeze blowing in from the water kept him downwind for the moment and that did help a little. One of the boat crewmen looked over at the other and said, as he grimaced from the lingering aroma, "I guess that must be him, Fatscat."

When the scumsters reached the end of the pier, they grabbed their dogs and led them up to a hitching post behind the C-Town Tavern, which was about to open for business. Fatscat started rattling the front door and a middle-aged cat came hurriedly out from the kitchen to unlock it. He said, "Sorry, gentlemen, we don't usually open for a few more minutes. Take a seat over here." He led them to a table in the front corner, only steps away from the dock, and went back into the kitchen.

When the man came back out to the table, Fatscat, Bruno, Carlo and Hiram all ordered coffee and breakfast, and Fatscat demanded a bottle of the best Scatch in the house. Fatscat couldn't relax and constantly was looking back over his shoulders, out at the piers and all around the room, still convinced that they had been followed from the get-go. Even though the meeting technically was scheduled for sun-up, Fatscat also was starting to complain about Hardcrass not having surfaced yet. No one else at the table could get comfortable with him squirming and bitching the whole time.

The plates were a sight for sore eyes and, even better, they distracted Fatscat for a little while. They were really big and they were filled to the edges with bacon, eggs and potatoes, all covered in cheese. The man who repeatedly kept coming out to the table to refill coffee cups and then disappearing back into the kitchen obviously knew that something was up. He was the owner of the tavern and he had recognized Fatscat immediately. Though he made no mention of it, he hadn't seen Fatscat in the tavern in well over a year, and certainly never at the crack of dawn. He just tried to stay out of the way, and spoke only when he had been spoken to.

It took them quite a while to dispatch with breakfast, and after the last plate finally had been licked clean, Fatscat reached for the bottle of Scatch with his lone forepaw. He unplugged the top, poured some into each mug on the table, and lifted his own mug high in a victorious manner. He started to say something, but we'll never know what it was that he had on his mind. All you could hear was

BOOM! BOOM! BOOM! BOOM! BOOM!

It was five-thirty on the dot and the world's loudest alarm clock most definitely did not disappoint. The top of Aracat was no short distance, but you could hear the explosions like they were just down the street. The top of the sky was lighting up like a Christmas tree, and everything in the C-Town Tavern was shaking and rattling. Whether all of this was a good thing of course depends on which team you might be rooting for, but dwellers of the Tin Roof corner surely were sharing a common sentiment: "I guess we could have picked a better day to let the compound double as a munitions dump."

The nice man in the kitchen took cover under a table. The faces of his four cruddy guests smacked of alarm and disbelief, as they all looked around the room and at each other. All except Bruno. He had let out a grunt that no one could have heard over the bangs, and was slumped face-down on the table with blood streaming generously from his neck. Victim of a shot that likewise was inaudible, timed perfectly with the start of the fireworks show that now was underway at the top of the peaks.

Everyone likely assumed that the shattering of the glass that previously comprised the Tavern's huge front window also must have been a product of the explosions. Until that next shot went off. It rang out loud and clear, and it drilled Carlo right through the heart. He fell back in his chair as his mug slipped from his forepaw and crashed to the floor. Fatscat and Hiram didn't really know what was going on for sure, but they at least had the sense to make a move. They were across the room and through the door so fast that even Elvis didn't have time to re-cock his rifle.

He had set up sniper shop on a nearby rooftop, where he was in the prone position using some of Team Fatscat for target practice. As Fatscat and Hiram took off down the pier, Elvis jumped from the roof, drawing both pistols in mid-air. In the process of touching down, he shot Hiram dead in the back with his right, and with his left he then fired at Fatscat. It caught Fatscat in the left shoulder as he dived into the boat at Dock 23. Fatscat yelled at the guy at the steering wheel, "GO, GO, GO. NOW!" The boat darted out into the lane without hesitation, and Fatscat lie flat on the deck, hoping that by the time Elvis got to the slip, the boat would be too far out to reach.

Fatscat got his wish. Elvis probably could have made the jump if he had to, but instead he just turned and looked back up into the hills. It was too far away to tell for sure, but from all appearances, the entire compound looked to be engulfed in flames. The impending sunrise was surrendering just enough remnant light to make the heavy billows of smoke somewhat visible. From his vantage point, lying face down on the deck, all that Fatscat could see was the sky beginning to lighten and smoke rising in the distance. Surreal for sure, but more surreal was the feeling that he had. He'd made it. He'd really made it.

Not that being wounded yet again was cause for celebration, but it really didn't seem that bad. Nothing like the last time he'd taken fire from the Gunslinger, he thought. He tried in vain to feel bad for his partners, but he couldn't stop the emotion from drowning away in the realization that their demises had landed him another million and a half bucks. And Hardcrass, that punk. Fatscat had his share, too. Not bad for a guy whose home currently was on fire.

When he thought that the distance was safe enough, he peeked his head up over the stern. No, Elvis wasn't coming. He really wasn't. He was just standing there on the pier looking back up into the cliffs. Fatscat slid one of the chairs to the very back of the deck and pulled himself up into it. After he got himself situated, he commenced to barking out orders. His first words were, "FULL SPEED AHEAD. And no stopping until we need to reload that fuel box!"

The cat at the wheel yelled back, "AYE!" Then, he picked an oar up from the deck. In this world, there is no baseball or cricket. Maybe they would be invented someday, but surely not yet. You wouldn't have known it from the way Frank turned his hips when he came around with that oar. If he had hit a ball, it would have gone a long, long way. Instead, he nailed Fatscat flush in the face, and the only parts of Harold that didn't go sailing overboard were the fangs from the top of his mouth, which now were lodged securely in the flat part of that oar.

CHAPTER THIRTY-FOUR

HOW IN THE WORLD?

Yeah, good ol' Fatscat. He and his buddies had made some serious time coming down those trails. But, Elvis and Frank, they weren't exactly your everyday, plodding chumps. They didn't get hauled across the country in their fancy train cabin, with their silly little safe, to be thrust into the most sensitive matter currently underway in the entire country because they lacked resourcefulness.

Even if they were less familiar with the territory, they did have a two-hour head start, and they weren't carrying nearly the load that Fatscat and his thugs had to lug. They had come straight, and I mean straight, downhill along the telegraph line of sleaze. Fatscat had strung almost every bit of it all by himself well over a year ago. It was too important of a job to leave to anyone else. The irony of it all! A private trail that had been custom blazed by Fatscat, it ended up being the shortest of short-cuts. When they made bottom, they were only three miles north of Catina Town, and Daisy and Stella covered that distance at a dead run in just under seven minutes.

By Elvis' watch, it was just shy of three-thirty when they arrived. When they sneaked up to Dock 23, no one was there. Frank and Elvis figured that they'd have a quick snack (yeah, the canned stuff) just to kill some time. Not that they weren't hungry, but they could have waited if they had to. When the crew arrived at what they believed was the early hour – even for fishercats – of four o'clock, they were rather surprised to find their vessel occupied.

Frank and Elvis were sitting in chairs on the deck playing a hand of gin. Elvis was nice enough about the whole thing. He said,

"We hate to do this to you guys, but we've got a proposition and it's one of those take it or leave it jobs. Either you drive us out to sea a few miles right now, and we shoot both of you and toss you in for a swim, or you can do what we say." Elvis and Frank each drew a pistol and used it to wave the crew encouragingly onto the boat.

The guys were shivering as they stepped on board, and one of them asked in a broken voice, "Are you with Mr. Hardcrass?" Frank said, "Sorry to disappoint you, but no. We're not. I assume that he still has plans to be here sooner or later. And if he *does* show up, we'll almost certainly have to kill him. Don't hold me to that, though. It's not completely set in stone, but he surely won't be getting the "help us out" option that we're giving you fine gentlemen right now.

"And, if we don't kill him, either we'll be taking him with us or we'll be turning him over to some law enforcement professionals. Hopefully the latter, because we don't want that sort of responsibility. It's been a long week and we've got enough to do already. Plus, if we don't kill him, then we'll at least have to hurt him, and we aren't going to want him messing up all of our stuff. Do you like it when someone gets hurt out there fishing and messes up your boat? Or sick, that's worse, right?"

They looked at Frank like he was from another planet and Frank yelled, "DO YOU LIKE IT? I didn't hear your answer." They both shook their heads back and forth and said in tandem, "No, no." Then one said, "We hate it." The other said, "Yeah, it's horrible." Frank said, "That's what I thought. Well, same goes for us. Oh, by the way, what time did Hardcrass say he would be here?" One of them responded, "He said five-thirty, maybe five-forty-five." Frank said, "Perfect. Okay, I think we're almost done with the questions." Frank looked at Elvis and said, "E, am I forgetting anything?"

Elvis looked at the two guys and said, "Just one thing. Mr. Hardcrass, as you call him, did he say whether anyone would be joining him for the voyage today?" One of them said, "Yeah, he did say that somebody else was coming. Supposed to be here around sun-up. He didn't say any names. There could be more, but at least one. We can handle at least six passengers. Eight unless everyone is really big. We've got the best steam engine available, too. It's the fastest boat on the water." Elvis said, "Thanks. We'll keep that in mind if we ever need a charter. For now, let me tell you that I think I know who this other passenger is going to be."

Elvis continued, "If you smell him coming from halfway down the pier, you'll know it's him for sure. His name is Harold Fatscat." One of them said, "You mean the mob guy, the Tin Roof Gang guy?" Elvis said, "Yep, the one and only. In case you didn't know, he and a few scumbag friends of his supposedly are headed this way right now. You guys are taking him, or them, and Mr. Hardcrass far, far away somewhere in this boat. Did Hardcrass say you might be gone for a while?" One of them said, "Definitely. That's why he's paying us so much. He already gave us ten thousand bucks, and we've got another ten coming. We've got a load of extra fuel on the boat, too. Probably can stay out for days."

Elvis said, "See, we do know what we're talking about. Don't we? I'm sorry to ruin it for you kids, but we can't exactly let you go running off with them. Remember the part about dying or doing what we say?" They nodded and Elvis said, "Well, one of the things that we're saying is that you can't leave with them. Don't worry. We'll make it up to you, but you won't be going anywhere with Hardcrass or Fatscat. Far away or anywhere else. Now here's the deal."

Elvis handed one of them a stack of bills and said, "First, take this. That's ten grand. Count it if you want, but it's all there. And don't give me that look. It's real. We got it from the bank. So, you boys won't be missing out on anything. Okay?" They nodded and Elvis continued, "I'm going over there right now to get set up. You see that building?" Elvis pointed to a building and they nodded again, and then he said, "I'll be up on that rooftop with this rifle and I'm really good with it. I mean, I don't want to toot my own horn, but."

Elvis turned to Frank and said, "Frankie, am I good with this rifle or what?" Frank said, "Yeah, he's pretty good with it. I saw some guy shoot a little boar from really far away the other day. I don't know if this guy here is that good, but he can hit you two and this boat from up there, no problemo." Elvis said, "Give me a break.

I could have hit that pig with my pistol and you know it." Frank looked back and smirked. Elvis said, "Now, where was I? Oh yeah, so don't try anything funky.

"My buddy is going to jump into the galley of this boat next door here and lay low. I guarantee you that Fatscat and his cronies will be here first. That's just how he does things. If he told Hardcrass he'll be here at sun-up, then he's coming at least an hour before then. He's a paranoid dude. You don't believe me? I'll bet you that ten grand right now that he comes at least an hour early. Five o'clock at the latest. Whaddya say, are we on?" They both shook their heads "no" and Elvis said, "Good call. Don't worry, he'll be down here soon checking things out to make sure it's safe."

Elvis pointed at the tavern and said, "Then he'll probably go up there, look around inside and wait for Mr. Hardcrass to get here." Elvis looked down and shook his head back and forth, as he chuckled to himself and said with a grin, "Mister? You really call him *Mister* Hardcrass?" They both shrugged and nodded. Frank looked at them with a pained expression and said, "You know, Elvis is right about that. Don't call him that anymore. That doesn't make any sense."

Elvis continued, "You make sure to keep your bandanas on when you talk to Fatscat and his buddies, so they can't recognize you later on. These aren't the kind of guys you want coming after you if something goes wrong. Don't let yourselves get too worked up about it, though, because we're probably going to kill all of them also, but just in case. You know, you never can be too careful these days.

"Just go along with whatever Fatscat says. I mean, you can't pull away on the boat or anything like that. If he wants to go right away, then just make something up and jump off as fast as you can, because my friend here and I are going to blow them and this boat to smithereens. Other than leaving right away, just cooperate with him and, whatever he says, agree with it. After he leaves, you two slip off the side of the boat as soon as you can without them seeing. Leave one of your bandanas here for Frankie. He's going to get onboard and take over, and that's pretty much it."

Frank said, "Swim to another boat or somewhere else safe, or get back to shore and run. Do whatever you need to. Just get away and out of sight however you can. If something happens to your boat, we'll get it fixed. We might even buy you a new one if it gets messed up really bad. So, you boys got it?"

The crewmen stood there nodding their heads. Frank grabbed his rifle and, as promised, jumped into the boat at Dock 24 and slid into the galley to wait. Elvis ran down the pier with his rifle slung over his shoulder and scampered up the side of a building right next to the water's edge, alongside of the bulkhead. He crawled and scooted over to the corner of the roof nearest the C-Town Tavern, and lied down on his stomach with his rifle by his side. He was just over fifty yards from the tavern's front door.

In case you didn't notice, in addition to his other talents and idiosyncrasies, Frank was an amateur explosives enthusiast. And a good one at that. Better than most pros. Except for his cans of food, some water-filled canteens, the portable spit and a few other absolute necessities, virtually the entire payload that Amos had left Elvis' barn with the other day consisted of dynamite and a bunch of nifty little timers. A lover of all things time, making the timers was one of Frank's favorite pastimes.

While they were hiding out on the edge of the compound the night before, there was a brief period when everyone but Frank was catching a few after-dinner winks as they waited for the dark of night. What was it that he was doing? Winding and synchronizing his timers. He had at least thirty of them. Then, while Elvis and Calli were out making their rounds at the barn and the telegraph room, Frank and Eddie were running all over the compound, digging holes, stashing TNT, affixing fuses and setting timers. By the time they were through, every building in the compound was teed up to be blown apart at five-thirty sharp.

Back to live action.

- - -

Frank turned the boat around and started laughing out loud as he passed back by Fatscat and waved. As Frank proudly watched the fruits of his labor light up the sky, all he could hear was Fatscat grumbling and splashing, with the gentle hum of the boat motor playing softly in the background. If things weren't bad enough for Harold already, forced bathing was an absolute clincher. It was his worst nightmare.

Frank drove back to the pier, past Dock 23 and all the way up to the first slip, which was wide open. Elvis was standing there with Daisy and Stella, who had been hiding in the nearby woods. Frank jumped out of the boat and they tied it off, and he and Elvis proceeded to unload saddlebags filled with almost four and a half million dollars and pile them onto the dogs.

Elvis ran into the tavern to make sure that everything was okay. He introduced himself to the man inside, told him that Calli had said wonderful things about him, and gave him a thousand dollars to cover the damage to the building. It was more than twice what the repairs likely would cost and the man tried to give it back. He said, "Please, please. This is too much."

Elvis said, "I'll make a deal with you. You keep that money, but you let us use one of your dogs for a few days. Ours have been up all night and they already have to carry us all the way back to South Sebastian. We definitely could use some help lugging all of this stuff that we have. We'll get your dog back to you by early next week."

Elvis continued, "Oh, and one more thing, if you don't mind." The man said, "What's that?" Elvis said, "My friend and I, we sure could use a proper breakfast before we ride up the road, and we'd also like to take that bottle of Scatch sitting over there on that table if you don't mind." The man said, with a wink and a big smile, "You've got yourself a deal."

CHAPTER THIRTY-FIVE

TO THE VICTORS GO THE SPOILS

It was almost dark and, as usual, Kathy Barncat was the last one to leave the building. As she locked the back door, you could hear her sniffling. Still, no one anywhere near sea level knew for sure what had transpired up in those peaks. Assuming that Eddie and Calli did make it out, they'd still be far from home, even with locals like Tomboy and Felaine to lead the way. No matter who you are, there still is a natural limit to the velocity with which you effectively can shepherd fifty or sixty dogs down a mountain range, and a steep one at that. Unless they had left the dogs behind at the compound – not likely for dog lovers, they'd surely be making camp tonight and wouldn't arrive until tomorrow afternoon at the earliest.

Warren, Benji, Burt and Timmy all had arrived safely late that morning with the former hostages parked up on Amos' back. But, none of them had any idea who was responsible for all of that noise up in the hills or what the upshot was.

She was wiping a few tears from her eyes as she started to turn away from the door, when a snide voice rang out: "Isn't it a little early for the boss to be leaving?" As she finished her turn, a smile came over her face. She looked at Elvis and said, "You little son of a bitch. If I wasn't so glad to see you, I'd come over there and knock you right off of that pup of yours. Don't you know that you can give someone a heart attack sneaking up like that?" Frank said, "We thought about that, but we figured that the Director of East Coast Operations could handle a little bit of a scare."

Kathy said, "I assume you boys want to come inside?" Elvis said, "Well, we probably should. It doesn't look like there's anybody left over there at the bank, and we really would like to find a safer place for all of this money. I guess we shouldn't have ridden all the way here with it for starters, but we didn't know what else to do." Kathy said, "You've got a point there." Then she unlocked the door, waved them in and said, "Well, come on."

Elvis and Frank put Daisy, Stella and Tammy (who they had borrowed from the tavern's owner) in the barn, gave them some food and water, and brought in the saddlebags. It was a mystery what had happened to the missing half million, but if anyone could absorb that kind of a hit, the Pusserschmotts were them. Maybe it would turn up, maybe not, but everyone knew that Morris likely couldn't care less now that his boy was home safe. A mere rounding error on the Pusserschmott balance sheet. Elvis ultimately would try to return to the family the twenty-six grand that he hadn't expended for bribes and repairs, but the old man and his daughters wouldn't hear of it.

It took them the better part of three hours, and most of that bottle of Scatch, to swap stories about everything that had happened since they last saw each other. Elvis and Frank decided to spend the night on couches at HQ. The Barncat was about to zip home to tend to her own family and dogs, and catch up on some shut eye before having to open up the next morning. Just before she left, Frank and Elvis asked if she would mind doing them one small favor and she was happy to oblige.

The following morning, Burt and Timmy were the first ones in. Like everyone else who would surface throughout the remainder of the day, they were anxious to know if anyone had heard from Elvis and Frank. She told them the same thing that she would tell anyone else who asked. She told them exactly what happened. The trip to the compound, the fireworks, the run-in with Fatscat and his crew at the marina, the money (most of it anyway) back in the bank, and everything else worth telling.

She also told the slightly bad news. That Frank and Elvis, they couldn't stay. Something big was going on back on the West

Coast and they had to take the first train out that morning. Everyone was so disappointed. The folks at HQ, the Pusserschmotts, Warren, Eddie and Calli. Everyone. The Barncat said, "I don't know what else to tell you. There's work to do, you know. That's just how it goes sometimes."

- - -

No one knows whether Fatscat ever made it out of the water alive. Knowing him, he probably did, but there would be no coming back from the brink this time. He was too old and too beat up. And even if he hadn't been, he was too tired of it all to care enough to start over. If he did live, he'd surely find some way to survive. Maybe he'd reconnect with his pal, Treeclimb. Or maybe not. Either way, Fatscat's days of wreaking major havoc had come to an end.

Speaking of Treeclimb, he had gotten so nervous the night before that he finally gave in to his urges just after four-thirty. He went to plead with Fatscat for sounding the alarm at five instead of seven. He kept telling himself that it was the right thing to do, as he rehearsed while walking uphill. When he couldn't find anyone in the quarters, he went straight to the office, where he found the cash and the note. He threw it into a sack and promptly started downhill. He didn't even chance being seen going to the barn for a dog. He knew that he'd make it to the bottom sooner or later, and he surely could afford one when he got there. He was glad he left when he did.

Hardcrass would have done some hard time, but after Calli confirmed everything that Elvis had told the Barncat about the original murder plan, the Barncat made Hardcrass an offer he couldn't refuse. In exchange for his cooperation, Hardcrass was left to his own devices, on pain of death (as the Barncat told him) should he ever find trouble again. He was true to his commitment and lived out his years very comfortably on the thirty-ish grand he still hadn't spent.

No one wanted to make a big stink out of it and attract a bunch of attention to the family, so they kept it on the way down low, but the vows of Clevin and Melba quickly were dissolved. Anyone else would have strung her up and left her for the flies and vultures to tend to, which is exactly what she deserved, but that isn't how the Pusserschmotts did things. The family bought her a house in the middle of nowhere, gave her just enough cash to live on and told her never to set paw in town again, leaving her to wallow in lifelong regret knowing what she had left behind.

It was late Saturday morning and two extremely attractive young ladies were giving their bags to a bellhop, bemoaning the end of their stay. Instead of heading down the steps toward the lobby, he climbed two flights and proceeded to the end of the hall. The ladies told him that there must be some mistake, but he assured them that there was not.

The bellhop opened the doors to an absurdly large suite, more resembling a small home than a hotel room. He led them over to the balcony, pointed down at the beachside swimming pool and said, "Those two gentlemen down there say you'll be staying another week here in the Presidential Suite with them." Elvis the Gunslinger and his trusty sidekick looked up from their lounge chairs, smiled and waved at Kelly and Melissa. They were sipping on fancy morning beverages, complete with midget umbrellas.

THE END

THANK YOU!

To the Reader:

Thank you so much for taking your time to read *Elvis the Gunslinger*. I hope you enjoyed reading it as much as I enjoyed writing it. I would LOVE to hear from you if you have any questions, comments, criticisms, remarks or any other kind of feedback. It really is important to me to find out what you think.

Feel free to email me at romey@elvisthegunslinger.com. And, please visit our web site at www.elvisthegunslinger.com, where you can join our mailing list, read a little bit about the real Elvis (who no longer is with us and to whom this book is dedicated), even find some ETG merchandise if that tickles your fancy!

I also would like to ask you for a favor. Nothing is more helpful these days for a book than getting a review. For first time authors like myself, it can be especially difficult to get them. If you have the time and the inclination, I would be ever so grateful if you would be willing to take a few minutes to review *Elvis the Gunslinger* and post it on Amazon, Goodreads or any other site that you review on.

Again, thank you for spending your time with my book. I really, really appreciate it.

Romey

ABOUT THE AUTHOR

The oldest of four children, Romey Connell grew up in a suburban waterfront community in the Baltimore/Annapolis area, and moved with his family to their nearby horse farm at the age of 14. He graduated from the Auburn University School of Business in 1985 and the Cornell Law School in 1988, whereupon he moved to Atlanta, Georgia.

He began his professional career as an attorney at Kilpatrick & Cody, a large law firm now known as Kilpatrick, Townsend & Stockton. After nearly 11 years there, he left to travel and begin writing. In 2000, Romey began working as an in-house attorney for Atlanta-based EyeWonder, Inc. and in 2006 he became that company's Chief Operating Officer.

Romey has been married to his lovely wife, Gretchen (an extremely talented artist and photographer), for nearly fifteen years and they are blessed with two wonderful children, Jerry (12) and Jamie (10). In 2010, after EyeWonder was sold, Romey left the working world for a while, so that he could spend as much time as possible with his family. They live in the Lake Claire neighborhood on the east side of Atlanta.

Though spending time with family is foremost these days, Romey's interests include travel, sports, the outdoors, beer and food, not necessarily in that order. He firmly believes that you should be wary of persons who do not get along well with children or animals. Romey is a fan of nearly all genres of music, although he is partial to those in which the artists actually play instruments, and he considers dancing all night to be the greatest form of recreation.

Romey began writing *Elvis the Gunslinger* in the spring of 2000. Distractions of work, family and fun somehow interfered with its completion for many, many years. He hopes dearly that others will enjoy reading it as much as he enjoyed writing it, and that writing will be the final entry in his admittedly short list of careers.